I0680776

Pride Publishing books by M.C. Roth

Single Books
The Drumbeat of His Heart
A Song for His Heart
Karma's Kiss
Greedy Boy

It's a Kink Thing
Kinked Up
Unkinked
Kinks and Crosshairs

It's a Kink Thing

KINKED UP

M.C. ROTH

Kinked Up
ISBN # 978-1-80250-968-7
©Copyright M.C. Roth 2022
Cover Art by Kelly Martin ©Copyright August 2022
Interior text design by Claire Siemaszkiewicz
Pride Publishing

Published in 2022 by Pride Publishing, United Kingdom.

KINKED UP

Dedication

For Q.

Chapter One

Nav

Nav's apartment key tumbled from his hand as his phone vibrated, rattling his change and his plastic swipe card from work. He fumbled in his pocket, pulling his phone out and groaning at the name on the display.

"This is *not* a good time," he said as he accepted the call, sighing at the laughter that burst against his eardrum. He glanced down, searching for his key that had somehow made it halfway under his apartment door, only the jagged edge visible beneath the crack.

He really needed to get a keychain so the thing didn't disappear on him again. He'd already gone through three keys in the last month, and the hardware store was starting to get suspicious as to why he needed so many spares. There just didn't seem to be much point to getting a sparkly keychain if he wasn't going to keep it for all that long.

"How did it go, Nav?" asked Sasha through the speaker.

No matter how many times Nav lost his things or moved, Sasha always seemed to track him down. He was Nav's self-appointed best friend and number one annoyance.

Nav let out a sigh, leaning his back against the door as he looked down the hall. There were a dozen doors that were identical to his, with grungy numbers barely clinging onto their hastily painted surfaces. At one point, the doors must've been a dreadful forest green, but someone had decided to paint over them with a thin layer of white primer. The results were pale lime rectangles with dark corners where the primer had been rubbed raw. The red apartment numbers completed the nightmarish Christmas look with tacky gusto.

"It went great. Better than great, actually. Everette never wants to see me again, and he got his brother to throw me out of the house." Nav rubbed at his shoulder where he was sure there was a bruise. They'd taken the throwing part a touch too literally, and Nav had found out first-hand how hard concrete sidewalks were.

"Ouch. Not unexpected, though," said Sasha, his laughter booming through the tiny speaker. "Maybe you shouldn't have hit on their dad?"

Nav ran a hand through his hair before he leaned back and let his head rest against the thin door. It sounded hollow to the touch, and it nearly bowed under his weight. "Maybe their dad shouldn't have been so hot. I mean, who the hell walks around in just their boxers then gets offended when they get hit on? I didn't know guys his age could even *have* abs like that. His body was just rocking."

"Gross... I don't need the details," said Sasha, the phone rustling. "How many is that now, though?"

"This year or this month?" asked Nav, sliding down the door until his ass met the thin and filthy carpet. A light flickered overhead, and somewhere a baby screamed. His neighbor down the hall was making their weekly batch of boiled cabbage, if the smell was anything to go by. And who the hell had crushed packets of ketchup at the end of the hall?

"You're such an asshole," said Sasha. "I've never met someone who has as many ex-boyfriends as you have. You must run into one at every bar."

Nav laughed, letting the grief of the situation roll off his shoulders and down the ratty hallway to find a sewer out on the street somewhere. There was hardly any grief there at all, if he were honest with himself. He'd only dated Everette for three weeks, which was two weeks longer than his usual attention span. The guy had been cute, but nothing compared to his dad.

"Most bars are out. Restaurants, too. I ran into Josh the other day, and I swear to God he spit on my salad," said Nav. He'd still eaten the salad, of course. A little spit never turned him off a good meal.

"So, you won't come out for drinks with us tonight?" asked Sasha. "Katie already did her hair up real nice, and I can't wait to fuck it up."

"Your straightness disgusts me," said Nav, letting his eyes drift shut. It had been a long week of too many hours at work and even more wasted on another guy he knew would never work out. His shower was calling to him, and he could definitely hear the cries of his lonely pillow.

"I dunno. I'm really tired, Sash." He leaned his head to the side to cradle his phone against his ear. A noise at the end of the hall made him startle, but he kept his eyes closed. It was probably just one of his asshole neighbors getting home after their day job. They would be able to step by him just fine.

"All the more reason to come out with us. You're in a rut, Nav. You need to relax and stop trying to fuck your way through every gay bedroom in the city. Come out with us tonight for drinks, keep your dick to yourself and I guarantee you'll feel better."

"Drinks do sound good," said Nav, pulling his feet closer when the squeak of shuffling footsteps approached him on the carpet. "Okay, I'll be there tonight. Don't let me fuck up again, okay?"

"Deal." Sasha chuckled. Nav could almost see his best friend's smirk through the phone. "I'll keep you surrounded by women so your dick shrivels up and dies. Then I'll get you so wasted that you forget about Tray."

"Tray was last month, before Scott and Paul, remember? Everette was the guy whose dad I just fucked," said Nav, lowering his voice as the footsteps came closer. He already got enough flack in his life for being gay and he didn't need any more shit from anyone.

"You are fucked up, man. I'll see you tonight. Nine sharp at Pinty's. Bring your long underwear and a chastity belt." Sasha ended the call with a click and Nav sighed, letting his phone slide to the ground with a hollow thump. He could sleep against the door, even with the floor jamming into the bruises on his ass.

Who *actually* threw someone? Concrete was not a fun place for his skinny ass to land. At least they had tossed him his pants.

"You okay?"

Nav's opened his eyes and cursed to himself, scrambling to get up to his feet.

Of course, the person to see him crumpled outside of his door had to be his smoking-hot and totally unreachable neighbor. He was gorgeous, with short blond hair that models would die for, and the softest blue eyes Nav had ever seen. Top that with thick shoulders, strong arms and thighs that could kill and he was everything Nav dreamed of.

The guy was also completely and totally unavailable. His boyfriend was the most average person in the world but had something that Nav couldn't even fathom—commitment. Every time Nav saw his him, the boyfriend was usually close by.

"Sorry… I just lost my key," said Nav as he pushed back against his door, his knees wobbling as his neighbor got closer. His mouth went dry, his throat constricting like nobody's business. His palms went damp as he suddenly began to sweat, his face flushing. Hunger evaporated in his gut like he'd just gotten a whiff of fresh ass, and his priorities had spun one-hundred-and-eighty degrees.

He was also the only one who did *that* to Nav. The beautiful blond specimen transformed him from a bonified slut who was proud of it into a blushing virgin.

Nav had fucked and been fucked by more guys than he could remember, but something about that tall, built frame and those crystal-blue eyes sent him back to his high school days when he'd seen his first cock and decided he was gay for life.

"Oh crap, that sucks," he said, running a hand through his blond locks that were probably softer than actual silk. "Did you call the superintendent?" He shifted a brown paper grocery bag in his hands, reaching into his pocket for something.

Of course he was environmentally aware, too, which made Nav want to drool. There was nothing worse than a hot guy who used plastic bags and drove a car that guzzled more fuel than a loaded transport truck. *Can you be any more perfect?*

Nav shook his head. "N-not yet. I think I probably just dropped it somewhere." Nav wanted to crumple into a ball. His voice was so soft and weak that he probably *sounded* like a virgin, too.

Virgins were the literal enemy. Clingy, flustered and nervous, Nav always steered well clear. He'd been there, done that and returned the T-shirt.

Knowing how thin the walls were in the building, Nav guessed the guy had probably heard his sex adventures from across the hall, which was probably why he was looking at Nav with confusion and concern etched onto his perfectly sculpted face. Statues were probably made of this guy — hopefully the ones with the big dicks and not the little ones.

Nav slid his foot sideways to where he remembered dropping the key, hopefully concealing it. He was such a fucking idiot, but he couldn't even think straight with his neighbor staring at him, his gaze piercing straight through his defenses.

"Did you need a hand? Just let me put my groceries in the fridge and I'll help you look for it." A soft smile settled on his lips as he pulled his own key out before opening his door with one hand.

"No, it's okay," said Nav, his face burning. He slapped his hands to his cheeks as the guy looked away, hoping to draw the heat out with his frigid fingertips. The sight of his wide, strong back had Nav flushing all over again. He looked away and into the apartment instead, his jaw dropping as something caught his eye.

There, on the wall, and hidden in the most unlikely of places, was a painting that he'd never thought he would see again.

"Oh my God, you have one of Brian Maeckery's paintings?" He stumbled across the hall, his key and his bag forgotten as the art drew him through the open door.

Seeing it again was the same as seeing it for the first time. The piece was one that had caught Nav's eye when it had been in the studio. His breath stuck in his throat as his cock swelled against his will, his groin pulling tight.

He couldn't help it. The brushstrokes were perfection, each one laid with such sensual purpose that Nav could almost feel them against his skin. The lovers on the canvas were wrapped around each other in an intimate embrace that made Nav's blood boil. They looked at each other in the peak of their pleasure, love and commitment frozen on their features. It was as unreal as a dream.

But what was his favorite painting of all time doing in a run-down apartment building? Sure, his neighbor had spruced up his place from what Nav could tell, but the painting didn't belong.

"Yeah." He set his grocery bag on the counter, before turning to Nav. "He's actually a friend of mine. He owed me a favor, so he gave this to me as payment. It's a beautiful piece." He shifted, flickering his gaze over Nav once before he turned and started unloading his groceries.

Butterflies erupted in Nav's belly. Brian Maeckery was nearly famous—like a shiny, untouchable doll on television. Nav would have worshiped the ground that he walked on, if only he had been able to find his house.

"I'm so jealous. I'm such a huge fan of his." He let out a sigh, reaching for the muddled color where the lovers' legs met. He hovered a few inches away, his hand trembling. The last price tag he'd seen on it was over one-hundred-thousand dollars. "It must've been one hell of a favor."

It still smelled fresh, the flavors of the paint rolling over his tongue as he inhaled sharply. The wooden frame was pristine, without a hint of dust or fingerprints, but how long would that last? It was something that should have been hanging in a temperature-controlled gallery for the rest of its life behind a pane of thick glass, not in a shitty apartment building soaking up the faint smell of cigarettes and cat piss.

His neighbor paused, a tray of chicken breasts clutched in his fingers. He furrowed his forehead before he let out a small laugh, his eyes lighting up. "Not really, no. My fiancé and I modeled for the painting, so Brian thought it was best if we were the ones to get it."

"Wait...what?" Nav took a step back, his gaze flashing between him and the painting. The faces on the canvas were in shadow, with only their lips visible and a hint of their partially closed eyes. But it *did* look like them, and the hair color was spot-on. And their bodies...*oh God.* Was that really hiding beneath the guy's T-shirt and jeans?

"Shit, I've jerked off to this painting," said Nav, flushing as he smacked his hand to his forehead. "I-I mean, shit. You're Theo?"

His boss had relayed the entire story as they'd hung

the painting in the gallery together—how Brian had claimed that Theo was his muse and how he had called to him with each brush stroke. Nav had agreed from the bottom of his balls. That had been the first time the painting made him hard—but not the last.

Nav dropped his gaze, flushing so fiercely that he wasn't sure his cheeks would ever cool again. He couldn't look at him. In fact, it was probably best if he turned around and crawled back to his apartment before begging for forgiveness through the door.

Nav started as his neighbor chuckled. His gaze was dragged back to the gorgeous blond, his heart thudding as he stared at the man with his head tilted back and his lips curled and open as the beautiful sound emerged.

"Theo's my fiancé," he said, wiping the gathering tears from his eyes as he continued to chuckle. "I'm Maverick, but everyone calls me Trick. Thanks for the compliment." He let out another laugh, his body shaking as his chest heaved.

"I'm so sorry. I'm just really tired, and I always say things I'm not supposed to when I'm tired." He bit his tongue as Trick laughed even harder. Trick was stunning when he was silent, but when he laughed, he transformed into an actual Adonis.

Nav looked at the painting again, something new surging from the base of his gut.

As much as he had longed to be the one in the painting in the past, it had always remained an unattainable figment of Brian's imagination. It had been fitting that the only thing that he would ever love was an imaginary scene with a fictional man.

But they were *real*...and the man he'd been fantasizing about was Trick. His heart rate picked up, his chest rising and falling like he'd just run a marathon.

Trick was obviously in love with Theo. He'd smiled, the corners of his eyes crinkling when he'd said Theo's name. And the painting…? Nav hadn't known what true love looked like until he had seen the canvas.

An ugly green monster twisted in his gut, leaving a foul taste in his mouth. It seemed that everyone could fall in love except him, even the not-so-fictional characters in a painting. He was going to be cursed to chase brief hookups for the rest of his life, ditching them before they lost their new boyfriend smell and shine.

"Sorry. I didn't mean to upset you by laughing at you. I was just surprised," said Trick, his humor falling away. "You sure you don't want me to help you find your key? Or I can get you a drink if you want to call the super and wait here."

"No, it's okay. I don't want to intrude," said Nav. He looked back to the painting, but the magic that had enthralled him for months was gone. His stomach lurched as he took a step back.

I'm just overtired. Alcohol required STAT.

"Well, it was nice meeting you…" Trick paused as if he were waiting for something.

"Nav." He shrugged, filling the uncomfortable silence.

"Nav. Just knock if you need something or if you change your mind." He smiled, parting his full lips to reveal white teeth that were perfectly straight. His smile was dazzling, pulling a wave of fresh heat from Nav's core.

"Thanks. Bye." Nav rushed into the hall, shutting the door before Trick could say anything further. His heart was still pounding, and for some strange reason, he felt the first prickling of tears at the corner of his eyes.

M.C. Roth

He took a deep breath and pinched the base of his nose. He must've been more exhausted than he'd thought if he was already starting to get teary-eyed. He usually didn't hit that level until he'd worked sixty hours in one week. He'd only done fifty-five hours in the last five days, so he should have still been in the glaringly frustrated and angry phase.

He reached for his key, easing it out from where it had squirmed through the crack under the thin door. He grabbed his bag, hauling it over his shoulder and turning the key in the lock before pushing inside.

Unlike Trick, he hadn't spiffed up his floors or counters in his apartment. There really was no point if his stay was going to be brief.

The paint was the original faded ivory with a few cracks around the corners and a smudge of purple along one baseboard. The floors were roll-on linoleum with a few holes in the kitchen where someone had repeatedly dropped a sharp knife. It could have been anyone's apartment.

Except for the art that he'd hung on the walls. The art was all his. Most of the paintings were little pieces he'd picked up in estate and garage sales in the city, with a few originals from up-and-coming artists. His work in the studio gallery put him in reach of a few artists who hadn't hit it big yet and had prices that were within his reach.

He stepped up to one of his favorites. The artist was known simply as *Rachel*, and they had a way with traditional techniques that wasn't too common anymore. A frog on a lily pad would have made most artists scoff, but Rachel had elevated the simple idea and done something beyond anything Nav could have imagined himself. The frog was made of stars, and the

17

lily pad was the cosmos, according to the gods. It always managed to take his breath away.

All the works he had managed to collect were beautiful and unique, but nothing like the scandalous and sensual canvas of Brian's work. It was so far beyond his price range that he didn't *deserve* to be close enough to touch it.

His throat clogged as he thought of the painting in its dismal setting across the hall.

"Christ, I need a drink." He pulled his clothes from his body, letting them trail on the ground on his way to the shower. As the water cascaded over him, he tried to push the painting and Trick from his thoughts.

Chapter Two

Nav

The bar was packed with sweaty bodies and a mixture of cologne and perfume that almost covered the scents of want and sex. The music was loud enough to get lost in, with a steady thrumming beat that pounded against his sternum and made it feel like there was a chickadee trapped in his chest. The lights were low, and the shadows long, concealing naked flesh and creeping hands as people hovered close on the dance floor, their legs entwined.

Normally, Nav would have been out in the press of bodies and heat, lost in the desperate craving for sex — maybe not in a regular bar, just in case a few assholes decided that he was a little too gay for their tits and ass party. He didn't even mind dancing with women, because they could *move,* and if he were lucky, their boyfriends would become awful jealous and decide that Nav needed to be taught a lesson on how to take a cock.

Nav was an 'A' student in that class. He could take cock like a horny teacher's assistant, and his blowing skills were good enough to make any straight man doubt himself. He was proud of the number of men who had flocked to the right side of wrong after he'd shown them what was on offer.

But not *here*. He was sitting on a stool to get wasted and drown in his single sorrows. Sasha had already almost chained him to his bar stool, which was between two ladies who were probably both hookers. That could have been the only reason that they were hitting on him when he emitted gay vibes like a fifty-foot transmitter.

Taking another sip of his drink, he glanced both ways. They still looked like chicks, and they were both still smiling at him like they knew something he didn't. *Maybe Sasha hired them to guard me?*

He knocked another beer back, just in case it made a difference. He couldn't remember what number that was, but he was feeling the buzz, even if he was still far from drunk.

"You hanging in there?" asked Sasha, planting himself between the prettier woman and Nav. She quirked her glossy lips into a frown before she caught sight of Sasha, giving him a once-over that made Nav want to roll his eyes.

His best friend *was* good looking, but not in a way that made him the slightest bit attractive to Nav. It was probably a good thing, because Nav could hardly stand Sasha on a good day. He wasn't sure if it was the backwards ball cap or the unlaced Nikes that turned him off — or perhaps the entire undersized and bulging ensemble.

Sasha panted as he leaned against the bar, sweat

beading on his forehead and tanned collar bone. His T-shirt was at least one size too small, but it wasn't as tight as his pants, which were blatantly displaying his too-obvious bulge.

Nav gulped and looked away. He must've been drunker than he thought if he was eyeing up his friend like that. The first and last time he'd kissed Sasha, he'd ended up gagging and going through an entire tube of toothpaste before he'd finally gotten rid of the lingering taste of Cool Ranch Doritos.

"I still don't get it," said Nav, slamming his empty glass down on the bar. His words weren't slurred yet and the room was still steady.

"Nothing to 'get', man. If you fuck some guy's dad, they are going to break up with you." Sasha shook his head, laughing as he flagged down the bartender. The woman on his right sighed and slipped from the barstool, heading onto the dance floor. Sasha slid onto the vacated seat, resting his elbows on the surface of the bar.

"Nah, I don't care about that asshole." Nav looked into the sea of bodies. "What does he have that I don't?" *What does Theo have that makes Trick love him?* Nav growled, picking up his empty glass and trying to drink. He blinked in confusion when his lips remained dry. He could have sworn there was another swallow or two.

"Lines, borders and maybe a hint of commitment," said Sasha, obviously thinking that they were still talking about Everette. Nav didn't give a shit about his most recent ex. It had been over before it had begun.

"I mean, come on, Nav. You've broken more hearts than anyone I've ever known combined, and you don't give a shit." Sasha grabbed Nav's empty glass, sharing a few words with the bartender while eyeing Nav out of the corner of his eye.

Was it so terrible that Nav didn't care about a single one of his exes? Maybe it was a bit harsh. Not one of them had looked at him the same way Trick had looked at his fiancé in that painting. No one had loved him so much that his chest ached.

"His fiancé isn't even that good looking. He's completely fucking average. I could probably even pass for him," said Nav, looking down at himself. "I'm about the same height, same weight and same hair color. But he doesn't look at me like that. Nobody fucking does."

"Nav, is something going on?" asked Sasha, his voice losing its humored edge. He leaned in closer, until Nav could smell his Gain laundry detergent over the cherry perfume from the woman on his other side. Sasha's beer was half gone, but Nav couldn't remember seeing him drink.

The floor wobbled as Nav stepped off his chair too quickly. Somebody must've cranked the heat in the bar as a joke, because he suddenly felt like he was dripping sweat. It was so loud that he couldn't even hear himself think over the barrage of noise.

How could Sasha stand it? He just sat there, drinking his beer as if it were just another night out — like his chest wasn't aching and his throat wasn't swollen shut so much that he could scarcely breathe.

It's never going to happen. The big L word would never make it into Nav's vocabulary. He might as well stop looking, because as soon as he'd seen that painting, it had been decided.

"I have to go get some air," said Nav, turning away from the bar. His friend called out for him, but he pushed through the crowd toward the rear exit, refusing to look back.

The alley called to him, along with its putrid-scented garbage bins and the stray cat that probably thought it got paid to mark its territory. He didn't want to face the brightly lit street or the line of people waiting to get into the club. They all had what he didn't.

He pushed the door wide, ignoring the warning sign that an alarm would sound if he did. Most of those signs were fake, and no one would hear anything over the music, anyway.

Cool spring air struck his face, drying the sweat and scents from his skin immediately. He stepped into the cold, taking a deep breath as the sounds of the club sank away through the closing door. It latched shut, the steady beat the only thing that made it through the thick steel.

He'd been in alleys more times than he could count, but never alone. No matter what part of the city he was in, they were all relatively identical. They smelled the same, at least, and all had a feeling of open privacy. They made for a great place for a no-questions-asked kind of fuck—his specialty.

The alley behind the dance club was better than most, with a single light that flickered a few times before stuttering into silence. The moon was tucked behind a few clouds, leaving him in almost complete darkness that was occasionally interrupted as the bulb fluttered to life for a few moments before dying again. It smelled like the cats had been steering clear, which was a nice change.

He turned to the wall, resting his forehead against the rough brick. The porous surface prickled his flesh, the cool masonry soaking the remaining heat from his skin. It pulsed from the beat, as if the building itself were alive.

Dragging in a deep breath, he nearly choked at the scent of trash. It smelled so similar to his usual relationships — sour and disposable.

It doesn't matter. They don't matter. The corner of his eyes prickled, his nose aching as he held back his tears. In truth, Nav was just as disposable as his lovers. He probably wasn't even worth an ear-marked page in a romance novel.

He dragged his hands down the brick, dipping over each ridge and bump. He let his eyes fall shut, placing his cheek against the cool surface. He could almost imagine the roughness was the stubble of an unshaven lover — not a fuck or a hookup, but an actual lover.

Suddenly, the peace of the night was torn away from him. Air burst from his lungs as something heavy struck his back, slamming him hard into the wall. He grunted, scrambling to turn around, but hands clamped over his wrists, stopping him in his tracks. He pulled against the grip, but the hands were so strong that he felt like a doll next to their power.

The scent of cologne and fresh sweat overwhelmed him as someone pressed against his back, covering his body with theirs. He shuddered as a thrill ran up his spine. Had someone been eyeing him all night, just waiting for him to step into the alley? He rocked his ass back, more out of habit than desire.

"What's your safeword, slut?" asked a low voice that was distorted by a deep growl. He didn't recognize the voice, but his heart was pounding, sending blood whooshing through his ears.

What? It took him a moment to understand the question. He'd had a brief encounter with a man who had liked to get rough in the bedroom. He had given Nav a safeword before he'd spanked his ass red.

Struggling to find his grip on the wall, Nav racked his brain for what the word had been. It had been *years*. But he didn't want this to end. Someone was touching him, and they were so strong that he couldn't have gotten free, even if he had tried. He'd never felt so alive—not since he'd had his ass spanked while he'd sobbed and writhed on the guy's lap as they'd hurt him.

"R-red." His voice wavered and he bit his lip, his cheek smarting as he was pushed harder against the brick. The memory surged to the front of his mind. *Red for stop, yellow for slow down and green for keep going.* The ache prickled against his nerves, lighting up something inside him that had been dormant for a long time.

"You going to scream, slut?"

Nav jerked when he felt something against his clothed ass. It was hot, hard and felt absolutely massive as it ground against him, prodding between his cheeks. The guy was already like steel. How long had he been watching and waiting?

Nav shook his head, pushing his ass back against the hardness.

"Good choice, but you can scream if you want. They would all come running back here to find you pressed against the wall with your ass out like the slut you are. Would you suck me off with them watching? Would you let them watch as I fuck you? You'd moan for them, and whimper when I hit your spot."

Holy fuck. Nav gasped as he flushed, his cock filling out. That sounded like a fantasy out of his wildest dreams. He wanted—no, needed more, even though his mind was struggling to keep up.

"That's my slut," said the stranger. "Keep your hands on the wall and don't fucking move." His tone left no room for argument, not that Nav would've.

Nav could hardly breathe, let alone speak or scream, as if the stranger had his hands around Nav's neck and not his wrists. He kept his palms flat against the wall as his wrists were released. He didn't move, even as the stranger swept down his body, leaving trails of prickling flesh that left him panting for more.

Groaning, he let his eyes fall shut as the light above the alley flickered once before dying again. The stranger smelled so good, and his body felt even better against him. He hadn't *asked* Nav to stay still. He had demanded it. His toes curled in his shoes as he bit his lip. He didn't want it to end.

He jumped as the stranger fumbled with the button on Nav's jeans, flicking it open and dropping the zipper in a move that seemed so easy that it had to have been practiced. Cool air struck his heated groin and he bit back the sounds that threatened to escape.

He wasn't wearing any underwear because he hardly ever did. No underwear meant easy access for a quick fuck, and it had become almost a habit. The spring air was almost freezing as it touched him, especially since he kept his curls trimmed short.

The stranger dipped into his open jeans, scraping his nails along Nav's belly until he met the first few hairs. He split his fingers wide, avoiding Nav's throbbing cock and pressing on either side instead, cupping around him and pulling Nav back to grind his hard shaft against Nav's ass.

The stranger made a low sound of approval in his throat. "You trimmed yourself for me. Good boy."

"Fuck," said Nav, his voice so distorted with need

that he didn't even recognize himself. His cock throbbed, untouched but not forgotten, and arching to the wall as if begging for the stranger to claim him.

He ground back against the hard cock touching his ass as his pants were quickly lowered. Cold air seeped between their bodies, goosebumps breaking over his skin as a shudder worked its way up his spine. The stranger cupped his ass, squeezing and kneading until Nav was sure he would be bruised.

"You're being so good for me, slut," said the stranger, dragging his nails over Nav's flesh. "But you can't fool me. I know you're a needy whore that will beg for anyone's cock. You were waiting for me here and wondering how long I would make you wait until I filled your hole, weren't you? You can answer."

Nav *couldn't* answer except with a nod. He was floating on the edge of euphoria and starting to drift away, as if he were standing back from himself and watching as he was taken.

No one had ever treated him like that. As much as he was a disposable piece of ass, no one had ever treated him like he was nothing more than a fuck hole that needed to be filled. No one had called him a slut — at least, not to his face.

He should have probably pushed the guy away before slamming a fist into his jaw. But he wasn't going to deny himself the first thing that felt right in so many years of wrong.

Fuck me. Fuck me. He couldn't say it. He could only think it and hope that he was understood.

The stranger released his grip on Nav's ass, only to bring his hand down in a slap that was hard enough to make his ears ring and his chest constrict. Nav's cock throbbed, the head tapping the concrete wall as he jerked in surprise. A startled gasp pushed through his lips as pre-cum painted the wall, probably dripping in the dark.

It was so fucking dirty.

"Look at this. You must really want to hurt tonight," said the stranger, his voice dropping as he dipped a finger between Nav's ass cheeks. He tapped at Nav's sensitive hole, sending a bolt up Nav's spine. "Where's your plug? I told you I wasn't going to prep you."

Nav gasped, his mind racing as he spread his legs as far as he could with his jeans still trapping him. *How did I miss that memo? Was it on a coaster or a napkin?* He hadn't exactly been paying attention to anyone or anything in the club. And he could barely focus with that finger tapping his furl over and over with only a hint of pressure.

He couldn't think. *Fuck*, he couldn't even breathe.

"Fucking slut. You didn't even slick yourself up for me. I'll make you fucking scream if that's what you want." The stranger bit the top of his ear, his teeth scraping over the lobe as Nav gasped.

The voice was vaguely familiar. Someone he had spoken to in the bar? He could only remember the two women clearly...and Sasha. Or was it just another ex from his long, long list? None of his ex-fucks had ever made him feel like he was going to burst from his skin.

Nav shuddered at the sound of a belt being undone moments after the stranger pulled away. All his usual meticulous thoughts about condoms, prep and lube were out of reach. No one had ever made him feel so complete and so willing.

He heard the stranger spit, then felt something slide over his entrance. His skin buzzed, his face flushing until he was sure he was on fire. He tried to relax as the stranger's thick fingers circled his rim, spreading his spit like it was lube. He couldn't help but tense when something much larger than fingers pressed against his tight hole as the man settled against his back.

He'd taken guys without prep before, but it hadn't exactly been fun. They hadn't been as big as this guy felt, either.

The first hint of uneasiness trickled into his mind as Nav slid his hands from their fixed position. He didn't make it more than an inch before the stranger grabbed his wrists, slamming them against the wall in a harsh grip.

"Don't fucking move," he said, his voice thick. "Or I'll hold you down and fuck you. I'll hurt you so fucking good that you won't be able to hold back your screams."

Smoothing his palms back over the ragged surface, Nav let the tension drain from his body. The stranger had him and Nav wouldn't be able to screw it up.

He didn't have a choice—well he *did*. He had his safewords, and he knew that if he said 'red', everything would stop. But the *illusion* of not having a choice was making his head swim and his cock throb. He let out a long groan, pushing his ass out and leaning on his hands, planting them to the surface so he wouldn't move again.

"What's your color, slut?" the stranger asked, his voice tight, presumably from holding himself back from forcing his way inside Nav's tight hole. Nav knew that had to be the reason, because it was the same thing that he was craving. *Take me, fuck me, hold me.*

Green. So fucking green. Nav's thoughts whirled, his cock throbbing and draining the last of the blood from his brain. He had to say it. The stranger couldn't read his mind.

"G-green," said Nav, his voice still strangled with his face squished against the wall. He'd never been more green or so fucking turned on. He wanted to say more and beg the stranger to fuck him hard so he would ache for days, but his lungs were burning for air, even as he panted.

The pressure on his hole peaked and Nav forced himself to relax, pushing against the intrusion to try to welcome it into his body. For a moment, there was only pleasure as the stranger's cockhead throbbed, slowly spreading him wider and wider. Scrambling against the brick, he took a deep breath, his body going as tense as his unstretched hole.

Agony pierced him as the head finally breeched his ring, sinking inside a few inches and splitting him wide. He gritted his teeth and held on, knowing the ache would be brief and oh so worth it.

"So fucking tight," said the stranger, pausing with what felt like just the tip of his cock inside of Nav. "I hope you're ready, slut."

Nav was ready—so fucking ready. He was ready to be taken away from the club, mind and soul, and be fucked by one of the biggest cocks he'd ever felt. He was ready for anything the stranger dared to give him.

The stranger eased forward, burying his cock slowly inside Nav in one smooth thrust of blinding white pain. Nav arched, trying to pull away from the intrusion as it threatened to split him apart. His heart pounded, a scream dying in his throat as a wave of pleasure washed over him that he hadn't fully expected. It shouldn't have felt good so soon. It should have hurt so much worse.

Nav hadn't moved his hands, digging his palms into the surface in an effort to keep still, even as he longed to writhe. He wasn't sure if he wanted to pull away or get the cock deeper inside him. He just needed to move.

"Fuck, slut, you feel so good on my cock," said the stranger, his hips thankfully still against Nav's ass and giving him a few seconds to adjust.

Nav's cock throbbed from the mixture of pain and pleasure, the line between the two so thin that it had nearly faded. The stillness was killing him as something bubbled up from his core. It was like the hidden monster under his bed that only revealed itself after he'd finally stopped believing in it.

"More," said Nav, his voice barely a whisper. He couldn't say anything else.

He lurched back, slamming onto the stranger's cock and driving it an extra inch inside his body. It fucking hurt, with an ache that spread deep within him. He knew he would be feeling it and regretting it later, but he couldn't bring himself to care. He wanted more, harder and faster. He wanted everything.

"Shut up, slut. I didn't say you could talk," said the stranger as he gripped Nav's hips, pulling out then slamming back inside with enough force that it drove Nav's breath from his body. He dug his fingers into Nav's hips, tugging him onto his cock over and over. He slammed into Nav's prostate, causing a streak of pre-cum to erupt from Nav's cock.

"More," said Nav again, completely unafraid of what the stranger might do to him for disobeying. He craved the punishment and the strength that would rain down on him. He wanted to break.

"More." The word scattered into a warbled scream as the stranger finally conceded, hilting inside of him ferociously.

Nav's breath caught as he started to come, spurting onto the wall completely untouched. Shudders racked his frame as he soared higher, his orgasm stretching for what felt like an eternity.

The stranger roared, grabbing Nav's cock in a painful grip and biting into his neck like an animal. "Did I say you could come?"

Nav's orgasm slammed to an abrupt halt, his balls aching and his cock flexing in the brutal grip. The pleasure hadn't stopped, though. He cried out, driving back into the cock that was carving a place inside him, lighting up nerves he didn't even know he had. He didn't need to keep coming. He only needed his stranger's pleasure.

"Fuck." The stranger growled one last time, biting him fiercely as he stilled his hips and ground himself even deeper.

Nav felt the warm rush of cum inside him, a sensation that had been reserved for his dirtiest dreams. He'd never had a partner who he trusted enough to go bare, but he trusted this stranger.

"I should lock you in a cage. You don't deserve to come," he said, panting against Nav's neck. He squeezed Nav's cock one last time before he released his grip, dipping his hand under Nav's shirt.

"I'm going to pierce that cock of yours and chain it to this—"

The stranger went stiff as he touched Nav's peaked nipple. Nav shivered as those warm fingertips hesitated over his bud. He was still throbbing, his interrupted orgasm building as if it had never started.

"Where is… What?"

The stranger grasped his shoulder, spinning Nav

around until his back was pressed to the rough brick. His shirt had ridden up, his lower back scraping against the raw surface. He groaned as the stranger's thick cock was tugged from his hole, leaving him aching and empty. Cum dribbled from it, slicking his thighs and soaking into his pants that were still trapped around his knees.

The light in the alley flickered, then buzzed to life, casting a warm glow in the darkness. An ache crept up Nav's spine as his eyes went wide.

"T-Trick," Nav stuttered, his mouth dropping open. His beautiful, kind and quiet neighbor, who had barely said more than a few sentences to him in his entire life, was pinning him to the wall. His blond hair was mussed, with sweat beaded at his temples as he panted, his minty breath dancing over Nav's skin. His beautiful blue eyes were wide, and his mouth was agape with a look of absolute shock.

How? What? Nav struggled to comprehend what he was seeing. He couldn't believe that the best fuck of his life had come from the man he'd been crushing on since he'd moved into his apartment. But if Trick had been watching and waiting for him to go into the alley, then why the hell did he look so shocked?

Nav's stomach sank.

The door to the alley slammed open, shattering the relative silence with a burst of dance music. Trick jumped, clutching at Nav's waist as he turned to the sound. His cock was still poking out of his jeans, the head glistening with a pearl of cum that hadn't shot itself into Nav. Nav's cock was nearly touching Trick's, pre-cum beaded at the surface as it strained toward his lover.

Nav finally looked to the open door when Trick's breath quickened into absolute panic. He recognized the person in the door, whose slim build was so similar to his own. In the darkness, they could have been the same person, him and Theo.

Trick's fiancé took a step into the alley, his shocked expression settling on them as the light flickered above. His gaze snapped from Trick to Nav, then to their bare cocks that were nearly touching.

"What the fuck?" Theo yelled, the sound echoing in the tiny alley. His face crumpled as he turned back to the club, the door slamming behind him as he fled into the thrumming music.

Nav wavered as Trick stepped back. Trick's hands had been the only thing keeping him from hitting the ground, and without them, he was powerless. He whimpered as his ass hit the mottled concrete, the ache monumental. Trick's gaze never strayed from the door as he took a stumbling step toward it.

The door opened and slammed a second time as Trick disappeared through it, leaving Nav alone with the dim whisper of music. The alley light spluttered and went out.

Chapter Three

Nav

Nav's phone vibrated again, humming on the thin wood of his cheap nightstand. That was the third time it had hummed since he'd blinked awake to the frigid light of dawn. The first two times, he hadn't even considered moving.

Flopping his hand toward the sound, he brushed his phone, accidentally pushing it off his nightstand. It thumped onto the linoleum, turning end over end before it settled back on the floor, buzzing again as it came to a halt. The sound was worse than a hammer against the jagged rumbling of his thoughts.

He scooted toward the sound, determined to silence it before his aching body split itself in two.

"Fuck," he shouted, curling in on himself as agony made itself known in every part of his body. His head throbbed with the beginnings of a hangover, his mouth dryer than it should have been after three beers.

Perhaps the five shots he'd pounded back after he'd dragged himself home had been the culprit.

Either way, the pain in his head was nothing to the pain in his ass. It felt like he'd been fucked to within an inch of his life with next-to-no lube — which was exactly what had happened.

Despite the additional drinks, he remembered every moment in the dark alley that had smelled of garbage and sex. He could still feel Trick's hands on him, pushing him to the wall and clamping down on his cock as he'd begun to come. He remembered the feeling of Trick's cum dribbling out of his ass and slicking his thighs.

He remembered the freedom and the stillness in his thoughts.

It had been like Trick had given him a joint and he'd taken the biggest hit of his life. His thoughts had been so clear and his mind quiet as Trick had sunk into him. Then it had come crashing down.

What the hell is wrong with me?

He'd let Trick do *that* to him and take total control. He hadn't even *known* it was Trick. How could he give himself to a stranger like that and let himself be marked, inside and out?

Trick's cum was still there, a crusted flakiness on his thighs that he hadn't been able to bring himself to wash. Just thinking about it made his heart beat faster and his chest go tight.

What the hell is wrong with me?

He slid his hand down his body, tracing the bruises left by Trick. A spot on his hip was swollen and warm to the touch, but his cock was the place that ached, the shaft bruised from Trick's fierce grip. Nav shuddered, his memory alone sending a rush of blood to his cock.

Something is seriously wrong with me. He didn't want to know how hard he would get if he touched his hole.

The phone buzzed again and Nav leaned over, swallowing dryly as his stomach twisted. He grasped the phone, accepting the call and putting it on speaker before carefully rolling back until his head hit the pillow. Taking a deep breath, he let his eyes fall shut, waiting for the earth to stabilize.

He needed to invest in better black-out curtains once he could move again.

"Hello?" Nav asked, his voice brittle and cracked, like his throat had been fucked and not his ass.

"Holy shit, man, are you okay? You disappeared last night, then you ghosted me." Sasha's voice rang out into the room, his voice still deep with layers of sleep.

"Sorry, Sash," said Nav, running a hand through his hair before turning his head into the pillow. He'd never been more grateful that he'd had the sense to splurge on a high-end pillow. If he tried hard enough, he could probably disappear onto its softness and wait it out until he was magically clean and healed.

Unable to hold back any longer, he shifted, moving a hand under his boxers that he'd put on before bed, and down to his rim before delicately tracing over himself with one fingertip. He bit back a whimper. He was swollen, and wet too, still full of cum from the night before. And he hadn't been that sore since he'd signed up for an orgy and things had gotten a little carried away.

"I'm okay," said Nav, forcing the words past his gritted teeth. The last thing he wanted was for Sasha to storm over to his place and play nurse or bodyguard. The last time Sasha had made him food, Nav had ended up with food poisoning. He could only dread his other nursing skills. "The bar was too much for me last night, so I came home to drown my sorrows in shitty whiskey and passed out on the floor. I'm so fucking hungover."

"Shit. I should've cut you off sooner," said Sasha, letting out a sigh. "I didn't think you'd be so determined to get hammered, because you usually don't give a shit when you break it off with someone. Everette must've been something else."

"Yeah, I guess so," said Nav, retreating from his pillow and rolling over to the edge of the bed. His bladder was primed to explode, and he would never live that down. "His dad was hot as fuck, and he took cock like a champ." He *had* taken Nav's cock like a winner, but he could barely remember his orgasm.

His ass twinged and he bit back his gasp. He hadn't come the night before, and it was still more memorable than any fucks he'd had in the past year.

"I did *not* need to know that," said Sasha with a groan. "If you fuck his sister, or even his mom, then you can tell me all about it, but leave the dicks out of it."

"You are so fucking straight," said Nav, grabbing the phone and easing slowly off the bed. He was breathing shallowly, and his head swam as he glanced down at himself. He was a mess in more ways than one.

He shuffled across the bedroom, leaning against the doorway until the room settled back on its axis. The rough trim scraped against his over-sensitized flesh as he trembled.

"And you are so gay," said Sasha, letting out a snort. "But that's why I love you, man. We are made for each other. With my pussy skills and your cock ones, we will take over the world."

Nav grunted, gripping the wall before taking another step. Even his balls were throbbing, like he was suffering from the biggest case of blue balls in history. His cock swelled at the memory of Trick's unforgiving grip that had strangled his orgasm as he'd started to shoot. *Wrong, so fucking wrong.* His chest went tight.

"I'm gonna let you go, man," said Sasha on the edge of a yawn. "Call me later and we can chat."

Nav nodded, despite the fact that Sasha couldn't see him, before the call ended with a click. He should have been thrilled about another wicked round of sex under his belt, but he couldn't feel anything past the weight in his chest.

He forced himself to swallow as he stumbled into the bathroom, his tongue sticking to the nasty film on the roof of his mouth. Reaching for the glass by the sink, he filled it from the tap and brought it to his lips. No matter how long he ran it, it never really got cold, and it always tasted stale.

He forced two full glasses past his lips as he relieved himself, before filling a third and carrying it out to the living room. He flinched as he lowered himself to the sofa. The couch was soft, with some of the fluffiest cushions that could be found on a sofa, but it was still too firm. Maybe he should have parked his ass on an actual goose. It was bound to be softer than feather pillows.

Pulling himself back to his feet, he let out a resigned sigh. He'd been sore after rough fucks before, but this was something beyond. He hoped he wasn't actually damaged in any way, because that was a trip to the doctor that he was not willing to make. He was determined to keep the doctor away from his ass until his first prostate exam was due at the ripe age of fifty.

Standing in the living room, he slowly looked around. His clothes were spread around, and a few shot glasses were still sitting out on the counter. The bottle of whiskey was open, its contents tainting the air.

"What's your color, slut?"

A shiver swept down his body and his cock throbbed, his balls already aching and full. That name, *slut*, should have pissed him off, but instead it gave him a dark thrill that made his groin pulse and his knees tremble.

He wanted it again—every bit of it—the fear, the helplessness and the pain. Was it wrong? Well, it certainly wasn't right. But how could something wrong feel so much like perfection?

A gentle tap on his door pulled him from his thoughts. He blinked, looking toward the sound. How long had he been standing there reliving something that he probably should have been trying to forget?

He adjusted himself in his boxers, not even bothering to retrieve a shirt. His cock was still a bit swollen, but the delivery people were used to him answering the door in all states of undress. One had even approved by sucking Nav's cock before Nav signed for his package. That had been one hell of a delivery.

The superintendent hadn't been quite as impressed, giving him her patented raised eyebrow. She'd pursed her lips before she'd given him a look that should have been reserved for street pigeons.

"Coming," he called out as the quiet knock came again. Limping to the door, he fumbled with the lock as it jammed halfway. He wiggled the latch, twisting it until it finally came free, before spinning the knob under his hand and pulling the door wide.

Light from the hallway rushed in, temporarily blinding him and sending a fresh throb into his skull. He clutched at the door frame as the floor tilted and spots danced in his vision. He took a deep breath, willing it to fade. The strong smell of the neighbor-down-the-hall's cooking did nothing to quell his sudden burst of nausea.

"Trick," he said, his voice barely a whisper as he took in the sight of his neighbor standing at his door, his hand still raised halfway through a knock.

Trick looked terrible, with black bags under his eyes and skin so pale that it was nearly transparent. His bloodshot and swollen eyes made it look like he was either stoned or he'd been crying for most of the night. He looked almost as bad as Nav felt.

Nav shifted, a throb curling up the base of his spine. *Almost.*

"Can I come in?" asked Trick. His eyes went wider as he gave Nav a once-over.

Nav had tried to picture what their next meeting would have been like, but he never would have imagined that it would have happened so soon. If Trick wanted seconds, it was not happening, no matter what Nav's cock had to say about it.

"I understand if you're not comfortable with me in your apartment," said Trick, looking up and down the hall. "I can leave if that's what you want, but I just needed to make sure you were okay."

Am I okay? Nav had no idea how to even go about answering that. The night before hadn't been just sex. Sex never left him feeling so out of control — so lost. But Trick seemed to *care.* And it didn't sound like he was coming around for seconds.

"Yeah," said Nav, stepping back and waving Trick in. His heart picked up as the blond stepped into his apartment, self-consciousness slamming into him, which hadn't happened since high school. "Just let me grab some clothes."

He limped to the bedroom, grabbing the nearest pair of pajama pants. He didn't wear them except for when

Sasha was over, which was probably why they were almost new.

He grunted as he lifted his legs into the pants before pulling the drawstring as tight as he dared. The next few days were going to be hell.

When he staggered his way back to the living room, Trick was still standing two steps inside the door. He wasn't even looking around with curiosity or judgement, or nosily peering at any of Nav's paintings. The moment Nav entered the room, Trick's gaze fixed on him, his eyes wide and frightened.

Nav stuttered to a halt. *How could Trick be afraid of me?* Trick was so much bigger and stronger. Nav had nothing on him.

"You should call the police," said Trick, clenching his fists at his sides. His arms flexed under his thin long-sleeve shirt, giving Nav a peek of how much power Trick contained.

That would explain the fear.

Nav had wanted it—every single fucking second of blissful agony. He'd had a safeword, and he hadn't used it for a reason. Hell, he wanted it again, only not until his ass felt better and definitely with an extra-large side order of lube.

"Why?" asked Nav, shuffling over to the couch before remembering that he couldn't sit. He looked down at himself as Trick's gaze dropped to his chest. The bruises on his hips stood out like vivid ink against a fair background. He was painted with them.

"Have a seat and I'll get you a coffee," said Nav, needing the escape that the kitchen provided. Morning afters were the bane of his existence. But whatever Trick thought had happened—Nav had to clear the air.

Trick looked at the couch as if he had no idea what it was. Maybe it was the shiny red pleather upholstery, or the fact that it looked like Nav had pulled it out of a dumpster. He *had* pulled it out of a dumpster, actually. But he hadn't been able to let it stay in the trash when it was the most beautifully tacky couch he'd ever seen. And it fit his décor like a penguin in the jungle, so of course he'd instantly fallen in love with it.

"W-why?" Trick stammered, grasping the edge of the couch as he started to waver. "I-I...I f-forced—"

"No, you didn't." Nav slammed a mug down on the counter, a tiny crack piercing the shiny porcelain. "What we did...it wasn't that." It was the one thing that he was certain of. He had wanted it, and he hadn't even put up a fight. He knew he would have done the exact same thing again if he had the chance.

"Fuck." Trick crumpled onto the couch, dropping his head onto his hands. He carved his fingers through his hair, a few blond hairs pulling free and falling to the cushion.

"I'm okay," said Nav, slowly inching his way back into the living room. His chest constricted and he grasped his hands together. He was used to dealing with heartache. Breaking up with a shit-ton of people had given him that skill, but no one had ever acted like Trick before. He wasn't sure if a hug would have been the right move, but it looked as if Trick was about to start crying at any second.

"I'm okay," Nav said again. Trick looked up at his words, his bloodshot eyes shimmering.

"I'm so fucking sorry, Nav. I don't know how I could have thought that you were him." He shook his head, his voice wavering. "He's never made noises like that. He's never begged for more...for pain. I should have known something was wrong right away, but it was just so fucking hot. I didn't even realize until I touched your nipple and it wasn't pierced." He swallowed, the

43

click of his throat loud in the room. "But it wasn't him —
It was you, and I forced you. *Fuck*."

Nav stepped to the couch as his stomach
plummeted. He dropped to his knees and clasped
Tricks shaking hands in his. He wasn't sure why his
own hands were so steady when his heart was beating
so fast or why he was kneeling in front of Trick, his
knees aching on his hard floors. It just felt right. It was
the only thing that had felt right since he'd woken up
alone.

"I wanted it," said Nav, trying to look Trick in the
eye. It was harder than it should have been. "You
checked in with me twice, remember? You asked me
what my safeword was, and my color. I could have
stopped you but I didn't, because I didn't want you to
stop." His toes curled against his will, and he dropped
his gaze, unable to keep eye contact as his face flushed.

Nav hadn't known that Trick hadn't realized who he
was until Theo had shouted at them in surprise and
shock.

"Shit. How is your fiancé?" *I shouldn't be here.* The
floor was suddenly too hard and his heart beating too
fast. *It was a mistake. Trick didn't want me after all because
I was supposed to be Theo. Just another fucking mistake.*

Nav shoved himself to his feet, wincing as he
accidentally smacked his ass against the edge of the
couch in his haste. A whimper escaped through his lips
as he reached back automatically. How could every
little touch hurt so fucking much when it had felt so
good the night before?

"You're hurt," said Trick, standing from the couch
much smoother than Nav had. "I hurt you." His gaze
darkened as Nav winced again as he found another
bruise along his lower back just above his tailbone.

"Nothing I didn't ask for," said Nav, forcing his lips into a smile. It didn't last long.

"Part of what should have happened last night was aftercare," said Trick, his voice sounding steady for the first time. "You can still call the cops…or kick me out. Say the word and you won't see me again, but can I just make sure you're okay first? Can I give that to you, at least?"

Nav took a step back. The term 'aftercare' sounded vaguely familiar, but he wasn't really sure what it was. He tried to recall what had happened after his epic spanking years earlier but came up blank.

"What would that entail?" He shifted back another step. He should have grabbed a shirt, and maybe a housecoat, too. Trick saw every bruise and mark. It was too much.

"Have you had a scene like that before? Something that was that intense?" Trick asked, holding his ground and thankfully not stepping toward him. The small amount of space between them made it a touch easier to breathe, even if Nav longed to close the distance.

"I've never scened before." The word felt foreign in his mouth. Was that what the spanking had been? It sounded like some sort of film term, not what had happened in the alley. The word did nothing to describe the strange rush of euphoria.

Trick froze before he let out a soft 'oh'.

"After a scene, particularly an intense one, I like to hold my partner and speak with them about what happened and how we both felt about it. I offer anything they need and check them for injuries if they are comfortable. It helps to bring both of us down." The way he spoke sounded like he'd read it in a book a thousand times. There was none of the emotion that

Nav knew was hiding behind his carefully constructed mask.

"Like snuggling? I'm not much of a snuggler," said Nav. He was more of a fuck and flee kind of guy. Sleeping in someone's bed or sticking around after sex was too dangerous. The longer he stayed with someone, the more likely their feelings would become contagious.

"It's more than that," said Trick, his expression unreadable. "Scenes can heighten your emotions and leave you raw and ragged, emotionally and physically. Aftercare helps with stability for both partners."

"You want to make sure I'm okay. No—you *need* to make sure I'm okay, because you aren't," said Nav.

It suddenly made sense. Nav and Theo weren't the only ones who had gotten a shock. Trick had, too. And instead of Trick's usual routine, he was apparently descending into some kind of emotional spiral.

"Is that why...?" Nav trailed off and slid a hand over his chest. Is that why his chest felt so heavy and everything around him was dull? The moments in the alley were so vivid that everything else paled in comparison.

"Yes," said Trick, taking a step.

Nav let him. He was willing to do anything to get the weight off his chest that was making it harder and harder to breathe. His skin prickled, and he could almost feel Trick's gaze against his skin, so much softer than his hands had been.

"I feel it too, Nav." Trick took another step until he was close enough to touch. He touched his own chest along his sternum, tapping the same spot where Nav ached. "Let me give you aftercare. Please."

Nav let out a breath, shutting his eyes. "Okay."

Chapter Four

Trick

"Can I touch you?" Trick couldn't believe how steady his voice was. Inside, he was crumbling, his narrow grip on his control slipping.

His stomach flopped. He still couldn't believe that he'd had sex with Nav, his cute neighbor who had caught his eye on more than one occasion. He was allowed to look, and sometimes, Theo encouraged him to do just that, but he'd never imagined putting his hands on anyone else — especially Nav.

"I've never scened before." The words played over in his head, hammering another nail in his coffin with each word. The dark pit threatening to consume him grew larger, something that had never happened with Theo. But they had never done something so *extreme*.

He couldn't imagine how Nav was feeling. Unlike Trick, he hadn't signed up for anything, and he hadn't had someone to support him as he came down. Trick had left him there — alone.

How could I be so fucking stupid?

Nav didn't even look like Theo. Their hair was close, and they were about the same height and build, but Nav was soft everywhere that Theo was hard. Theo was all lean muscle from his time at the gym. His hands were callused, and he had the grin of someone who had seen too much but had pushed through it, anyway.

When Nav had touched him, with hands so soft they couldn't have been real, Trick had almost lost it. The sounds Nav had made and the way he'd submitted, asking for *more*, was something that he never could have imagined with Theo.

Trick had never felt so fucking high — and he'd never crashed so hard, either.

"Did you shower already?" asked Trick. He hadn't been able to stop himself from looking at Nav's body when Nav had answered the door in nothing but a tight pair of boxers. He'd seen every bruise, every scratch and every stain he'd left. He refused to admit how beautiful his marks looked on Nav's pale skin.

Nav shook his head with the tiniest movement. He furrowed his forehead and rested a hand on his pale hip where a particularly dark bruise lay.

Finally giving in to his need for contact, Trick reached for him, sliding his fingers onto Nav's delicate palm. The change was immediate as Nav relaxed before his eyes, dropping his shoulders and fluttering his eyelids shut.

Trick caught the scent of unwashed flesh that matched the stickiness on his own skin. He had refused to shower, even after Theo had screamed at him for it. He didn't want to wash the evidence away if Nav did want to press charges. He wasn't going to hide.

"I was too drunk to shower last night, and I woke up just before you knocked," said Nav, opening his eyes but keeping his gaze fixed on the floor.

Trick's stomach dropped even further. He'd smelled alcohol in the alley but had shrugged it off. They had been outside of a bar, after all.

"You'd been drinking?" asked Trick, his voice sharpening. He cringed as Nav flinched. "Jesus." He took a deep breath, trying to calm himself. There was a reason that he didn't allow alcohol or drugs anywhere near a scene. The tally of his fuck-ups was getting bigger.

"Would you be okay if I bathe you? I think that would be good for both of us, but only if you're comfortable. You say the word, and I'll get out of here." Trick really hoped Nav didn't kick him out. He couldn't allow Nav to be alone until he had stabilized.

Nav nodded again, his gaze never lifting from the floor. He was so fucking submissive, and it seemed to come naturally for him. There was no hesitance in his eyes or disgust as Trick squeezed his hand, leading him farther into the apartment.

The layout looked almost identical to his own place, even though the floors and walls were completely different. Trick glanced at a massive canvas perched on the wall next to where he assumed the bathroom door was.

Landscapes weren't usually something that caught his eye, but this one was exceptional. The trees were twisted and desolate with stripped bark and bare branches that forked their way into the pale sky. Between the uncovered roots, and almost hidden from view, was a fawn. It was the only thing on the canvas that had any life, but it spoke of such hope that it infused the entire canvas with unparalleled vibrance.

Tearing his eyes away, he dropped Nav's hand as they entered the small bathroom. It was tight with two people in the tiny floorspace. As much as his skin crawled, begging to be clean, Nav came first.

Nav glanced between the pale ivory tub and Trick, biting his lip with a frown.

"Bath or shower?" asked Trick, scooting along the wall to give Nav more space.

Nav hadn't seemed to be worried about his near-nudity when he'd answered the door. He'd either had enough confidence that it simply hadn't mattered — or he was hiding himself beneath too many layers for Trick to see.

"Shower, I think. The bath really isn't big enough for anyone taller than five foot five," said Nav, letting out a breath before he dropped his hands to the waistband of his pajama pants. He looked over his shoulder to meet Trick's gaze, and Trick caught the first flicker of worry.

"Did you want me to undress you?" asked Trick, trying to keep the eagerness out of his voice. He needed to touch and hold, but he wasn't going to do anything Nav wasn't comfortable with. He'd already done too much.

Trick enjoyed bathing his sub after any scene. It was the only time Trick wanted to be on his knees, as he stripped his sub's clothes from their body, worshiping each flawed inch with wonder and awe.

"I don't know," said Nav, chewing at his lip. He played with the drawstrings on his pants. They had come untied, and the pajamas were just barely holding onto his hips.

"If you need me to stop, just say so and I will." Trick took a step forward, leaving the door open behind him so the room didn't feel any smaller than it already was. Sliding his hands over Nav's, he tugged the waistband of the pajamas down. As they crept over Nav's pale hips, he looped his thumbs in the elastic of Nav's boxers, inching them down at the same time.

Time slowed as Nav was revealed in all his glory — a perfection that Trick hadn't had a chance to admire. Nav's hips were narrow, and fit perfectly in his hands, and his skin was smoother than anything Trick had ever felt. Swallowing back his urge to explore, Trick kept his hands on Nav's clothes.

His gaze dropped to Nav's groin as it was slowly bared to the open air. He should have looked away and tried to keep his attentions professional and limited, but his instincts were screaming at him to do the opposite. Nav didn't need his indifference. He needed a gentle touch, so he would know that he could be loved just as easily as he could be broken.

Nav's pubic hair was neatly trimmed, and shorter than Theo usually kept his. Trick had always preferred a bit of hair as opposed to the smooth landscape that some men kept. It gave him something he could run his hands through or feel against his nose when he went down on his partner.

Nav's cock was fucking perfect. He was cut and completely soft, lying against his sac that was a few shades darker than his pale thighs. Trick bit back his desire to see what Nav looked like when he was erect, with pre-cum pearling at the tip of his cock and leaking down the shaft.

I have a fiancé. His relationship was not open, even if they liked to pretend every once and a while. He took a slow breath, shuddering when the thick smell of Nav filled his senses.

"Does it hurt?" asked Trick, his words failing him as he stared at Nav's cock. He remembered squeezing it when he'd felt him start to come, Nav's walls clamping down to milk his cock. He had been so high and so far gone that he had probably squeezed too hard. He never would have dreamed of being that rough with Theo.

"Not too bad, actually. I'm surprised it doesn't feel worse," said Nav, his voice eerily calm. A trembling breath gave him away, though.

Trick dropped his focus lower, to the crusted white stains on Nav's thighs. "Fuck." He traced them with his fingertips, the patch of dried cum rough against the otherwise-smooth skin. Nav shivered at his touch, his cock swelling before Trick's eyes.

Let go. Don't touch him like that. He couldn't stop. That was *his* cum on those pristine thighs, and probably still inside Nav, owning every part of him. Trick's cock throbbed, caught in his tight jeans that he'd worn to the bar.

"I'll start the water," said Trick, finally managing to force his hands away. His fingertips burned, begging to return to Nav's skin. "Is it okay if I take my shirt off?"

Nav nodded, letting out a soft sigh as Trick turned the tap and the sound of rushing water flooded the room. It didn't take long before steam started to rise, condensing against the cool tiles and mirror.

Trick pulled his shirt from his body and Nav stepped under the spray, the first burst of water ricocheting gently off his chest and splattering against Trick's naked chest. Goosebumps speckled along Nav's skin, his nipples peaking from the sensation.

"Can I wash you?" asked Trick, waiting for Nav's nod before grabbing a blue loofa from the hook in the shower and squirting a dollop of body wash on it. It smelled sweet with a hint of coconut that brought memories of sunshine and the beach.

The first touch to Nav's damp skin was Trick's undoing.

Nav was attractive enough when he was dry, but with water dripping over every naked inch of his body, Trick's cock went completely solid in his jeans. There was even a distant pang of loss as he gently scrubbed Nav's thighs, cleaning the flakes of dried cum from his skin.

What I would give to paint him white again, over his thighs and in his ass. Trick shook his head, pressing the heel of his hand against his groin to try to squish it into submission. Moisture from his damp hand soaked into his jeans, painting the material dark.

Nav had tilted his head back, water rushing over his hair and rinsing the suds from his body. Trick bit his lip at the sight, wondering how long he had before Nav noticed the tent in his jeans. How long until he kicked Trick to the curb? *Get a hold of yourself.*

"Turn around," said Trick, his voice thick, even to his own ears. Nav turned without hesitation, brushing his hair back from his forehead before facing the wall. Moving his hands to the surface, Nav slid his palms against the tile with his fingers stretched wide. He shifted, spreading his legs until Trick was gifted a quick glimpse of his puckered hole.

Nav's ass was even more beautiful than his cock, with pert cheeks that looked perfect for squeezing. Bruises dotted each globe with darker prints along his hips and a bright scrape over his lower back.

Keep control. Trick palmed his cock, adjusting it so it tucked up under his waistband. He remembered gripping Nav's ass, kneading the pert flesh and wondering when Theo had gained the extra bit of softness. It had quickly slipped his mind when he'd found an unstretched and unlubed hole to sink his cock into.

He passed the loofa down Nav's back, trailing a line of scented bubbles over his wet skin. He heard the little gasp as Nav shifted, spreading his thighs wider until the view of his hole was clear.

"Oh fuck." Trick let out a groan. Nav's entrance was swollen and pink, with a blush of vibrant red in the middle.

The loofa slipped from Trick's fingers as he let his instincts take full control. He couldn't be a good Dom and hold himself back from what he needed and what his body was telling him Nav needed as well. Trailing a fingertip over Nav's swollen bud, Trick let out a second groan. It was hot to the touch and so soft that he just wanted to slip inside and *feel*. Nav let out a loud gasp, his back arching as he slid his hands on the wall, shifting his legs even wider.

"Does it hurt?" Trick asked, rubbing the red furl ever so gently, and watching as it flinched and relaxed under his touch. He licked his lips, moving as close as the edge of the tub would allow. Water struck him, dripping from his arms down to his sides and soaking into the top of his jeans.

"Fuck, yes. I don't think I've ever hurt this bad," said Nav, arching his back farther as Trick continued his slow caress.

"Did you want me to stop?" Trick asked, unable to look away.

Nav pushed his ass out, meeting Trick's touch. "Don't stop."

Trick let loose a feral groan, dipping his fingertip slowly into the center of Nav's furl. Nav parted as he eased inside, the red flush flaring bright as he moved deeper. Curling his finger, he probed along Nav's inner walls, shuddering as the swollen flesh clung to every bit of him. "I have to check to make sure I didn't damage anything."

Is that what I'm doing? He was only certain that he wasn't able to stop. And as Nav pushed back, meeting every movement, Trick knew that it was exactly what Nav needed. An earthquake could have brought the apartment down around them, and the rescue team would have found Trick's finger still jammed into Nav's ass.

He moved so slowly that he was sure his cock would expire by the time he was knuckle-deep. Nav throbbed around him, squeezing him so tight that his finger tingled. He couldn't imagine his cock fitting in Nav's hole. How had Nav ever taken him?

But he had.

A whine cut into the room over the sound of the shower as Trick pulled out until only the very tip of his finger was left inside. He stared at the spot where they were connected, looking for any sign of blood. There was no blood, but there was a hint of something white in the furl of his knuckle.

It was his cum, still wet and still inside.

"Fuck," said Trick, dropping to his knees before he licked the exposed part of his finger, sucking his own cum from the surface. Nav whimpered, bucking back when Trick flicked his tongue over the edge of his hole. Nav's cock caught his eye, bouncing as he bucked. Nav was rock-hard, his veined shaft red and the head a purplish hue with a bead of pre-cum clinging to it.

"Where's your room?" asked Trick, pulling his fingertip free and reaching to shut the water off. His own taste, mixed with one that he could only presume was Nav's, slid across his tongue, trapping his mind in an unshaking grip.

Grabbing a towel, he wrapped it around Nav's trembling body as Nav started to shiver in earnest. Goosebumps prickled over his pale skin, begging for Trick's touch. Nav looked over his shoulder, his pupils blown wide and his lower lip red where it was caught between his teeth.

Trick dipped down, breathing in the scent of Nav's skin. "Let me take you to bed."

Chapter Five

Nav

Trick's finger in his ass had stung so fucking much that Nav thought he was going to split apart all over again. Then Trick had leaned in and sucked his own cum from Nav's ass, like he was a fucking candy dispenser.

Nav trembled with arousal as he was wrapped in a towel, stumbling to the bed with Trick's scent enveloping him. He couldn't bear the thought of being fucked, but he still followed Trick to the bed. He could barely speak through the want echoing in his body.

Something bloomed in his chest, a calmness settling over him in the same way it had in the alley. *Why do I trust him?* Even when Trick had been a stranger, Nav had still trusted him. He let himself sink into the feeling, refusing to let go of it, even as Trick pushed him to the bed.

Hurt me. He couldn't say it. *But how can I?* How could he even begin to explain that he wanted Trick inside him again, even if it was just his finger? He needed that raw edge of pain to send him even higher, until every hollow bit of him was filled to the brim.

"Lie back," said Trick as he pulled at his jeans, tossing the sodden clothing on the floor with a *splat*. Nav's gaze dropped to Trick's barely contained cock that was straining against the black fabric of his boxers. He looked as big as Nav had imagined, with a watery stain near the hidden head that didn't look like it had come from the shower.

Swallowing, Nav scooted back, letting his head drop against his pillow. His aches faded as his thoughts sharpened, his headache drifting away, until he knew exactly what he wanted.

"Will you fuck me again?" Nav asked, his voice coming from somewhere else. Trick frowned, then shook his head, even as his eyes went dark. "Did I do something wrong?" asked Nav. His heart picked up, his skin prickling from the sudden chill as his towel fell away.

Trick caressed his body, searing his flesh. "You are being so good for me. Did you know that?" He slipped his hands around Nav, pulling him close as he lowered himself on the bed. "You've already given me so much. Let me take care of you now."

Nav sank into the embrace, nuzzling into Trick's chest. The man was built, with a body to die for and perfectly tanned skin that smelled as delicious as it looked. The last of his control started to slip as a haziness fogged his thoughts.

"You think I'm good?" asked Nav, furrowing his forehead as he tried to concentrate. Sure, he was a hard worker, a decent artist and had an eye for detail that others envied, but he wasn't *good*.

Trick hummed, sweeping up Nav's damp back before settling his hand in Nav's dripping hair. He tugged softly, pulling Nav by his tresses until their gazes met. Trick's blue eyes looked so much clearer than they had when he'd first knocked on the door. His pale pallor had given way to his natural tan, and his lips were bright and wet.

"You are good," said Trick, holding Nav's hair tight. "Last night, you took me so well, and gave me more than I could have ever hoped for. When I pushed inside you, I hurt you, but you took it all for me. I know you'd let me fuck you again, and you'd take every bit of pain and pleasure I gave you, simply because it's mine to give."

"Yes," said Nav, his mouth dry and his eyes watering.

"Good boy," said Trick, the words sending a warm glow straight to Nav's belly. It sucked in the darkness, rendering it null and void. It didn't give him the same rush of endorphins that the sex had, but something else entirely — something so much deeper.

"Good boys get to come," said Trick, his voice dipping lower.

Nav shuddered as Trick leaned back just enough to move his hand between their heated bodies. Nav's cock flexed, begging for attention and already dripping. *When did I get hard?* The moments in the shower had gone blurry.

"You said sluts don't get to come," said Nav, his words shaky and quiet. "Am I still a slut?" That word gave him a different kind of thrill that was closer to the freedom that he had tasted in the alley. *Can I be both?*

"You are what I say you are," said Trick, moving his rough palms down Nav's flat belly to his trimmed groin. He scratched at the short hairs there, sending shivers of pleasure up Nav's body. Nav bucked, his cock smacking the back of Trick's hand.

"That's my good boy. You listen so well. Tell me... Could you come again without my hand on your cock? You tried to in the alley." Trick circled the base of Nav's cock, caressing his groin, but never touching the shaft. Nav jerked his hips again.

"Please," said Nav, biting his lip and pressing his face into Trick's chest. He took a deep breath, relishing the deep scent of Trick's skin. He was so warm, so hard and so fucking perfect. Nav's imagination had never come close to the real man in his bed.

"Answer, slut," said Trick, his words sending Nav higher. "Don't make me repeat myself."

"I can come with one finger in my ass," said Nav, flushing. "That's all I need."

It was a skill, and he was proud of it, but saying it out loud had a sudden shyness curling around him. What if Trick didn't think it was a good thing?

"Good boy. Such a sweet boy for me." Trick rolled them until Nav was pinned under his weight, his legs wide on either side of Trick's hips. Nav bucked up, aiming for Trick's covered cock that hovered so close to his own, but Trick laughed, leaning away and shaking his head.

"Take what I give you, good boy, and I'll let you come. You deserve it, for being so good for me." Trick dropped down, mouthing at Nav's neck as he moved his hand between Nav's ass cheeks. "What's your color?"

"Green," Nav immediately breathed out with a burst of air. He didn't even have to think about it. He just *knew*.

A moment later, Trick prodded at his rim, sinking his finger inside with a burst of fire and an ache that made his toes curl. Whining, Nav fisted the sheets as he tried to relax.

"Does it hurt?" asked Trick, sucking the sensitive spot above Nav's collar bone.

Nav nodded, staggered breaths bursting from his lips as Trick moved inside of him, dragging against his bruised walls. He felt so stretched and full, even with a single finger.

"Good. You are so beautiful when you hurt for me," said Trick. His eyes sparkled as his face flushed with arousal.

"More," said Nav, unable to hold himself back. His cock throbbed, the head nearly purple and weeping steadily.

"You'll take what I give you—no more, no less. I can't listen to a slut like you. You could have hurt yourself last night, but I won't let any harm come to you now that you're mine."

Nav arched, a ragged scream tearing itself from his throat as his orgasm ripped through him. Milky cum shot over his belly, a few stray beads spurting onto Trick's chest and cut abs, tangling in the coarse blond hair.

"Good boy," said Trick, rumbling in Nav's ear as he closed his eyes and panted through his release.

Nav lolled in a haze as Trick withdrew before pulling him close. Trick spoke, but Nav could barely keep up with the words or what they could possibly mean. He shuddered when Trick moved away for a moment, grabbing the discarded towel and wiping them both clean.

The bed shifted and a blanket fluttered under Nav's chin. "Stay?"

"As long as you need." Trick settled back against him as Nav let himself go.

Chapter Six

Trick

Trick glanced at his phone as it vibrated on the arm of the stiff couch, the melodic buzz making his heart flutter. Theo was next to him, looking comfier than necessary on the rigid cushions, leaving only a few options as to who the caller was.

He slid his hand toward the phone, lifting it up while sending Theo a quick glance. His fiancé was sharp and would catch him if his gaze lingered too long.

Swallowing dryly, he looked down at his lap. He shouldn't have to feel guilty that he'd made a friend, even if their friendship had started because of an accidental fuck. It was only later that he'd found out that Nav was one of the easiest people to talk to that he'd ever met.

He glanced at the screen, a smile sneaking onto his face as he saw Nav's text.

Just got home. How do people do this nine-to-five shit?

Sending a second glance at Theo, who was still mesmerized by the baking show on the screen, Trick typed out his response. Usually Trick would have been enthralled right along with Theo, but not when his thoughts were fifty feet away in a different apartment.

Not all of us are workaholics like you. Anything exciting?

One of the many things that Trick had learned about Nav was that his work schedule was enough to make a trucker weep. Nav had been complaining daily since his boss had cut his hours nearly in half.

Trick stared as three dots appeared, wishing he could hear Nav's voice instead of seeing his words appear on a lifeless screen.

Trick shuddered. Nav's voice had carved its own special place in his memory, which would hopefully never fade. The way he'd sounded as Trick had hugged him close in bed, his body sated and his mind finally at peace, still resounded in his soul.

But he had to shove those memories away. It had been a one-time thing, and he had Theo beside him — sweet, beautiful and strong Theo, who had forgiven him as if it had been easier than breathing.

He *adored* Theo and the things they did together in and out of the bedroom. Theo was his sub in every sense of the word, and Trick was his Dom. They didn't have a twenty-four-seven power exchange like some couples but kept their kinky interactions to the spare room, which Trick had converted into a dungeon.

But Theo had never sounded like *that*. Even in the midst of passion or during a scene, that seemed to happen less and less the longer they were together.

Aftercare had never felt better than the main event before.

It was as if a new part of himself had suddenly made itself known. Even after more than ten years in the lifestyle, he had never felt as balanced as he had in Nav's bed, holding Nav close and kissing his neck.

He'd stayed in Nav's apartment for more than six hours, cuddling and talking until he finally felt whole again. He'd asked for Nav's cell number before he'd left, with every intention of texting him for several days. But even though two weeks had passed, they still texted daily.

He read Nav's new text, frowning to himself.

Nah. Just some bullshit. Boss wants to cut back my hours even more until the next gala, so I'll be 'well rested'. I still have the same shit to do but less time to do it. Your day okay?

He typed back, glancing up at the screen as a baking disaster was revealed.

Good. Watching "Nailed It".

"Is work bothering you again? I thought you talked to them about that."

Trick started at Theo's voice. He hadn't even noticed that Theo had abandoned the show to watch him text. A flush spread over his face as he struggled to respond. A lie was already on his tongue, but he bit down, a hint of copper filling his mouth.

"I was texting Nav," said Trick, swallowing thickly when Theo's lighthearted glare turned serious.

"Is he okay?" asked Theo, crossing his arms. His eyes narrowed with concern, his lips thinning.

Trick wanted to smack himself in the face on behalf of Theo. Guilt crawled up his throat, attempting to suffocate him.

"He's fine. He just got home from work. See?" said Trick, handing his phone to Theo. His heart pounded as his fiancé looked down at the screen, biting his lip. Theo's lips were full and darker than Nav's, and Trick wondered if Nav's would have felt the same as Theo's did, or if they would have been completely different, just like everything else was.

He shook his head. He would never find out. Theo was his fiancé and had everything he would ever need.

"I don't understand," said Theo, his fingers frozen on the screen. He didn't scroll or look up, as if he couldn't read the words that were plain in front of him.

From a distance, Trick saw a fresh line of text appear. He itched to grab the phone to see what Nav had written.

"I thought you were checking in on him to make sure that he was doing okay after what happened. I didn't know you guys were chatting," said Theo, handing the phone back to Trick. "It sounds like he likes this show, too." A tiny smile flickered on his lips, but it was gone in an instant.

Trick looked down at the screen.

Fuck, I love that show. Makes me feel like I can actually bake.

"I'm glad he's doing okay," said Theo. He looked back to the show, but his eyes had glazed over as if he wasn't really seeing what was in front of him.

Trick slid his phone to the side, turning the screen down so he wouldn't be tempted to look again. "I'm sorry," said Trick, swallowing again. His mouth was so fucking dry. He reached for his glass, taking a sip of cold water.

"You don't have to apologize," said Theo with a shake of his head. "You're only being a good Dom. You were really shaken after what happened, and I'm glad you're feeling better...both of you."

Trick's stomach dropped. Theo was too good for him. Sure, he had been angry at first, but he had allowed Trick to stumble through a tear-filled apology, and he had let him give Nav aftercare.

At some point after that, the lines had blurred.

Theo reached for the remote, flicking the television off. "What do you say to an early night?" He waggled his eyebrows. "We haven't played in a while, and I wouldn't mind being a bit sore tomorrow."

Trick's cock swelled as his mind filled with possibilities. He hadn't pulled out the flogger in a while, and Theo's moans always had to be muffled behind a gag when he brought that out. One day, when they could afford a house, he would listen to every sound that Theo made without a gag in the way.

A line of ice trickled down his back second later and he shook his head. "I don't want to do anything — not until I get tested. I don't want to put you at risk."

He had trusted Nav when Nav had told him that he got tested regularly and was always careful, but it wasn't something that he wanted to fuck around with. He'd thought about it a lot over the last two weeks, but work had been crazy and he hadn't had time to go to the clinic.

"I thought you were going to do that last week," said Theo, pulling back with a frown.

"I've been busy." Trick bit his tongue. Anger bubbled beneath the surface of his skin, but he didn't let it go any further. "If you think you're the only one who's frustrated, then you're wrong." He gripped the arm of the couch, his fingers touching the edge of his phone. It vibrated, sending a hum across the arm.

"You've been busy texting our neighbor," said Theo, his fists going tight under his crossed arms.

"N-no. I..." Trick trailed off and thought back through the last week. His lunches and breaks had been filled with text messages and laughter instead of the errands he would have usually run. "I'm not cheating on you."

Two weeks before, he wouldn't have dreamed that he would have had to say those words...or even think them.

"I never thought you were," said Theo, standing and throwing his arms wide as his voice rose. "But the fact that you jumped to that has me worried. I trust you, Trick. I wouldn't be with you if I didn't, and I wouldn't agree to scene with you if I didn't trust you. Tell me what's wrong."

Trick crumpled, running his hands through his hair as his chest went tight. Theo knelt in front of him, his beautiful brown eyes wide as he gripped Trick's hands in his own. His palms were rough and callused, and not for the first time, Trick longed for someone softer. Trick used to be able to lose himself in Theo's eyes, but at some point, that had changed. He felt almost...nothing.

It will pass.

"I can't get it out of my head." Trick pulled his hands free as his memories of Nav played over in his mind. He had reminisced about the moments so many times, but the thrill never seemed to fade. His cock started to fill, pressing against his zipper.

"What can't you get out of your head?" asked Theo, touching Trick's leg as if he hadn't noticed Trick's subtle rejection.

"The scene."

"You didn't force him, Trick, and what happened wasn't your fault. It was a misunderstanding." Theo kissed Trick's knee and Trick's heart nearly broke.

"That's not it." He could hardly say it. Every bit of his self-confidence had shattered under the weight of his uncertainty. "I want to do it again, even though I know I can't. I would never betray you like that, but it was just so real. The sounds he made, and the way he took it and begged for more... I just can't stop thinking about it." Trick took a deep breath, his guilt piling higher when Theo stayed silent. "Fuck, I'm so sorry. I'll put it out of my mind, and I'll stop texting him. Please forgive me."

"Forgiven," said Theo without hesitation.

Trick pulled Theo into his arms, clutching his strong, lithe body. Theo was always there for him, no matter how badly he managed to fuck up. His favorite part of the day was sinking next to Theo in bed before twining their fingers together and letting himself breathe. Only Theo had the strength to forgive him.

Then why don't I feel better?

Chapter Seven

Nav

Dating was worse than going to the dentist. There were so many unwritten rules that were different for each one. Was he allowed to swear? Did he really have to listen to a thirty-minute lecture about some political party that he knew nothing about?

The only thing he didn't wonder while at the dentist was if they going to get to the point any time soon or was he wasting his Saturday afternoon with a supreme asshole who had no intention of taking his clothes off? It helped that his dentist was a seventy-year-old man. The asshat in front of him was not, though.

"Is your burger okay?" his date asked him at the same time he shoved his own into his mouth. *Can someone chew that loudly?* Bits of desiccated grossness were visible, and he didn't seem to notice the grease dribbling down his arm.

His profile had looked so promising. *Athlete, self-employed and a big cock.* It was like playing the guessing game Two Lies and One Truth. If self-employed meant un-employed, then that was the only truthful thing on his profile.

Nav shuddered. Those hands were *not* touching him later without a good scrubbing. Bleach and hand sanitizer probably wouldn't cut it.

Nav looked down at his untouched burger. It smelled overpoweringly greasy, and the visible edge of the lettuce was beyond wilted and looking closer to half-decomposed. It was probably one of the least appetizing burgers he'd ever seen, and he had lived off fast food during his first year on his own.

"I'm a vegetarian, but I make an exception for sausage," said Nav, plastering what he hoped, was an alluring smile on his face. Maybe he could convince the guy to fuck him hands-free. Nav could put the condom on himself so everything stayed greaseless.

"Why did you order a burger if you don't eat meat?" his date asked through a mouthful of food. What was his name again? Dennis? Dino? He was pretty sure it had started with a D.

"It was a joke," said Nav slowly. He looked back down at his burger. *Nope.* He was not eating that. Hopefully Mr. D's cock had more intelligence than the man himself. "I'm trying to say that the only meat I like to put in my mouth is a big, girthy sausage."

"I don't get it," D-whatever said, a piece of tomato flapping out of his mouth and smacking down on the plate.

When did my standards get so low? When he was desperate...really fucking desperate.

"Cock," said Nav, a touch too loud for a public place. "I'd rather suck cock than eat a fucking burger. Get it?" The guy nodded slowly, as if he had to think about each word a few times before he managed to catch up. A leering grin broke over his face a few seconds later.

"Why the fuck are we still here, then? I'll settle up and you can meet me out back." The leer twisted his somewhat-handsome face, the last of his attractiveness draining away.

"In the alley?" Nav asked, lowering his voice. He couldn't in the alley. Alleys were fucking sacred. They were for him and…*someone* who had stopped returning his texts the week before.

They had been texting about a hilarious television show, and the next thing he had known, he'd been fucking ghosted.

"Well, yeah. I'm not taking you home when my mom's there. She would tell my girlfriend," said D. He cleared his throat, chomping on a chunk of phlegm before wiping his hands on his shirt.

"You know what? Sure. Give me a minute, and I'll meet you back there." Nav stood, his chair squeaking as he shoved it back. Giving D a quick smile and nod, he turned and headed to the front door. The guy would probably wait for half-an-hour before his tiny brain figured out that Nav had left.

A warm breeze struck Nav's face as he stepped out of the door, the spring day one of the warmest of the year so far. He blinked against the sudden onslaught of light, spots blotting out his vision. As for first dates, that one hadn't been the worst he'd had.

That is just sad.

There was no way that he was telling Sasha that he'd struck out again, because his friend would just torment him for it. Apparently, Nav was setting his standards too high, according to his best friend.

The breeze picked up, sending a wash of freshness over him that almost cancelled out the smell of the restaurant. Summer wasn't his favorite season — mostly because of all the sweat — but spring? Spring was the best time of the year.

Pulling his phone from his pocket, he brought up D's contact info, blocking his number with a satisfying click. He glanced at the name. *Huh, Deralt. Sounds like a screwdriver.* In hindsight, his name had probably been the reason Nav had agreed to the date. A screwdriver was exactly what he needed.

No, it isn't.

"Shut up. Shut up," he hissed at himself as he picked up his pace. His building was only a few blocks away, which was either incredibly convenient or creepy, since Deralt had picked the restaurant.

Nav shrugged it off. It was probably just a coincidence, seeing as the place had been one of the cheapest restaurants in the city, if not *the* cheapest.

A blow job was worth a five-dollar burger with a side of fries these days. Nav's small Pepsi had upgraded it to a fuck.

As he approached his building, his breath caught in his throat, all his thoughts about burgers and sausages slamming to a halt. Trick was at the main door, balancing two paper bags filled to the brim with groceries while struggling to pull his key from his pocket.

Nav watched as a box tumbled out of Trick's bag, pinging off the door before it settled on the ground between his legs. Trick let out a low curse, trying to brace the bags against the wall as he continued to search in his pocket.

Building security was great, until your hands were full.

"Trick, let me help you," yelled Nav, running the last few paces to the entrance. His stomach fluttered as Trick turned to him, his blue eyes going wide. The sight of him so close took Nav's breath away. Had his skin always been so perfect and golden, with his short blond hair fluttering in the breeze? And his hands...they were flawless, down to the slightly chaffed knuckles and the puffy skin around the hangnail on his pinky.

"I've got it," said Trick, shaking his head as Nav held his arms out to take a bag.

"Come on. Let me help. Or at least let me open the door for you," said Nav. He dipped down, grabbing the box that had tumbled to the ground. He almost dropped it again as soon as he looked at the packaging. Condoms — extra-large condoms.

Don't I know it. Don't blush. Shit, I'm blushing.

Trick took a step back, giving Nav room to unlock the door and hold it wide. Clutching the box of condoms tightly as Trick passed him, Nav let out the breath he'd been holding. He'd packed regulars for his date with D, and they were starting to burn a hole in his pocket.

Nav followed, catching the scent of Trick's body wash as he passed. He let the door slide shut and lock automatically.

"How have you been doing?" asked Nav, keeping his voice low as Trick headed up the staircase. Normally Nav would have used the elevator, but the excellent view of Trick's ass was worth a few lost calories.

He'd never had the chance to really look at it before. The black jeans hugging Trick's slight curves made his mouth water more than any burger had in the history of his life.

"Great," said Trick, not turning around to answer. His voice sounded strained, even with the slight echo from the enclosed space.

"You don't sound great, and you don't look great, either," said Nav. He couldn't let himself hope that Trick was missing him as much as he was missing Trick, but he'd noticed the dark shadows under Trick's eyes the moment he'd run up to the building.

The tension thickened to cold molasses as Trick's shoulders went tight.

"Is it my fault?" asked Nav.

Nav's thoughts spiraled faster than the staircase. Was Trick still doubting himself about what had happened? They had talked about the risks of an intense scene as they'd cuddled in Nav's bed together. Trick had said that sometimes the doubts started right away, but sometimes they took days to evolve into negativity.

Trick whirled, pinning Nav to the step with narrowed eyes. "This is not your fault." His voice came out as a deep growl that sent a shiver up Nav's spine.

Nav gripped the extra-large condoms as his cock began to swell.

Ten dates in seven days and he'd hardly had a flicker of interest below the belt. But one glare from Trick, and it was as if he were back in bed again with those powerful arms easing the aches from his body and mind and making him whole.

"Then why did you ghost me?" asked Nav, dropping his gaze to the box. "I texted you three times because I had questions for you, but you never got back to me, even when you promised you would."

It was partially true at best. Trick had told him that he would reply any time day or night if Nav had negative thoughts about what had happened. That hadn't exactly been what he'd texted Trick about.

Trick let out a sigh before he shuffled the bags in his hands. "I'm sorry, but I couldn't reply to you. It didn't feel right."

"Oh." Nav's gaze dropped to Trick's feet. He was wearing well-broken-in running shoes with the laces pulled so tight that they resembled the laces on hockey skates.

It shouldn't have been surprising that Trick was having second thoughts. Most guys were pretty quick to decide that Nav wasn't good for anything more than a quick fuck to let off steam. *At least I can let him go now, right? There are hundreds of guys out there calling my name, and another hundred cursing it.*

"Here…you dropped this." Nav set the condoms on the top of the closest bag before he pushed past Trick, making his way up the stairs two at a time.

His lungs burned, and he almost fell flat on his face as he reached his floor. His next apartment was going to be on the first floor and not the eighth. Taking a deep breath, he reached for the handle, bracing himself as his head swam for a moment. *Low blood sugar is a bitch.*

Trick's footsteps echoed behind him as Trick called out, but Nav was far past caring.

It was just another day in his life as a lonely gay man. If only breasts got him hard. There had to be a chick out there somewhere who would put up with him, seeing as no man would.

"Nav, stop," Trick yelled again, but Nav pushed his way through the door. His feet hit the grungy carpet, his sandals slipping on the surface. *How does it feel to be ignored, motherfucker?* Nav gritted his teeth.

Nav didn't make it another step before Trick grabbed his arm and spun him, slamming his back into the wall with enough force that the drywall quaked beneath him in protest. Panting, he stared at the man who had caught him, Trick's eyes wide and almost feral.

"I said stop." Trick's voice was a low growl, the same tone that managed to send shivers directly to Nav's cock. "I do not repeat myself — period." He flexed his hand, digging into Nav's arm until Nav had to cut back a whimper.

The painful touch rushed past his head, then straight to his cock. It was so fucking good, and it was everything he'd been missing. They weren't even in a scene, but Trick was controlling him and making him listen.

"I'm going to put my groceries away, then I will come to your apartment. You will ask me your questions, and I may or may not answer them. Is that understood?" His blue eyes sparkled as Nav nodded, barely able to lift his gaze to meet Trick's. His pulse fluttered, his heart pounding.

Trick turned away, picking up his bags from where he had tossed them to the ground before disappearing into his apartment, leaving the door open a crack. The sound of him putting his groceries away carried into the hall through the gap. The fridge door closed with a jingle of glass, and a cupboard thudded shut before Trick's footsteps grew louder.

"Why are you still in the hall?" Trick hissed as he rounded the door frame, his voice dripping dangerous calm.

Nav could barely keep himself from melting to the floor and presenting his mouth for Trick to use in any way he wanted.

Trick closed the distance between them. Nav flinched, sucking in a breath as Trick raised his hand, only to relax against the wall when Trick dug his hand into Nav's jeans pocket, fishing out his key. Trick unlocked Nav's door before he turned back, gripping Nav by the back of the neck and pushing him through the threshold.

The second the door slammed shut, Nav went to his knees. He wasn't even sure what possessed him to do it, but he knew it was exactly where he belonged. From the level of Trick's shin, he looked up, biting his lip as Trick's expression faltered with a hint of uncertainty, a curse pushing through his lips.

"I can't do this with you," said Trick, his fury dropping away until his exhaustion shone through. His gaze tracked the walls, as if he was seeing the paintings for the first time.

"Why?" Nav breathed out, his skin tingling as his knees started to ache.

"I can't betray Theo. He is my fiancé and my sub." Trick dropped into a crouch, cupping Nav's chin in his rough fingers. "I can't be your Dom, Nav, and I can't scene with you. You were so perfect for me, but our first time together has to be our last." His blue eyes were shiny and bloodshot, the dark smudges under them even worse from up close. He looked like he was barely hanging on—as if he were struggling just as much as Nav was.

"Okay," said Nav, swallowing the lump as it formed in his throat. His skin broke out in goosebumps where

Trick was touching him, the only thing keeping him from crashing down. *He's a good man. I have to let him go.*

"Ask me your questions, and I'll answer them." Standing, Trick offered Nav his hand, helping him up and leading him to the couch. A frown touched Trick's lips as he drew his hand back, sliding to the opposite end of the couch and leaving a cavernous space between them.

Nav settled on the cushion, his stomach bubbling as he looked at his hands. There was something tumbling around the back of his mind, but his courage was only hanging on by a thread. A month ago, he wouldn't have been able to put two sentences together with Trick looking at him. He was unlike any man Nav had ever met.

But it was now or never. Chances were that Trick would ghost him the moment he walked out of the door, and Nav's time in the apartment would probably come to an end. He always ended up moving sooner or later. *Usually sooner.*

"I want to do it again…what happened between us," said Nav, pausing as he heard Trick suck in a breath. "I get that you don't want to, but I just can't get it out of my head. That was the first time that sex felt like *more* to me, and I need to know where I go from here."

The wall clock continued its rhythmic ticks as Trick remained silent, his gaze burning into Nav's skin. Nav swallowed, his throat dry and his stomach so tight that he wasn't sure if he'd ever be able to eat again. The scents from the greasy diner still clung to him, but Trick smelled so good, his body wash lingering in the apartment and soaking into the cushions of his couch. But how long would it stay? Probably not much longer than Trick himself.

"Do you think it's the pain or the submission that you want again?" asked Trick softly, finally breaking his silence.

"I don't know," said Nav, shaking his head and taking a peek at Trick's face to see his reaction. "Both maybe. I want to feel powerless, as if I don't have any control, but I don't know if I want to hurt quite like that again."

In the alley, the ache had hummed under his skin, sparking pleasure from deep within him, coming from a place he hadn't recognized. But when the equal measure of pleasure had faded and he'd been alone, that same pain had been almost unbearable.

"Sceneing is something you should do with someone you trust. We should have had days of communication and discussions about limits before we even started to plan what was going to happen. It isn't something that should be done spontaneously. So, start by speaking with someone you trust that would consider giving that to you." Trick's voice was soft and soothing, but every syllable grated on Nav's nerves.

"I trust you," said Nav. Why didn't Trick understand? "I don't know anyone else who I'd even dream of asking. I'm a single guy, and most of my friends are straight. In the last ten years I've dated too many guys to count, but I never would've trusted any of them with... *that*."

Silence stretched, and Trick was unmoving except for his slow, deep breaths. Just when Nav had started to give up hope, he finally spoke.

"I can help you find someone. I've been a part of the lifestyle for more than ten years, and I know a few people. I can make a few inquiries on your behalf."

Nav should have felt elated by the news, but his stomach plummeted instead. Would someone else be the same as Trick? Would someone else hold him down if he tried to get away? Trick was powerful, his lean body built for exactly that. In a real struggle, Nav wouldn't stand a chance, and that was exactly how he wanted it be.

"Will you be there?" *I don't know if I can with anyone else. I'm so scared.* Nav bit his tongue, keeping the rest of his words locked away. It would be fine. *He* would be fine.

"There's a shibari demonstration at Unkinked this weekend. Theo and I were going to check it out anyway, so I can bring you along as our guest." Trick's hand twitched, the only sign of his internal struggle.

"I like sushi," said Nav. That one was the truth, even if he had lied about being a vegetarian. Although fish were cute, and he preferred them served with chips.

Trick froze, a smile quirking the edges of his lips before he started to laugh. Tiny wrinkles formed at the corners of his eyes, and they practically sparkled. Nav couldn't look away.

"Sorry... I don't mean to laugh," he said through a chuckle. "Shibari is a type of rope bondage, not food."

"Oh," said Nav, flushing until he was sure he matched the couch. "I have a feeling I'm going to mix stuff up a lot. I don't have much experience other than what I've seen in porn."

The porn was *hot*, but it was rare to find videos that were realistic. Even in the amateur clips, too much happened off screen for it to be reality. He thought it was best not to mention his spanking experience. That relationship had only lasted a short time, anyway.

"That's okay. I know a few Doms who would love to show a newbie the ropes, pun intended." Trick's smile was broad, and it melted a bit of Nav's doubt away. "I'll pick you up at seven on Saturday."

Nav leaned his back against his closed door as soon as Trick left, sliding down the wooden surface until his ass touched the floor. Saturday was only two days away. He could wait that long. And by then, maybe he would be able to get Trick out of his dreams.

Not likely.

Chapter Eight

Trick

Trick's belly had fluttered with nerves as he'd strode across the hall to find Theo already home and pulling the milk out of the cupboard and the cookies out of the fridge. Trick had swallowed, looking at the disaster that he'd made of the groceries in his frantic rush to get to Nav.

Theo hadn't asked where Trick had been or why the milk was in the cupboard, and he hadn't seemed to notice Trick's obvious erection either.

I have to tell him.

Instead of reacting with anger and jealousy, Theo had accepted Nav's invitation the same way he accepted every other part of Trick — with a sweet smile and a tiny nod.

"You should absolutely help Nav find a new play partner. You said he's new to the scene, and there's no one better than you to find him a match," Theo had said as he'd wiped a few stray breadcrumbs from the counter after salvaging

what had been left of a package of crushed hotdog buns.

How would I survive without him?

But an hour later, Trick realized that something had changed between them. The television had remained silent as Theo had wandered off to the bedroom, grabbing a novel as he went. When Trick had joined him an hour later, Theo had rolled away from him in bed, burying his face into his own pillow instead of Trick's chest like he normally did.

Two nights had passed, and the box of condoms remained unused, taking up more space than they were worth in the dresser. Trick wasn't even sure if he would get the chance to use them before his test results came back.

Sighing, he tugged on his tightest pair of jeans, pulling a thick leather belt through the loops for show alone. A night at the club was exactly what they both needed, and a bit of leather could go a long way with a sub like Theo.

A demonstration would hopefully get them through the rough patch of Trick's own making. The sensuality of a sub bound with silken rope and completely at the mercy of their Dom never failed to turn him on.

"Ready?" Theo asked, gripping the door handle and pushing his way into the hall. It was the first thing he'd said since dinner.

Trick nearly stumbled into the door when Theo let go of the handle before Trick was all the way through the doorway. He slapped his palm against the wood before it could slam into his nose, staring after Theo with wide eyes.

Theo knocked on Nav's door, not even looking back over his shoulder as he tapped three times. Nav's door swung wide immediately, revealing a flushed Nav, whose gaze dropped to the floor the second he spied Theo.

Trick's breath faltered, one hand still gripped on the knob and his key in his palm, poised to lock the door. His mouth dropped open, and his cock immediately thickened.

Nav was gorgeous, squeezed into a pair of dark jeans that were so tight they looked like they'd been painted onto his thin figure. He wore a dark T-shirt with an image of crisscrossing chains along the front. It hugged his chest the same way his pants hugged his cock, showing off every bit of hard and soft flesh.

I am so fucked. Trick shook his head, forcing his gaze back to Theo, who was watching him with a calculating gaze. Theo's usual smile was gone, along with his laugh lines.

"It's nice to meet you, Theo," said Nav, his blush disappearing as he held out his hand. It looked like he was trembling, but Trick wasn't sure if it was from nervousness or excitement. Hopefully the latter. Trick hadn't been this excited in…well, *years.*

"You as well," said Theo, shaking Nav's hand as if there was no animosity between them. "Let's go then. Trick, you ready?"

The trip passed in an awkward silence that blanketed the car with enough angst that nobody spoke. Even Trick's favorite song on the radio did nothing to quell the mood. His palms were slick on the steering wheel by the time they arrived, and he wouldn't have been surprised if there had been an actual hole in the side of his head from Theo's glare.

The street was lined with cars of all sorts from a polished Lamborghini to a rust-bucket that looked like it hadn't had an oil change in three years. Knowing the owner, it probably hadn't. The street was unusually well-lit, but other than an Office Depot, there were no other businesses close by. The club was unlabeled, with a plain white door that could only be accessed with a key card.

Ninety percent of the population didn't have any idea that behind the door was one of the best kink clubs in the country. Trick had been one of them, until he'd met the owner and had dived into a new world with everything he'd had. He even made his rounds as dungeon master once a month—a gig that was as exciting as it was frustrating.

Tapping his key card, Trick held the door wide, letting Nav take in the first view of the club. Most might think that the tiny curtained-off closet with a single bouncer was anti-climactic, but it was one-hundred-percent necessary for the privacy of the patrons.

"Hey, Ned," said Trick, nodding to the bouncer who looked at Nav with bright interest. Trick squashed the jealousy that instantly tried to surge, only then noticing that Theo had already slipped through the curtain. "Can we get Nav checked in as a guest?"

Ned nodded, quickly producing a plethora of non-disclosure agreements and waivers. It was probably the least exciting part of kink, but absolutely necessary. The rules alone were enough that they'd almost turned Trick off ten years before. It had taken him a while before he fully understood that they were there for a reason.

Nav looked as overwhelmed as Trick had felt, but it was nothing to the way his eyes went wide when Trick pulled the curtain to the side and led him into the club.

"I thought there would be more naked people," said Nav, his gaze jumping around the room like a kid with ADHD. *Maybe he didn't notice the two naked subs at table four?* Nav's eyes widened when he looked that way and Trick let out a chuckle, nodding as they passed by Rowan, who appeared to be the dungeon master for the night.

"We usually save that for the private rooms on regular nights. In a scene, everyone has to consent, including the onlookers," said Trick, watching as Nav blinked. "Come on. I have a room reserved for us. Derreck is going to meet us there."

Trick had spent too many hours trying to pinpoint the perfect Dom who could lead Nav to where it sounded like he wanted to go. Philip was more mature, but he had a sadistic streak that was probably a bit too extreme for a beginner like Nav, and Trick was almost completely sure he was straight. Henley was sexy as hell, but he had a heart for his own version of primal fucking. The rest were taking a break, not looking for a newbie, had kinks that didn't seem to line up with Nav's or were in closed relationships.

Trick moved past the bar and lounge, avoiding another curtained area that led to the main stage that was used for open play when there were no events scheduled. The private rooms were tucked at the back of the club and out of the way, with an ample seating area outside for couples to come down after they'd left their room.

"Hey, Derreck," said Trick as he spotted Derreck loitering outside the hall that led to the private rooms. All of them were named after the implements and the kinksters who were probably inside. They were unlocked with the same swipe cards as the front door that linked to the reservation system. If a door was left open, voyeurs were welcome.

"Maverick," said Derreck, taking Trick's hand in a shake that would have taken a lesser man to his knees. "Long time no scene." Derreck's thick lips split into a rare grin as he spied Nav, who had trailed Trick like a loyal dog.

Nav's eyes lit up, his face flushing when he got his first good look at Derreck. Trick had had the same reaction to Derreck the first time they'd met, along with every other gay man and straight woman.

Derreck was built and broad, with caramel skin and a strength that still made Trick hard. He could probably dead lift twice the amount Trick could, and he could fuck up most body builders in a heartbeat. There was a touch of terror that always clung to Derreck, so most newbies steered well clear. Luckily, Trick had known him from almost the beginning, so he was only moderately afraid of him.

"You guys want to chat, and I'll take off?" Trick asked, his stomach twisting as he thought about leaving. He should have probably been looking for Theo, but how could he turn away from Nav? He longed to watch Nav's face as Derreck played. Derreck never gave demos anymore, and his subs had been few and far between as of late. It was a privilege to see him at work. *Just keep telling yourself that.*

"Can you stay?" asked Nav, shifting from foot to foot. How could anyone be more perfect? *Theo… Theo is perfect too!*

"He can stay, and he can join," said Derreck, his almond eyes sparkling. His pink T-shirt stretched over his chest, showing off his pecs and a six pack that you could do laundry on.

Derreck turned down the hall, pulling out the swipe card and tapping it against the door with *Impact* written across it inlaid gold cursive. It would have been the room that Trick would have picked as well, but one he rarely strayed into with Theo.

He'd almost forgotten what it looked like inside. It was simple, with a comfortable-looking couch to one side that was made of some sort of material that looked easy to clean. There was a cupboard with fresh folded towels, washcloths and sanitizing spray in the corner of the room, plus a small sink. Next to the sink was a small basket with complimentary items like lube and condoms.

In the middle of the room there was a restraint bench with padded leather that was echoed in several of the other rooms. On one wall there was a cross, also meant for restraint, but the back wall was where a few dozen floggers, paddles, whips and canes that hung on a large rack.

The air had the lingering scent of antiseptic, but Trick could still smell Nav's body spray as he passed by, Nav's eyes going wide as he took in the sight of the implements.

"Holy shit," said Nav as he blanched, biting his lip hard.

Trick shut the door as soon as Nav crossed the threshold, effectively cutting off his escape. There was no lock from inside, so Nav would have been able to leave at any point, but the symbolism of it struck a chord and Trick's cock started to swell. *What is Nav thinking right now?* Trick would have done anything to immerse himself in Nav's thoughts as he eyed one of the whips with wide eyes.

Nav took a step back, his ass brushing against Trick and his chest rising fast as he panted. His skin-tight pants gave nothing away. Either his cock was truly squished beneath the denim or he wasn't hard yet.

Trick tilted his head. *Interesting.* He would have thought that Nav would get off on fear, the same way he had in the alley.

"Let sit and talk limits," said Derreck, taking control seamlessly. There was a reason that he was sought after as much as he was feared. Derreck scratched his neck, a tiny flake of sand dropping to the ground.

"Okay," said Nav, looking anything but *okay*. Trick felt a grin spread over his face as he caught Derreck's predatory gaze. There was nothing better than a fresh sub that was as unsure as he was willing. Watching them writhe was usually twice as hot.

Derreck listed his limits, before he started firing off questions to Nav as if he were reading from a list. Nav stuttered through the first few, gaining confidence as he set his limits against pissing. They hadn't booked the right room for that, anyway.

"I don't really know," said Nav for the fourth time, his face so flushed that he was nearly red when Derreck inquired about restraint.

A brief smile flitted over Derreck's lips before he patted his lap. Nav slowly lifted himself from his side of the couch before moving to Derreck's lap, perching like a bird ready to leap off a mountain for its first flight.

Trick shifted against the wall. They looked good together, with Nav's pale skin and Derreck's darker complexion like yin and yang. Nav was the same height as Theo, but Derreck still had a few inches on Trick — and an overwhelming amount of muscle.

"Do you like this?" asked Derreck, as he moved his hands up Nav's body, sliding one to the middle of his chest and the other around his throat. His fingers wrapped nearly all the way around Nav's thin neck, like a dark brand against his skin.

Nav took a deep shuddering breath, his gaze meeting Trick's before he slid his eyes shut. "Yes."

Trick went rock hard, his cock straining against the zipper of his jeans as Derreck clutched Nav's throat— not squeezing but caressing...warning. Nav tilted his head back, giving Derreck better access as he sucked in a breath.

"So responsive," said Derreck, his voice dropping into a rumble. "Tell me when it's too much." He moved his other hand up Nav's chest, finding a nipple through his thin T-shirt. He clamped down on the bud with his fingertips, looking as if he were gradually increasing the pressure.

Nav let out a loud gasp, his back arching and his lashes fluttering against his cheeks. He was so beautiful and so responsive, even as a furrow built on his forehead as Derreck continued to increase the pressure.

"Ahh." Nav let out a gasp and a small burst of sound, but nothing more. Derreck relaxed his grip and Nav's body folded like a balloon suddenly bursting into nothingness.

"Good boy," said Derreck, dropping his hands.

Nav stood, his eyes locking with Trick as he adjusted himself, now obviously hard. Was he regretting wearing pants that tight? Trick suppressed his smirk. Did Nav even know that his pants wouldn't be on for much longer?

"Take your pants off, then face the wall," said Derreck as he moved from the couch, stalking to the display and eyeing up the implements. "Any suggestions, Trick?" He looked over his shoulder.

Trick swallowed as a barrage of suggestions came forth, trapped behind his teeth. He hadn't told Derreck everything about what had happened, only that Nav had scened with him once and wanted more—even though it had been a one-time thing.

I shouldn't be here. His cock was too hard, and his heart was pounding too fast for him to be able to think straight.

He'd always managed to keep a clear head with Theo, never taking things too far. Why was it so different with Nav?

Why not? I'm not cheating. Trick strolled to the display, taking his time as Nav turned away and slowly peeled his pants from his legs, his ass trembling along with the rest of him. Skimming his hands along a few floggers, Trick settled on one. It had thin strips that would sting more than thud, as well as spread the hit all along Nav's ass with each strike. He could imagine the glowing mark it would leave against Nav's pale skin. "This to start."

Derreck grunted his affirmative, accepting the flogger and giving it a few practice swipes against his wrist. He turned back, his gaze narrowing as he watched Nav trying to get his legs out of his too-tight jeans. *How did he even get into them?* Nav was facing the wall, struggling to get the material past his thighs.

His bruises were gone, Trick's fingerprints nothing but a memory. Trick blinked. *Of course they are.*

"Did I say you could turn away from me?" asked Derreck, his voice quiet in the small room. Nav jerked, turning to them with a scowl and seemingly unafraid of Derreck's tone.

"You told me to take my pants off and face the wall," said Nav, his voice dripping with barely concealed sarcasm.

Trick grinned as Derreck strolled across the room, the flog hanging from his fingertips as a threat. Thrusting his hand into Nav's hair, Derreck used his grip to push him against the wall. "Would you care to rephrase that?" asked Derreck softly, the flogger's fibers tickling against Nav's belly where his shirt had ridden up.

"Um." Nav bit his lip, his gaze flickering to Trick's, then back to the floor when he must've realized that Trick wasn't going to step in. "I was only doing what you asked me to do." He said it much quieter, arching his back as Derreck tugged and twisted his fingers through Nav's tresses.

"Take your pants off, then face the wall. I want to see that cock of yours to know if it's worth my time. So far, I'm not impressed." Derreck's voice was brutal, his grin nothing but a distant memory. That was the man that subs feared.

Trick shifted, his cock throbbing. Nav hadn't set humiliation as a limit, and Derreck was digging his claws into it, probably testing the waters for Nav's reaction.

Nav shivered, his eyes sliding closed again and a flush spreading over his cheeks. Dropping his hands back to his stalled jeans, he pushed, the fabric sliding over his skin and exposing every untarnished inch. Derreck stepped back as Nav freed himself, tossing his pants to the side with his cock bobbing from every movement.

"That's better," said Derreck. "You have a nice small cock, perfect for getting fucked. I'm not sure it would be of much use for anything else, especially not for fucking someone."

That was probably the most Trick had ever heard Derreck say, and for a moment, Trick wondered if he had made the wrong choice. Derreck fucked with a sub's mind as much as he fucked with their body.

But then Trick noticed Nav's cock, a bead of pearly pre-cum dripping down the tip as it flushed near-purple. Obviously, Nav was still on board, and he had his safewords if that changed.

Trick pressed against the wall, folding his arms and hoping that he wouldn't try to interfere.

Nav let out a breath before slowly turning to face the wall, slapping his palms on the reinforced drywall with a thud. His back was arched, his legs spread like a man who had no shame about his nudity. His sac hung between his legs, dark, soft and nearly hairless.

The posture was so familiar that it made Trick's mouth run dry. *No. No! Just watch. You can't touch him.*

"I'll start you off easy. What do you say if it's too much and you want to stop?" asked Derreck, taking his position behind Nav, his feet shoulder-width apart.

"Red."

"And if you want to slow down?" Derreck flicked the flogger against his palm, quirking his lips at the sting.

"Yellow," said Nav, moving his palms down the wall until they were level with his head.

"Good boy." Derreck drew his arm back, his biceps flexing as he tightened his grip on the flogger. With no warning, he let it fly. It sailed through the air, nearly soundless, until it struck Nav's ass with a burst of noise that must have felt like agony and fire.

Nav let out a strangled yell, startling the moment the leather strands touched his skin. He shifted, his feet shuffling on the ground as he turned his head to look at them, his eyes wide and filled with surprise more than pain.

I am so fucked. Nothing had ever looked that good before, and Trick had never been so hard in his life. Derreck looked unaffected so far, his cock silent in his leather pants.

"I don't know if I liked that," said Nav, his gaze never leaving Trick. A furrow creased his forehead before he bit his lip, the pale pink flesh flushing bright.

"Is that your safeword?" asked Derreck, pausing with his arm cocked back for a second blow. Seconds stretched, but Nav remained silent. Derreck let out a quiet huff before he brought the flogger down a second time, hitting the same spot with expert precision.

Nav cried out, shifting his hips away from the blow until he hit the wall cock-first. His eyes went wider, alarm bleeding into his expression as he pleaded with Trick with his eyes alone. Another hit and he called out, a pink blush bleeding across his ass from the hit.

Trick saw the safeword on Nav's lips before Nav probably even realized that he was going to say it. He knew it would be a color and that it definitely wouldn't be green. *It doesn't make sense.* Another hit followed by a tear-filled cry. *Nav won't let go like this.*

Nav was still so perfectly submissive, and the thud of the flog was nothing compared to what he had endured for Trick, but Nav was obviously starting to panic. Nav started to shift his hands, and Trick knew he only had seconds before the scene would be over before it began. Derreck must have sensed it, too, because he turned to Trick, a touch of worry on his usually stoic face.

Trick moved before he could stop himself. There was no looking back.

Chapter Nine

Nav

Fuck, it stung. The little thing that Trick had selected from the 'wall of pain' – as Nav had named it – that looked like a mop had made babies with a riding crop, had been so unassuming. But it fucking hit with the force of a bitch-slap and left a puddle of fire wider than his hand. The weight behind the blow should have been impossible for such a small thing.

Had Derreck used every bit of muscle behind the hit? It certainly felt like it. It was the complete opposite of what Nav had expected when he'd jammed himself into his tightest pair of pants.

When the second hit came, then the third, Nav realized that he had been wrong. Each blow was a bit harsher, and Derreck looked like he was barely even trying.

He couldn't take this. His ass stung, but not in a good way, and his cock was well on its way to withdrawing into his body.

He looked over his shoulder, catching sight of Trick, who was leaning against the wall and watching Derreck's every move. *Do something.* His gaze dropped to Trick's crossed arms then lower. *He's hard for this? How?*

I can do this. If it was turning Trick on, then he could do a lot more than take a couple of hits that were basically glorified spankings. He couldn't be a disappointment — not again.

The next hit sealed his fate. Nav barely held back a scream as his ass flared. *I can't.* Was he bleeding? Was he broken? He concentrated on his safeword, knowing that it was his only option. He wasn't sure if he could survive another hit.

He saw Trick move from his spot on the wall, and Nav turned so his forehead was resting on the cool surface. He slid his hands down the drywall, memorizing every little dip and imperfection as time seemed to slow. *Such a disappointment.* Trick was probably coming over to tell Nav to get out so the big boys could play.

A hand threaded through his hair and Nav stiffened, his face digging into the drywall as he was pinned. He shouldn't have looked away from the men behind him. Derreck's hands had been surprisingly gentle, even as he'd used Nav's hair to control him. But the hand that squished his face into the wall was like raw fury against him, unyielding and rough. *Trick.*

Trick's scent enveloped him, his spicy cologne nearly overpowering. Nav's mouth watered as Trick leaned against his back, the rough fabric of his jeans scraping against his ass. Tears prickled at the corner of his eyes.

"I can't do it," said Nav, his voice barely above a whisper. Trick's hand in his hair went tighter, a few strands pulling free from his scalp as his head was tugged, arching his back painfully. The air rushed from his lungs and he let out a harsh cry, his cock throbbing to life faster than he could comprehend.

"Do you think you have a choice, slut?" Trick's voice was dark and hot against his ear, and it plunged him straight back into the alley. His cock stiffened further, the sensitive head butting with the wall. Trick's cock was against his ass, poking him like the hardest steel.

All for me.

"You are going to take whatever Derreck wants to give you, then you are going to thank him for it. Do you understand?" Trick tugged, a few more strands breaking free. Nav scrambled to stay on his feet, blood rushing through his ears.

"Yes," Nav bit out with a whimper. "Whatever you want." He kept his hands on the wall, sinking into the surface as he started to pant. Sweat beaded on his chest, soaking into his shirt as his head swam.

The need for his safeword drifted away. Trick had him. Everything was fine—better than fine—because Trick would take care of him. He sank deeper, the sting in his ass throbbing.

"I want to beat you so hard that you can't help but come," said Trick in a low voice that only Nav could hear. "Then I want to press my cock into your hole and fuck you raw. Are you still tight? Or did I ruin you last time? No one likes a loose slut. I'm not sure you could even make me come with how much my cock stretched you out. You'll never be the same."

"Please," said Nav, grinding into the wall. The pressure in his groin was unreal and his mind was getting closer to that familiar startling awareness that he'd only ever felt with Trick.

Trick's cock rubbed the top of his ass, the blond just a touch taller than him and so much stronger. If Nav concentrated, he could almost feel the ridge of Trick's cock through his jeans. He knew how good it felt inside him. His own cock throbbed, getting ever closer, but not close enough.

"Such a slut," said Trick, dropping a hand to Nav's naked ass and spanking him hard. "Look at you rut against the wall like you're desperate. You want me to hold you down and make you come?"

Nav nodded, swallowing hard. *Yes*, his mind shouted at him. *Yes, yes, yes!*

"Take what Derreck has to give, and I'll let you come. Say your safeword and everything stops. Remember that."

Nav nodded, his movements slower than molasses. Dropping his grip, Trick moved to the corner of the room, placing himself directly in Nav's line of sight.

Renewed fire danced against his ass, but it was nothing to Trick's gaze. Nav's curled his toes, arching his back as he let out a long moan. He studied the flicker of a grin on Trick's lips, knowing that he was finally doing something right.

Joy surged through his chest. *Trick looks happy — pleased, even.*

"Harder," said Trick, never looking away from Nav.

The next hit made Nav cry out, and the one after it made his ass burn like it was truly on fire. He had to have been bleeding, but it could have been just sweat trickling down his ass cheeks from above. He would never sit again.

"Harder," said Trick again, molten lava lancing across Nav's ass.

"Do you think you have a choice, slut?"

Suddenly, it wasn't enough, and the pain transformed into something else entirely. Nav kept his hands firmly against the wall, despite his slippery palms, and he shifted his feet wider, silently asking for more. He didn't want a touch of fire. He wanted to fucking burn, and he wanted to Trick to watch.

"More," said Nav, after more strokes than he could count. Trick's lips curved, his grin sparkling as his pupils blew wide. "Please, more." He was almost there, although, he wasn't exactly sure where *there* was. His cock was hard, and his heart was racing. *Am I going to come?*

No, not until Trick says I can. Only good boys get to come. Be good.

Nav held on, willing his heart to slow as he let out a scream at the next strike. It hadn't even been as hard as some of the others. He needed more and he needed it *now*. He had to make Trick proud.

"Fucking harder," Nav snarled, clenching his teeth as he looked to Trick. His blue eyes were nearly black, his lips wet from him tracing them over and over with his tongue. Trick licked them again as Nav watched, before he reached down to adjust himself.

The blows ceased for a moment, until Trick nodded. For such a simple tilt of his head, it meant more than Nav could fathom.

The next hit was almost his undoing. It was brutal, merciless and tore into his ass with the force of a thousand knives that set him on fire. The sound had changed from the previous sparking thud, and the thin leather had been exchanged for something new and sinfully delicious.

Tears streamed down Nav's face as a sob erupted from his throat. He was soaked with sweat, his body slick and dripping.

I can't hold on.

Trick was suddenly there as Nav's palms slipped over the wall, threading his long fingers through Nav's hair before forcing their lips together.

Nav nearly blacked out as their lips touched, lust surging through him. He moaned, desperate for more, even as his head swam, his body aching for air. Trick tasted so much better than he had imagined, and he was instantly addicted.

He'd barely had a taste before Trick pulled back, their gazes meeting as the flogger rained down on his ass, pushing Nav beyond anything he'd ever felt. It was so much—too much. He was hanging on by a thread, but he was terrified to let go. He needed Trick.

"Come."

Nav screamed, his vision flickering as his body pulsed, his orgasm bursting from somewhere deep inside. He painted the wall with his seed, wave after wave tumbling from him as his cock ached and his balls drew up. He wobbled, his knees going soft as his energy drained, as if a plug had been pulled from his lifeforce.

Trick caught him, pulling Nav against his chest and gripping his ass with hands that had to have been made of needles. Trick let out a groan, his hips jerking as Nav fell against him, his cock throbbing and twitching between them.

"Good boy."

Chapter Ten

Trick

Trick was sure that he had just hit the peak of his kink career. Watching Nav lose himself and giving up the last of his control had been the hottest moment of his life. *I've been thinking that a lot lately.* Everything to do with Nav was better than the best.

Nav was the malleable clay that Trick molded into whatever he wanted for his pleasure. With Nav cradled to his chest, he could have done anything, and Nav would have let him, too far gone to even remember where he was. The pure trust was mind-boggling.

But all Trick wanted to do was hold Nav close as he came back down, ready to ease him back into reality.

Trick had never felt so fucking high before, and he'd been an onlooker for most of the scene. It should have been terrifying, with how close he had been to losing control, but it was liberating instead. He'd never let himself go so far, not even with Theo.

Beautiful, kind Theo, who would have let him do almost anything, but never would have let him do that. Theo would have safeworded long before he had reached the same state as Nav, and so would've most other subs out there.

Nav was special, and from the air of disbelief in Derreck's eyes, looking as if his control had fled the room at the same time as Trick's, Trick knew that he wasn't the only one who felt it. It was a wonder that Nav had barely dipped his toes into the waters of kink before, because he was made for it. He was made for Doms like Trick and Derreck.

He was made for me.

"Fuck," Derreck breathed out, his gaze meeting Trick's as he wiped the back of his hand over his mouth. "That was intense." Derreck turned away, grabbing a fresh towel from the cupboard before laying it out on the couch.

It had been intense—intense enough for Trick to shoot in his jeans the moment Nav touched him, his cum smearing the inside of his boxers like a dirty secret that would seep through soon and make itself known.

"Couch?" asked Trick, his voice surprisingly steady as he watched Derreck wobble. He'd never seen the other Dom so far gone, even with pain sluts who could take a beating like no other. But he wasn't hard. It was...different for Derreck. Kink had nothing to do with sex for him. *Which makes him perfect for Nav.*

"Yeah, I need to sit down. You got our subbie okay?" asked Derreck, looking like he wanted to lift Nav and carry him across the short space.

Trick only hummed, holding Nav that much tighter. He carried him bridal style to the couch, sitting next to

Derreck so their shoulders touched. There was lots of room, but Nav would need the closeness as he came to.

He turned Nav in his arms so they were chest to chest, Nav's red ass bared to the room and to Derreck, who gently touched the flaming skin. Nav's head lolled against Trick's neck, a whimper breaking through his lips at Derreck's touch.

He was conscious, but Trick knew it would be a while until Nav was really *there* again. He was soaring in a place where only the luckiest subs managed to go. They had to bring him down gently, easing him back to himself.

"Easy, Nav," said Trick as a second whimper pushed through his lips. "You were so good for us. Such a good boy. You took that so well, and you came so beautifully. You are so perfect for us."

Nav's whimper changed into a contented hum as he nuzzled his face into Trick's neck, sucking the warmth from his skin with a deep breath.

"You okay, Derreck?" Trick asked softly, barely able to tear his eyes away from Nav's beautiful ass. It looked so sore and so perfect. Nav had taken every lash and had asked for more, demanding it harder when Derreck had held back. Trick wasn't usually one for topping from the bottom, but Nav was a newbie, so he was willing to let it slide once.

The moment Derreck had finally unleashed himself, Trick had told Nav to come—and like magic, he had.

The welts were raised, a few of them bruised purple already from when Derreck had changed implements to something with a bit more bite. Trick had nearly lost it when Nav had taken the first hit, his eyes going wide when he realized that the leather flog wasn't the only thing that was going to be used on him.

It had been perfect.

Derreck let out a deep breath, his gaze fixed on the marks he had left. He closed his eyes as he trailed his fingers down one of the larger welts that had come close to breaking skin.

"He was perfect," said Derreck, letting out another shudder. "Where did you find such a perfect boy?" His eyes were still blown wide, and Trick knew he wasn't the only one who was still feeling the effects of the scene. They were all flying right now.

"Let me grab the cream," said Derreck, lifting himself off the couch. They may have been floating, but they were still good Doms. Nothing would get in their way when it came to looking after Nav, not even their own highs.

Nav stirred in Trick's arms as Derreck gently spread the cream over his ass. It would help with the sting, but the marks would remain when he woke up the next day. They would probably take more than a week to heal, especially against such pale skin.

A week of Nav thinking of them every time he had to sit down.

"How are you feeling?" asked Trick, blowing against Nav's ear as he stirred, his forehead furrowing as his body started to stiffen.

"It hurts," said Nav, his words on the edge of a sob that transformed into a shudder as Derreck spread another layer of cream over his ass.

"Did you like the scene?" asked Derreck, capping the bottle and scooting closer before lifting Nav over his lap so he was draped over both of them.

"Fuck, yes," said Nav, his snarky attitude starting to bleed back into his voice. Trick stroked Nav's sides, his palm rising with each slow breath. The simple rhythm of in and out was more calming than any meditation.

"What was your favorite part?" asked Trick, directing the question down to Nav. He grinned as a flush bloomed over Nav's cheeks. He was shy about the question, but not about being draped over them while nearly naked, his stomach still slick with a bit of cum that Derreck hadn't been able to reach with the cloth.

"I liked it when you called me a slut," Nav said softly, shoving his face back into Trick's neck. "I liked it when you told me I didn't have a choice."

"You know that you could have safeworded, and we would have stopped, right?" asked Trick. Nav nodded and Trick hummed with contentment. He was all for pushing boundaries, but consent was everything to him.

Derreck dipped beneath Nav's shirt before moving his hand up Nav's back. He leaned in, his shoulder touching Trick's and their breaths mingling. "I wondered what you said to him. Did you like the flogger?"

Nav purred, turning so he could look at Derreck. He hissed as his exposed ass touched Derreck, fluttering his eyes shut as his cock twitched. Trick watched as Nav squirmed between them, biting his lip.

"Yes," said Nav, finally stilling and taking a breath. "The second one was different, though — really intense. What was it?" He followed Derreck's gaze to the discarded flogger on the ground. It looked lethal — and its bite had been just as bad as its bark.

Nav paled when he caught sight of it. "Oh shit. No wonder it hurt so much." He reached back, skimming the edge of his reddened ass. "How could anyone take that?"

"You took it perfectly," said Derreck, his expression giving nothing away. "I only use that one on the most special subs."

Something creeped into Trick's belly at Derreck's words. The rational part of Trick warned him that he was just coming out of his haze a little too fast. But he couldn't turn off the twist of *something* in his belly that felt a lot like jealousy. *I can't be jealous. I set this up and it went...perfectly. I need to be happy for them.*

Nav and Derreck made the perfect partnership, their skin tones an elegant contrast and the marks on Nav's skin elevating it even further. It was a match made in kinky heaven. Derreck would look after Nav and treat him better than any sub could ask for. Derreck could break Nav's mind and body, then build him back up, fitting the tiny pieces back together until he was more whole than before.

But a niggling voice in the back of Trick's mind insisted that the marks on Nav's skin should have been made by him. Nav was supposed to look at *him* in wonder, like Trick had hung the moon, then colonized it, because Nav was *his*. He wanted to break Nav, then build him back to perfection and never leave him wanting.

Theo.

Trick cleared his throat. "Are you guys okay for a bit if I go check on Theo? I'll be back in a couple of minutes." He winced at how shaky his voice suddenly sounded. Derreck sent him a not-so-subtle glare, murder and confusion in his almond eyes. "I'll be back, I promise. I would never leave such a good boy. I'd be too worried someone might try to steal him away from me."

He sent the glare straight back at Derreck, and the tension mounted as he tightened his grip. There were going to be *words*, but not when Nav still needed them.

Nav giggled, squirming against Trick's chest before he wrapped his arms around Derreck's neck. Derreck let out a deep rumble, carding through Nav's hair and sucking up the affection as if he were starving. Nav looked so perfect in his arms, and he fit just so.

Trick stood before he could grab Nav and pull him back. He needed to get out of the room before he did something that would ruin his friendship with Derreck or jeopardize Nav's trust in him.

He grabbed his key card and let himself out of the door, shutting gently behind him. Running his hand through his hair, he took a deep breath of cool air, the sound of his own breathing washing over him.

The rooms were soundproofed, so he couldn't hear anything except for the distant music at the bar. The only one who could see within with the doors closed was the dungeon master, who had access to the security system.

He followed the noise, emerging from the hallway and into the wide space that had been littered with couples when they'd first arrived. The bar was nearly empty, which wasn't surprising when there was a strict one-drink maximum for people who wanted to play.

"Can I get three bottles of water?" Trick asked Clint as he approached the bar. He should have gotten them ahead of time, but he had been so laser-focused on Nav that some of his standard operating procedures had fallen through.

The bartender and owner, a blond-haired and gorgeous man named Clint, gave him a quick once-over before handing him three bottles. "I see you aren't the only one having fun tonight, but I don't think I've ever seen you this fucked out. I have to ask who the lucky guy is, seeing as your man is on stage right now."

Trick paused, eyeing himself in the mirror behind the bar. His hair was beyond help and his skin was coated in perspiration, a warm flush on his cheeks that had obviously come from a vigorous scene. He glanced down to see that his cum had soaked through the front of his jeans, leaving a sizable wet spot that had started to stiffen. He hadn't come that hard in a while, and his balls had obviously decided to make it known.

"I just wanted to check on Theo. Is he on the main stage?" he asked, expertly avoiding Clint's question. He wasn't quite ready to face flack from anyone but Theo. Clint had mentored Trick when he'd first dipped his toes into kink, and he still felt like a padawan learner next to him.

"Yeah," said Clint, grabbing a bar towel and wiping a stray droplet of liquid from the gleaming surface. "Harold probably has him pretty tied up by now." He let out a small smile. "He looking for ideas for you two?"

"Thanks for the water," said Trick, hurrying to the curtain that led to the main stage area. The place was warmer with so many people packed into the space that usually housed a few couples taking advantage of the equipment and the instruments, but it was near-silent. Every eye was on the stage where the dim lights highlighted something breathtakingly beautiful.

Harold was the most skilled shibari master that Trick had ever met. He took a simple rope and an attractive body and turned them into a piece of art unlike anything he'd ever seen. Trick had taken a few of his classes, loving the way the smooth rope felt as he wrapped Theo in it, but it wasn't his true passion.

Maybe I should re-evaluate that.

Theo was on stage on his knees, his head thrown back with a look of absolute ecstasy on his face. His naked arms were encased in soft-looking blue rope that twisted down to his wrists then looped around his ankles. It was a deceptively simple design, but beautiful, nonetheless, especially with someone like Theo. He was completely immobile and at the will of his Dom.

Trick smiled, letting out a sigh of relief. He would have felt terrible if Theo had been standing off somewhere waiting for him. Instead, he was on stage, getting exactly what he needed from a friend and fellow Dom. Theo's hard and naked cock was completely natural, given the situation.

Should I be jealous? I'm not.

Trick turned away, trying not to overthink it. He had a sub and a Dom calling his name. He left the room, letting the curtain fall behind him with a near-silent swish.

Chapter Eleven

Nav

Nav shoved his phone into his pocket as his boss approached him with a glare on her face. He was either about to get fired or promoted, but, as usual, it was impossible to tell. A smile probably didn't fit on her face—at least, he'd never seen one. How she could be so miserable surrounded by works of art all day probably had something to do with the fact that she had the skills of a three-year-old with a crayon.

"Can I help you, Ms. Morgan?" he asked carefully, sliding his fingers over his favorite pen out of habit. He made sure to put extra stress on the *Ms.* while lifting a piece of paper onto his desk from within the printer tray without looking away. He had slipped up and called her 'Mrs.' once, and he had thought she was going to castrate him.

"Explain something to me," she said, crossing her arms. Her dark blonde eyebrows pushed together, and she pursed her lips into a nearly invisible line. "Why is

Brian Maeckery leaving a voice message on my phone? Do I look like a secretary? For some strange reason, I thought that was what I hired you for."

She paused, her lipstick winking in and out of existence as she worked her jaw. She would have been truly terrifying if she had been taller than five-foot-one and had weighed more than a thirteen-year-old. But no matter how many times she yelled at Nav, he couldn't get the image of a tantruming child out of his head.

Not so pissed after all. When Nav had answered the phone and *the* Brian Maeckery had been on the other end, he'd almost had a heart attack. Brian was the man of his art dreams.

"Mr. Maeckery asked to leave a voicemail for you. He expressed an interest in doing another piece but was uncomfortable going into the details with me," said Nav, looking down at his boss and smothering the smile that was trying to creep onto his face. He watched as a vein bulged in her temple. She would start stamping her feet next—then came the screeching.

"That's the problem," she said, her face flushing as she clenched her tiny fists. "If my clients are uncomfortable with you, it's because they don't trust you. And how am I supposed to keep someone untrustworthy in my employ? Anything that can be said to me, they should be able to say to you."

A hint of dread seeped in, but Nav squashed it down. They'd had a similar conversation more times than he could count. She wasn't going to fire him…he hoped. The gallery had been failing when he'd arrived with bright eyes and big dreams of meeting famous artists. He hadn't cared that she'd already chomped through half of the personal assistants in the city. The art was worth it.

"I believe he was uncomfortable speaking with me because of the personal and sexual nature of the piece. It's the one you had commissioned for your lover and yourself." He bit back a laugh as she blanched.

"I-I didn't think you knew about that. I may have f-forgotten that it would be ready soon," she stammered, taking a small step back. Her tiny heels clicked on the floor.

Nav plastered his winning smile on his face. He knew everything about his boss and the gallery. He knew how much money she had in each of her accounts, because he did her banking and opened her mail. He knew what each painting sold for, and what had been offered. He knew that she had killed two goldfish because she kept putting pepper in the tank instead of fish food. Why the two shakers had been kept side by side was still a mystery to him.

"That's why you keep me around," he said, slamming the point home with no small amount of gusto. "So I can remember everything you tell me, even the things you've forgotten." A frown flickered on her face, and he backed off. He didn't want to push *too* far.

"I will call him back on your behalf immediately and let him know you'd like the piece delivered to your home." He wondered what her husband would think about the painting of his wife and his secretary.

"No, that's quite all right," she said, a touch too quickly. "Just have him bring it here. I would like to hang it in my office." She turned and marched away, the flaps on her suit jacket fluttering like tiny wings. If they ever caught a stiff breeze, she might just get blown away.

Nav chuckled, shaking his head. Perhaps he was a masochist, but he *loved* working with that woman. She was a hardass, but she'd taught him a lot and she had unreal connections in the art world...like Brian.

He groaned, thinking of the painting adorning Trick's front hall. Brian was an artistic genius, and he wasn't afraid or embarrassed of the human form and its imperfections — or perfections, in Trick's case.

He slipped his phone out of his pocket again, reading the last text from Trick.

There is a squirrel outside my window and she's carrying actual babies. OMG, they are so cute!

Nav rolled his eyes. Trick was one of the most confusing people he'd ever met, but he was eternally grateful that he'd been unghosted after the intense night at the club. The man was almost goofy outside of a scene, but the second he got a whiff of submission or sex, he transformed into a sadistic beast that was intent on driving Nav mad.

When Nav had looked in the mirror that morning, his heart had fallen to his feet. For the past week he'd traced the bruises and welts every morning, reliving the scene as he kneaded his own ass and jerked off into the bathroom sink.

But they'd finally faded from blue to purple, then yellow. The last of them had disappeared, leaving nothing but smooth and flawless skin behind. It was as if the scene had been erased, the last proof of it gone forever. *Did it really happen?* Nav wasn't so sure anymore, not without proof.

But through all their texts, Trick hadn't expressed any thoughts about doing it again. The man had been so hot that night at the club, and almost wild as he'd watched Nav take the beating.

Derreck was another matter. That man looked like a fucking god and had an arm that any baseball player would have been proud of. Nav could imagine himself pressed against the wall again with Derreck's hits raging down on him from above.

But when he opened his eyes in the vision, Trick was always looking at him. Would he be able to do it again without Trick? Could he get lost in his own head and trust Derreck enough to let go? There was only one way to find out.

I think I'm going to message Derreck.

He sent the text off to Trick, scrubbing his face with his hand. He was about to slide his phone back in his pocket when it vibrated.

Why? You doing okay? Are you feeling level?

Nav could almost feel the demand in Trick's texts. He would have laughed, if the man hadn't been so damn cute. He knew it was serious and he shouldn't make fun, but he was feeling fine — great, actually. He'd never felt so *whole*.

No worries, I'm good. I was wondering if he would scene with me again. My marks are gone, and I really miss them. I want them back.

He slid his phone back in his pocket this time, striding over to the wall where Brian's painting used to hang. There was a modern piece there of indistinguishable geometric shapes. It was beautiful — if not a touch strange. His phone buzzed against his ass, but he ignored it. His break had ended the moment his boss had started yelling at him, and he had phone calls to make.

* * * *

Three hours later, and after too many hours rushing around the studio with more preparations for the upcoming gala, he finally remembered to check his phone. Trick had sent him a message a minute after Nav's last communication.

Can I call you?

"Shit," he said, looking up and down the gallery entrance. It was almost quitting time anyway, and he had worked his ass off all day. He sent off a quick text, hoping Trick would still reply after the long wait.

Shit, sorry! Got busy at work and I just saw your text now. I can call you when I get home in an hour. That okay?

Trick answered right away, like he'd been waiting for Nav's reply the entire time. Nav shook his head. Who was he kidding? Trick was engaged to Theo, who looked like a model and was really sweet, apparently. Nav was only on Trick's radar because he'd accidentally planted himself in the middle of a scene.

Can I stop over tonight instead? Maybe around eight?

That sounded more than all right. Nav couldn't keep the smile off his face. Even if Trick was unavailable, he was still hot as fuck, and they'd shared things that he had never shared with anyone else, not even Derreck. Derreck had flogged him, but he had never taken control in the way Trick had.

Derreck expected submission, where Trick took it.

Sounds good. See you then!

Nav shoved his phone under a stack of papers and lifted the receiver of his work phone to his ear. The line was dead, with the drawling buzz of dial tone grating against his ear, but his boss didn't have to know that. From the corner of his eye, he watched her peek around the corner. He nodded to the phone, hanging it up with a small smile. To her, it would appear that he was just hanging up from a successful call.

Bullshitting was something they should have taught in school.

"Still here?" she asked as she marched up to his desk, eyeing the stack of papers. "Oh, and working hard. I like this." She grimaced, which was the closest she ever came to smiling.

She was always mellow when she saw the dollars in the bank at the end of the day and after Nav had assured her that they were still bankruptcy-free. It probably helped that Brian had delivered her painting that afternoon.

Nav had actually *met* him, and he'd almost had a spontaneous orgasm, even though Brian had turned out to be a fifty-something balding guy who thought a sweater vest was a fashion statement.

His orgasm had fizzled away to nothing when he'd caught sight of the canvas. He was never going into her office again, because no one should have to see that much of their boss.

"I was just about to head out. I'll lock up if you want," he said, sliding a stack of papers neatly into a folder that he could address on Monday before setting the landline to sleep mode.

"Nonsense. You get out of here, and I'll lock up. Have a good weekend."

Nav had to do a double take to make sure it was actually his boss looking back at him and not an alien doing a shitty impression. What had she been doing in her office all afternoon? Probably staring at the painting of herself getting it on with her husband's secretary. *No thank you.*

Banish my thoughts now before they can go into long-term memory.

Nav forced a smile on his face before booking it to the door and sending a wave over his shoulder. She was already making her way back to her office, a spring in her step that was too awkward for him to acknowledge.

Chapter Twelve

Trick

Trick stared at his phone, wondering what the hell he was supposed to say to Nav when he went to his apartment. *What can I say?* He shouldn't have even made any plans to go there. Theo hadn't said a thing when Trick had mentioned that he had started texting Nav again, but Trick wasn't sure if that was a good thing.

But Nav wanted to see Derreck again, and Trick couldn't let that happen. The twinge in his gut ate at him as he had stared at his screen for three hours, turning every possibility over in his mind. Morgan, one of his coworkers, had even tried to start up a conversation about his new dog, shoving a picture in Trick's face. Trick had snapped at him, sending the man scurrying away.

Most days he played the part for them. He was gay, so of course he loved animals, right? And he was always happy, spoke and dressed a certain way and stared at every man's ass in existence—at least according to his coworkers. He usually didn't mind indulging them because he didn't want to be an asshole about it, but, as he'd bit his nails closer and closer to the quick, he'd lost his patience completely.

Trick looked up as Theo slid into his spot on the couch next to him. If there was anyone in the world who could make sense of what was going on with him, it was Theo, even if he had been quiet lately.

"What did you want to watch?" asked Trick, reaching for the remote. Television usually helped take his mind off Nav, and it would make the hour go faster. "I'll even be nice and let you decide." He went to hand the remote over to Theo, but Theo shook his head, his gaze lowered as he chewed on his lip.

Trick had never seen Theo look so guilty, with his hands folded and his back stiff. He set the remote back down in the holder, turning to face his fiancé.

"What? Did you eat my chocolate bar that I hid in the fridge? I was going to share it with you anyway," said Trick. Theo's frown deepened and he slouched his shoulders as he let out a long sigh.

"There's something I have to tell you," said Theo, closing his eyes as he took a deep breath.

Oh God, he's dying. Trick's heart skipped a beat. What else could it be? Theo had always been cheerful and upbeat, and Trick had put his recent moodiness off as his own issues with Nav, but what if Theo had been sick the whole time? Struggling through it on his own while Trick had his head in kinky clouds?

"I did a scene without you last week," said Theo, cutting off Trick's thoughts like a brick wall in the middle of the highway.

So? Trick waited a few moments for the actual issue, but Theo stayed silent.

"I know," said Trick, his words slow as he tried to figure out what Theo was so upset about. "I saw you and you looked amazing. You're always beautiful, but decorated in rope like that and completely unable to move, you were gorgeous." Trick shifted as the memory alone made heat pool in his gut. He should have stayed longer, but Nav had needed him. Even the three minutes that he had been gone from the room had felt like ages.

"What do you mean, you know? Everyone said that you weren't there." Theo flushed, clenching his fists as he ground his teeth. Trick spiraled deeper into confusion, reaching for Theo before thinking better of it and dropping his hand back to the couch.

Some Doms coveted their subs, keeping them close so that no one could lay a hand on them, but he had never been like that with Theo. They'd been together for a long time, but they didn't have a contract or a relationship that was anywhere close to twenty-four-seven, even if that was what Trick sometimes needed. He'd thought Theo *knew* that.

"I saw you up on stage. I wanted to make sure you were okay because you seemed pissed off when we got to the club, and you looked great—blissful," said Trick, leaving out the rest of his side of the story. If Theo found out that he had watched a scene with Nav, he would have been pissed.

"And you're okay with that?" asked Theo, his brows almost disappearing into his dark hair. "Why the hell are you okay with that?"

"Why the hell shouldn't I be?" asked Trick, irritation seeping into his tone. First, Theo acted pissed off about

Nav—not that he didn't have a good reason—but for some reason he was pissed that Trick *wasn't* upset about him in a scene? It reminded Trick of the year that Theo had said that he hadn't wanted anything for Christmas. That had been the Christmas from hell.

"I'm not great at shibari, but I know it's one of your interests. Harold is a master and probably the best Dom out there to scene with you like that. He gave you what you wanted and needed when I couldn't. That makes me happy, not upset."

Theo threw up his hands, standing from the couch. "What the fuck is wrong with you, Trick? You're my fiancé and my Dom, and I didn't even ask you if I could scene with another man…and you're okay with it?"

Trick shook his head. The conversation was spiraling fast, and Theo looked like he was close to hyperventilation. Theo was strong, but he was just as vulnerable as anyone else.

"Did he not respect your safeword?" asked Trick. There was something more to what Theo was saying. If that were the case, Harold would never find a club that would let him in their doors again.

"I never safeworded. He was kind and gentle," said Theo. He looked away from Trick, his gaze stuck on his socks. His dark hair was mussed, with shadows under his eyes that Trick hadn't noticed before.

"Did he give you aftercare?" asked Trick, slowly getting up from the couch and putting his hands on Theo's shoulders. He dropped his hands away when Theo flinched from the touch. *That's new.* They hadn't been intimate lately, but Theo had never flinched away from him.

"Yes."

"Then he did everything that I would have. He's a good Dom and a friend, and you can scene with him if you like. You don't have to ask me permission for something like that. I expect you to scene with someone else if you need something I can't give you."

"You don't get it, do you?" asked Theo, standing from the couch and turning away. "I should have to ask you, but it's like you don't even care. Sometimes I wonder if you even want me as your sub. You're too busy with someone else."

"Is this about Nav?" Trick swallowed. Even with their engagement, their relationship had always been somewhat open, to a point. They had scened with others in the past, although they were both usually present at the time. They hadn't had sex with anyone else — at least, not deliberately.

"No, it's about us," said Theo, his voice soft. "I've been feeling unsure about our relationship, because over the past few weeks, it has been like we are living together as friends, not as lovers. Something changed between us and I'm worried that it's never going to go back to the way it was."

"Theo, you are the kindest, gentlest, kinkiest man out there, and you are *my* man. What happened between Nav and me was an accident, but I feel like it's my obligation to help him with what he's going through."

"Are you going to scene with him again, Trick? I don't know if I can hear it from someone else next time." His caramel eyes were watery and bloodshot from suppressed tears. A part of Trick broke at the sight, while a deeper part burst with rage. *So he already knew.*

"I won't if it is one of your limits." He forced the words out, even though each one caused him a visceral ache. "But he's my friend, too. I can't give up his friendship, Theo."

Theo let out a sigh. "You really just don't get it." His words were so soft that Trick wondered if he was supposed to hear them at all.

Theo walked away, slamming the bedroom door behind him and plunging the apartment into lonely silence. Trick ran his hand through his hair, tugging the strands.

He knew what he had to do, even if it made him wonder if it would truly break him. He had to let Nav go.

Chapter Thirteen

Nav

Nav rushed home, running a comb through his hair and splashing water on his face before he caught the sound of three knocks on his door. He rushed to open it, his hand nearly trembling with excitement. *This must be how dogs feel when their owners get home.* Nav shook his head. Trick was not his *owner.*

He had expected a smile—or any kind of acknowledgment, really—but Trick only blinked as Nav opened his door. He didn't give Nav a once-over, or even mention the skin-tight jeans Nav had jammed himself into. Trick seemed to be looking over his shoulder at an invisible spot on the wall instead.

"Everything okay?" asked Nav, managing to keep his voice even. "I made dinner. I wasn't sure if you'd already eaten." If grabbing takeout on his way home and going out of his way to get Trick's favorite counted as making dinner.

"No, thank you," said Trick, only briefly looking over Nav's face before he looked back at the wall. "Can we talk?"

"Yeah, sure, of course." Nav stopped himself before he said anything more. Trick's presence was so overwhelming that he often still felt like a blushing virgin.

Besides, that line was so familiar that he was surprised he didn't have a phobia to it. Nav had heard it a hundred different ways. It was usually 'we need to talk', or 'I've been thinking about something', which was usually followed by something along the lines of 'we need to break up'. Only Trick wasn't his boyfriend.

"I think you should call Derreck and ask him to be your Dom," said Trick, as he pinched the bridge of his nose and clenched his jaw.

Derreck — tall, dark and handsome personified, although the size of his cock was still unknown. Nav hadn't even realized until after the scene that he hadn't seen, felt or even cared about Derreck's cock through the whole experience.

"Yeah, okay. I actually already sent him a text while I was waiting for you. We are going to meet up tomorrow night and try another scene. He said that after our last one, he'd been thinking about a few things to try." Of course, he had refused to tell Nav what those things were, as if implements of pain were some kind of surprise birthday gifts.

"Oh," said Trick, his expression falling as he ran a hand through his hair.

"You sure you're okay? Are you having second thoughts about the scene at the club? I know I don't understand that much about aftercare, but you said it was something that Doms need, too."

Taking a risk, he slid his hand into Trick's, locking their fingers together. Trick shivered from the touch, the vibrations going up Nav's arm. *Is he coming down with something?*

"No, it's not that. It's just...Theo. We had a fight." Trick took a deep breath before squeezing Nav's hand tight.

"I'm sorry," said Nav, barely hesitating before he pulled Trick into a hug. Trick was rock solid with tension, and the hug didn't seem to be helping any. "People fight all the time, though. You guys love each other, so I'm sure you'll work it out."

"I don't think he wants me to see you anymore," said Trick, his voice soft.

"Oh." Nav pulled back, his heart plummeting as his throat clogged. "Is it still because of what happened in the alley? I can tell him it wasn't your fault. I was just in the wrong place at the wrong time."

"No, he forgave me for that weeks ago," said Trick, looking down at his hand where it was probably still warm from Nav's touch. "It was about the scene with you and Derreck. I think Theo believes I'm cheating on him."

Nav snorted, then slapped a hand over his mouth when Trick shot him an irritated glare. "You make it sound like we had some sort of sex marathon in that room. I mean, I was the only one who came — and that's probably pushing the line, but it's not like there was any penetration at all. It was fun." *And intense, and the pinnacle of anything sex-related in my life.*

"I came," said Trick, his pupils dilating.

"You did?" Nav sucked in a breath. How had he missed that? Probably because he had been out of his mind with pain and pleasure.

"Of course I did," said Trick. "How could I not? You're the perfect sub, and you took everything like you were made for it. Like you were made for—" He cut himself off, taking a step back. "I just wanted to let you know. I'm not ghosting you, but now that you have another Dom, I don't think we should hang out anymore. If you have any questions or if you need help, you can text me, but otherwise, I'm going to try to stay away. Theo means the world to me, and I can't fuck that up." Trick gripped the door handle, the knob shaking as he trembled.

"I'm sorry," said Nav, his feet frozen to the floor. He'd never been so torn. Trick meant something to him, but he'd managed to fuck it up, just like every other relationship in his life. None of his break-ups had felt so final before.

Trick didn't say anything. He just took another step back into the hall, letting the door fall shut with a soft click.

Nav was alone again in his tiny apartment surrounded by beautiful things that could never be less alive. Even Sasha was out of town for a convention and couldn't bomb Nav's place with his presence.

Grabbing his phone, he blinked back the tears that threatened to fall as he dialed Derreck's number. Derreck answered on the second ring, his deep timbre sending a shiver down Nav's spine.

"Hey, can we meet tonight instead?"

Chapter Fourteen

Trick

"Where were you?"

Trick struggled to lock the door as Theo's voice broke down the last of his carefully constructed defenses. The sound of Theo's disappointment was so much worse than yelling or screaming.

Theo was standing in the kitchen, leaning against the cupboard and gnawing at his lower lip. Trick wasn't sure how long Theo had been there, but from the state of his lip, it had to have been quite some time.

"At Nav's." He had no desire to half-lie to Theo anymore. "I told him to ask Derreck to be his Dom, and that it would be best if we didn't hang out anymore." He looked down at his hands. They didn't feel like his. It felt more like he was crashing after a scene, his mind and his body stretched far apart.

"You didn't have to do that, Trick." Theo's voice softened and he pushed off the kitchen counter before wrapping his arms around Trick's neck. Trick leaned into the embrace, letting Theo's warmth wash over him. It still didn't feel real — Theo's arms nothing more than a Band-Aid on a broken body.

"Yes, I did. I would do anything to keep you," said Trick, sinking his hands into Theo's hair and taking a deep breath.

"Even give up the best sub you've ever had?" asked Theo, his voice quiet. He tightened his grip, as if he were afraid that Trick might try to pull away. "He's good for you, and a better slut than I could ever be."

"Don't say that." Trick jerked away, breaking Theo's grip easily. His fiancé was lean and strong, but he was no match for Trick.

"I've been wondering if it's time for me to say goodbye to the lifestyle, and you've hardly touched me since that night in the alley. It's as if you already knew."

"Knew *what*?" asked Trick, his chest rising rapidly as everything started to crumble. Theo had never said anything about leaving kink behind...and as for their sex life? For Trick, there wasn't one without the other.

"That I wasn't going to show up," said Theo, steadying himself against the counter. "I couldn't do it. Consensual non-consent is just too far for me. I was almost ready to have a panic attack, so I waited inside the door at the bar, hoping you would come back in, but you didn't. When I opened the door, I was going to safeword as soon as I saw you. But...you were with him, and I've never seen you look so high before. You looked like a god who'd gotten his first taste of a sacrificial bull."

Trick swallowed, rage and betrayal surging through him faster than he could have imagined. Not only had he let Nav down, but Theo, too.

"Why didn't you say any of this? We talked about that scene for months and planned every little detail. Why did you stay quiet?" He clenched his fists.

"Because I wanted to be your perfect slut. But I know now that I can't be." Theo let out a sigh. "I don't want to do this anymore, Trick. I think it would be best for both of us if we broke up." Theo looked to Trick, his gaze shockingly fierce. He was so strong, even when Trick was breaking apart.

"I'll stay at my sister's until I can find a new place," said Theo, as he reached for the door.

"I don't need you to submit to me, Theo," said Trick, facing his fiancé with rage and fear nearly blinding him. "Kink isn't my life. You are." *I'm lying to him again. I can't live without kink.*

Theo shook his head as he held the doorknob. "You said it yourself, Trick. If you can't give me everything I need, then you would expect me to get it from someone else. You don't have what I need, and I won't ask you to force yourself to be that man. You're my best friend, but I've been putting this off for way too long. I'm sorry that I hurt you, but I don't think the pain will last as long as you think."

After that, the door shut so quietly that Trick wondered if it had really happened. Twenty minutes passed as he stared at the chipped paint on the door, his mouth dry. He touched his lips, turning to the canvas on the wall.

They were so beautiful in the painting, every brushstroke filled with love so fierce that it made his heart pound every time he looked at it. When Brian had shown them the completed piece, Trick had dropped to one knee and proposed to Theo right there.

Love wasn't something he'd ever thought would happen between him and Theo. They had been good for each other, but he'd had a feeling that they'd both been vaguely dissatisfied. But the painting had shown him that it had been right there in front of him the whole time. It had just taken Brian's skills to show him that.

Sure, being with Theo hadn't given him little chills or made his heart pound. He didn't admire the pale skin of Theo's wrist or the crinkle at the corner of his eyes when he smiled. He'd only noticed those little details on one person — the man across the hall who he'd just cut out of his life.

But Theo was good, kind and worthy of the deepest affection that Trick had to offer. And Theo had called Trick his best friend. *Not my lover, not my fiancé — my best friend. What am I supposed to do with that?*

Without taking his eyes off the painting, Trick pulled his phone from his pocket, typing Brian's number from memory. They had been more than just good friends at one time — long before he'd ever stumbled across Theo at a munch.

"Trick, how are you, my darling?" asked Brian.

When Brian had come out to his friends and family, he had dialed his flamboyancy to the max. Usually it made Trick smile, a little chuckle in his voice at Brian's absolute joy of finally being free to express his sexuality, but his lips hardly even twitched as he held the phone to his ear.

"I need you to tell me something," said Trick, tracing his finger over the frame of the painting. It was smooth, polished and as dustless as the day Brain had lugged it up the stairs.

"Anything for you, my dearest."

"The painting you did of Theo and me, did you paint exactly what you saw?" The question burned his lungs, his ears already ringing as he inhaled the scent of long-dried paint. The scratched autograph in the top corner called him away from the artistic expression of his own body.

"You guys were perfect models, honey. You held still for me for so long, and you didn't even pop a juicy hard one for me — which was a disappointment. But no one is that good," said Brian with a tinkling laugh. "I left out that little mole on your tooshie, and Theo had that terrible hangnail, the poor dear."

"I don't give a fuck about moles," Trick snapped into the phone, instantly feeling terrible for it. "Did we really look at each other like that?"

"Trick, sweetie," said Brian, letting out a slow sigh, "you've never looked at anyone like that — not even me. We were together for five years, but you look at Theo the same way you looked at me — like we are fancy pieces of furniture that sometimes you like to sit on. We are just stuck looking back at you, knowing that you have no idea that we are out of your price range."

"Shit." Trick ended the call and cut off whatever else Brian had to say to him. He could go on for hours if given the chance. "I need a fucking drink."

Did I ever love Theo? He wasn't so sure anymore. The only real proof he'd had was apparently an expensive forgery.

He grabbed his keys, pushing out of the door and stomping down the hall.

Chapter Fifteen

Nav

"I want to try something new tonight," said Derreck as he pulled Nav's shirt over his head. His hands were molten against Nav's skin, the calluses dragging against him. Were all the calluses from flogging the shit out of people? Nav could guess that a few were, at the very least.

"Yep, you said that," said Nav, shivering in the chilly room and pointedly ignoring the frown that Derreck sent his way. It was a different room than the last one, but Nav only gave it a cursory glance. He wasn't scared or nervous, but he just couldn't keep still.

Derreck squeezed the back of his neck gently and Nav fought the urge to shrug him off. He looked to the walls instead, trying to focus on what was before his eyes and not tumbling around in his mind.

Restraints of every kind lined the room named *Still*, from a familiar-looking cross, to ropes and actual manacles. There were hooks on the walls and a few hanging from the ceiling with attached chains at different heights. One of the ceiling fixtures appeared to be attached to an adjustable winch. Nav shuddered, looking down at his thin wrists.

"Address me as 'Sir' tonight," said Derreck as he tossed Nav's shirt on the couch. He smoothed his dark hands over Nav's sides, before moving to Nav's front and pinching his nipples. "I think I've earned that title."

"Um, okay?" Nav tilted his head as something that looked like a medieval stretcher caught his eye. He hadn't called anyone 'sir' in his life — not his father, his teachers or that one cop that gave him a speeding ticket, even though he was only going ten above the speed limit.

"Just okay?" Derreck clamped down on his nipples until the zing went all the way to Nav's toes.

"Okay, Sir," said Nav. The word felt strange in his mouth and almost artificial. It wasn't as bad as calling someone 'daddy'. He shuddered for real, even as Derreck eased the pressure. Nav's father had been an asshole, and he had no desire to bring those childhood memories back anytime soon.

"Good," said Derreck, soothing Nav's sore buds with his fingertips. "Now, do you remember what to say if you want to stop?"

"Red." Nav rolled his eyes. Did they have to do this every fucking time? He just wanted to forget about his shitty day and his new best friend walking out on him.

Maybe he should have just called Sasha and endured the immature gay jokes over the phone instead of in person.

"Red what?" Derreck said calmly, pinching Nav's nipples between his fingers. It was as if Derreck's hands were made of hardware vises and not flesh and bone. Did he bench press a hundred pounds with his pinkies?

Nav bucked, trying to push Derreck away as the ache sharpened into a sting. His nipples were sensitive to begin with, and they were going to be bruised as fuck if Derreck kept it up. It wouldn't have been as fun as having bruises on his ass that he could poke and admire in the mirror.

"Red, Sir," he bit out, whimpering when the pressure suddenly eased. His chest throbbed.

"Good. And if you need to slow down?"

"Yellow, Sir." Nav rubbed his nipples, flinching with each soothing stroke.

"Much better. I think you deserve a reward for that," said Derreck, leading Nav over to the wall.

Nav rolled his eyes. A reward? What was he, a dog? From what he'd seen in the club, some guys were into that, which was totally fine. It was also totally not for him. He had not been born to be collared or *tamed*.

"I'll let you choose for your first time. Rope or manacles?"

Is that the reward? Nav swallowed.

The rope looked like a fancy version of something he could use to tie a boat up, only it was crimson and had an ominous shimmer. The manacles were exactly what Nav expected manacles to look like, with a lining of padding probably for *comfort*—as if manacles could ever be comfortable. They were hooked through a loop in the wall and looked sturdy enough to hold a spooking horse.

Glancing between the two, Nav chewed his lip. Neither of them had any appeal. They didn't give him that freedom in his mind that he'd been hoping for.

What's the right answer? Which one would Derreck want to see him in?

"Choose or I'll make the choice for you," said Derreck, his voice gruff. The sound sent a shiver down Nat's spine, his cock swelling in response.

Now *that* was exactly what he'd been looking for. He stayed silent, closing his eyes and shaking his head. He didn't want to make the choice. He couldn't.

"You'll be sorry for that one," said Derreck, his deep voice carrying an edge. Nav's cock hardened further, starting to ache against the confines of his jeans. He knew he wasn't getting fucked — Derreck had made that clear on the phone — but his cock didn't know that.

Derreck grabbed him, dragging him away from the wall and over to a different set of restraints. They were cuffs, silver and merciless-looking, with no padding to speak of. They clicked around Nav's wrists one at a time, the cold of the metal biting into his bones.

His breath picked up as soon as they'd clicked into place. It was as if something had settled over his mouth, and he could only get half the amount of air, even with his mouth wide open. He tugged, testing the strength, half-heartedly trying to break free. They were solid and unyielding, cutting into his wrists and leaving bruises behind.

He didn't want to hurt himself by pulling harder on the cuffs. The whole idea of that made his cock shrivel and dread seep into his gut. But what was he going to say? He didn't want the scene to stop. He wanted to lose his fucking mind.

"Yellow," he said quietly as he tugged on the cuffs again. They were too cold, too hard, and he couldn't breathe.

Derreck was there in less than a breath, releasing the cuffs with a latch that Nav hadn't noticed. Nav sucked air into his lungs, flushing as he dropped his gaze to the ground. Three seconds in and he'd ruined everything.

"Is it the cuffs or the restraint itself?" asked Derreck, his voice soft and sweet as he gently rubbed Nav's wrists, soothing the small red lines.

"I think the cuffs. It was like I couldn't breathe." Nav touched his chest, rubbing along his sternum as the ache eased. His heart was still beating fast, and although Derreck's voice was probably supposed to be calming, it wasn't working.

I want Trick.

"Did you want to stop or try something else?" asked Derreck. "Don't feel pressured either way. Exploring kink has its ups and downs, but it's good we found this out now before we went any further."

"Something else. Don't tie me down." He couldn't walk out of this room yet. He needed to think about anything but Trick.

"There are ways to restrain someone without using ropes, chains or cuffs," said Derreck as he pressed his chest to Nav's back, nudging him closer to the wall. He closed his huge hands over Nav's wrists, pinning him with strength, muscle and nothing else.

Nav shuddered as his cock filled again, aching with confusion. He'd slept with a few men who had manhandled him, and it had always ended up as an intense round of fucking. It really was too bad that sex was off the table with Derreck.

"Color?" asked Derreck, breathing into his ear.

"Green." Nav arched his back, rubbing his ass against the front of Derreck's jeans. He wasn't sure if

Derreck was hard or not, but his pants certainly felt full of man.

"Excited?" Derreck chuckled, pressing Nav's cheek to the wall. Tugging Nav's arms behind his back, he restrained him with one hand alone.

"I can manipulate you in so many ways, until you'll hardly be able to move." He raised Nav's arms up his back, until Nav's shoulders started to ache from the angle. Derreck paused a moment before it became too painful.

Nav bit back a whimper, squirming in the grip. It was a lot, but it didn't bring him anywhere close to the headspace that he craved. Blinking, his spirits fell as he found himself seeking out Trick in the corner of the room. He bit his lips, wondering what it would take to have Trick there looking back at him. *I don't want Trick – I need him.*

"I don't know if I like this," said Nav. He was powerless, but not in a good way. Nav wanted to be taken, defiled and overpowered while Trick slammed his cock home, caring nothing for his pleasure or his comfort. He didn't want to be held. "I can't," said Nav, a few tears leaking from the corner of his eyes when Derreck didn't let up immediately. When had he started crying? *Fuck I'm a mess.* Why hadn't Derreck let go? What was he waiting for?

"Yellow. Fuck, yellow."

Derreck released him so quickly that Nav slid down the wall, his knees hitting the floor. Nav curled in on himself, wrapping his arms around his legs and pulling tight.

"Can I touch you?" Derreck asked softly, crouching down until he was at Nav's level.

Nav shook his head, wiping the second wave of tears away before they could fall. *Trick! Trick, I need you. Where are you?* But the corner was empty, and Trick wasn't coming.

"I don't think I can do this with you," said Nav as he pushed himself to his feet. Goosebumps broke out over his skin and his teeth chattered. His hands were trembling so bad that he wasn't sure if they would ever stop.

"That's okay," said Derreck, his voice so soft that it almost helped. Retrieving Nav's shirt, Derreck passed it to him while keeping well back. "You were good to tell me your safeword when you were uncomfortable."

Nav shook his head. He didn't want to be good for *Derreck*, even if he was one of the hottest guys he'd ever met.

"I'm going to go. I need to go," Nav stammered as he pulled his shirt on, not even caring that it was inside out. The design on the front stuck to his sweaty skin.

"That's fine, Nav, but I need you to call or text me if you're not feeling okay. Remember what we talked about. I trust you to reach out to me." Derreck let him pass, his eyes pinched with concern.

"Thank you." Nav forced a smile onto his face. "You're a good Dom, Derreck, but you aren't the Dom for me. I think there's only one person out there who I can scene with. Thank you for helping me figure that out." The worry lines on Derreck's face eased, even as Nav's stomach twisted. *The only man I want is the one I can't have.*

Nav pushed through the door, taking a deep breath of air as soon as he stepped into the hall. There was a bite of alcohol and sex in the air, along with the distant murmur of voices. He would have to walk by all of them to get to freedom.

The lights were low as he rounded the corner, ducking his head to try to conceal his face. His cheeks always went splotchy when he cried, and he imagined that his eyes would be completely bloodshot. He wiped his cheeks again, the back of his hand coming away wet. *Why can't I stop crying?*

A woman to his left was folded on her hands and knees next to a high-backed velvet chair. Her Dom took a long sip from a glass, before setting it in the middle of her sub's back. The sub looked so at ease, taking the weight of the glass and balancing it perfectly without having to shift or struggle. He couldn't help but stare as the sub blinked, a soft smile on her lips.

There were things that had happened in Unkinked that had blown his mind and opened up his sexuality in a way that he had never imagined. *I'm going to miss this.*

"Nav?"

He froze at the familiar voice, blond hair and blue eyes filling his vision. Every time he saw Trick was like the first time. His chest went tight, his heart pounding as sweat gathered beneath his hair. The tears on his face were obvious to anyone who cared to look.

He dropped his gaze back to the raw hardwood floor. Fate was cruel for dangling his favorite treat in front of him, knowing that he could never reach it.

Side-stepping Trick, Nav ran toward the door, pulling the curtain wide. The bouncer gave him a startled look before Nav pushed through the door and into the silent street.

Outside it was warm and thick with the first tease of summer, but he was shaking as if it were February and not May. The wind picked up, drying the sweat from his skin and cutting straight through him. His teeth chattered as he gripped the wall.

"Nav, wait! Are you okay?" Trick stumbled through the door, his shoes slapping against the concrete sidewalk. Grabbing Nav's shoulders, he spun him around, digging his fingertips into Nav's muscles.

Nav huffed out a laugh as the first sparkle of joy seeped into his night. "You never did have any boundaries, did you?" He shook his head and tried to turn away. Trick only gripped him harder, bruises probably stamping into Nav's skin.

"Tell Theo I'm sorry," said Nav, dropping his gaze to Trick's feet. He was wearing the scruffy runners again with the laces pulled so tight that his feet had to have gone numb. Nav's chest tightened further as he looked at them.

Trick touched Nav's chin, tilting his face until their gazes met. Nav smiled through the tears that clouded his vision. Why was he trying to kid himself? He was totally gone on Trick. *I've never been strong enough to do what's right.*

Wrapping his arms around Trick's neck, Nav lifted himself up on his toes until their lips were almost close enough to touch. Their breaths mingled, and Nav shuddered as mint mixed with a bite of something darker.

Trick's eyes had gone wide, but he hadn't pulled away, dropping his hands to Nav's hips instead. Trick was just so good and perfect. How could Nav ever resist? Giving in to the only thing that felt right, Nav brought their lips together.

Chapter Sixteen

Trick

How could one kiss mean more than a ten-year relationship? Nav's lips were so soft, just like his skin, and he tasted of peach gum and innocence. He swept his tongue out, longing to taste more of Nav. He'd only gotten a hint during their last scene, and he'd ached for it ever since.

He sank into the kiss, dipping into Nav's mouth and mapping out every ridge with his swirling tongue. His gut surged and his cock throbbed to life as Nav let out a tiny gasp, tilting his head back to meet his touch.

Trick spun them, pushing Nav against the wall before grabbing Nav's legs and wrapping them around his waist. Nav clung to him like a pro, crossing his ankles to hold on tight so Trick had his hands free to explore.

Trick shoved his hands under Nav's shirt, groaning at the first touch of soft skin. Nav was chilly and clammy with drying sweat, but Trick had never felt anything better. *I must be a saint if I've resisted this long.*

Rocking his hips, Trick moaned as he met Nav's hard cock that lined up perfectly with his own. Nav was smaller than him—most men were—but Trick knew he was thick and beautiful beneath his layers of clothing. If Trick hadn't had self-control, he would have already had Nav in his hand or his mouth so he could finally admire his perfect cock the way it deserved.

Going still, Trick took a deep breath through his nose, gentling his mouth until their kiss was almost sweet. His two beers were still too many drinks to give Nav what he really deserved.

"Trick?" asked Nav, as he turned his head to the side to break their connection. He was panting, his lips glistening, swollen and practically begging for another kiss. "What about Theo? I can't let you betray him for someone like me," said Nav, his voice barely a whisper. His eyes were still shimmering with tears, his cheeks damp.

"Don't," said Trick, capturing Nav's lips again as if he could draw every negative thought from Nav's mind with such a simple touch. "Don't say his name when we are together like this. He left me because I wasn't able to see what's been in front of me this whole time. Please let me have you."

Nav's breath tickled Trick's damp lips, each puff a promise that was just out of reach. Emotions flickered over Nav's face as he went from disbelief, confusion and something that looked like anger. When a smile finally touched Nav's lips, Trick's relief was nearly palpable.

"Your car or mine?" asked Nav, chewing on his lower lip as he dropped his gaze to Trick's shoes.

Cupping Nav's chin, Trick tilted his head up. There were times he needed submission and others that he needed a partner.

Sliding his hand down Nav's neck, he traced every shallow curve before clasping Nav's slim wrist. Nav let out a gasp, tugging where they were connected and furrowing his forehead. The pale column of Nav's wrist was tainted with thin, dark bruises and a touch of red.

"You okay?" asked Trick, something inside him aching as he traced the marks with his fingertips. He hadn't made them, but he knew exactly who had, and it nearly killed him. He didn't want to think about Nav moaning and writhing for someone else — getting hard and coming for someone else. But from Nav's bloodshot eyes and tear-streaked cheeks, the scene hadn't gone well.

"Did you use your safeword?" asked Trick. Nav had been so close to using his safeword last time, but Trick had stepped in and salvaged the scene. What had happened when he wasn't there? Anger boiled under his skin. If Derreck had ignored Nav's safeword, Trick didn't care that he didn't have a chance in a fight against him, he would find a way to kill him.

"Yeah." Nav's gaze dropped, and a tiny sob puffed through his lips. "Yeah, Derreck stopped right away, but I feel like a bit of an idiot. He barely touched me, and I freaked out."

Wrapping Nav in his arms, Trick pulled him to his chest. He couldn't hug away the hurt and embarrassment, but he could dull the memory. Nav shuddered, his tears dripping down Trick's collar and soaking into his T-shirt. Rubbing up and down Nav's back with soft strokes, Trick waited for him to calm. He would give him as long as he needed, then a bit longer.

It didn't matter that they were in a desolate span of sidewalk between two streetlamps, or that more than one person making their way into the club had given them worried looks. He just wanted to hold Nav and suck the sorrow from his soul.

"Can I take you home? We can come back for your car when you're feeling better," said Trick, after Nav's tears had finally stopped flowing. He waited for Nav's nod before he let his arms fall, reaching for Nav's hand and leading him to the car. He held Nav's gaze as they walked, ready to trip over his own feet as long as he didn't have to look away.

Nav chuckled as Trick almost tripped, wiping his cheeks with the back of his arm. "I'm okay, Trick. Just watch where you're going."

"It's okay to not be okay," said Trick, keeping an eye on a raised corner of sidewalk so he didn't fall and take them both to the ground by accident.

Trick released Nav's hand as they reached his car, opening the door for him and taking his hand to help him into his seat. Nav rolled his eyes as Trick leaned over and buckled him in, adjusting the straps over his lap and chest. Some Doms would have been upset at Nav's bratty behavior, but Trick sucked it in, absorbing another layer of everything that was Nav.

Thankful that he had sobered from his two beers, Trick scrambled over to his own seat and turned the key, his favorite song obliterated the silence of the car, leaving a comfortable relaxation behind. He glanced at Nav as he pulled away from the curb, licking his lips at what he saw.

Nav's dark hair looked almost black in the scattered light that came only from the lamp posts dotted down the street. His tears had dried, and his head was tilted back with his eyes shut and his long lashes against his cheeks. A smile quirked at his lips.

"I can feel you watching me," said Nav, opening his eyes as his smile went wide.

"Sorry," said Trick, clearing his throat and focusing on the road just in time to see someone cutting him off. "You just look so beautiful."

Nav wasn't beautiful in the same way Theo was. He wasn't made of perfection and rigid curves. But perfection was boring. There was something else about Nav that pulled Trick in, beckoning him to drown.

"You said Theo left," said Nav, cutting off Trick's thoughts. Did he always have to get right to the point? *He wouldn't be mine if he was any different.*

For once, Trick had hoped Nav would ease into the conversation. Theo had left a gaping hole in his life only a hours before, and his control was tenuous at best.

"Yes," said Trick, gripping the steering wheel. The calm in his voice surprised him. *Am I really that cold-hearted?*

"Are you upset?" asked Nav, his voice pitching higher as he turned to Trick. "You don't sound upset." He tugged at the seat belt that Trick had probably pulled a touch too tight.

"I don't...know," said Trick. He should have felt sick. At the very least, he should have been the one crying. He'd only had two drinks, but that couldn't have been enough to drown his sorrows.

"Maybe you're in shock?" asked Nav, leaning forward to adjust the air conditioning as the front window started to fog. Trick hadn't even noticed. "You came to the right guy if you're looking for a break-up cure. I have a tried and tested method."

Trick slammed the brakes, ignoring the commuter behind them that laid on their horn, their high beams flashing into the rear-view mirror. "You are not my rebound, Nav. Don't ever say that about yourself again. You are the only one I could think about when Theo told me he was leaving." His voice was nearly a snarl, and Nav's eyes flew wide, a flush rushing over his cheeks.

"Okay," Nav whispered, dropping his gaze.

Trick ran his fingers over Nav's jaw, tilting his face up. Nav's eyelashes fluttered over his flushed cheeks, just a hint of his pink tongue visible through his open mouth. "Okay."

Nodding, Trick released his hold and eased off the brake. He waited until Nav looked away before he reached down to adjust himself, hoping that his cock would get the hint and back off. He could keep a clear head, even though Nav had pushed him closer to losing control than anyone else. But the way Nav submitted to every tiny piece of him never failed to make him hard.

Even with his inexperience, Nav was a natural.

Trick started as Nav slid his hand over his thigh, a mischievous grin spreading over Nav's face. His cheeks were still tinted pink, mixing innocence with his debauchery.

"Eyes on the road," said Nav, sliding his hand higher until he fumbled with Trick's zipper. His hand was steady, his tremble long gone as he pulled Trick's cock from his jeans and exposed him to the air.

Trick couldn't protest, not when his cock throbbed at the first touch of Nav's cold hand to the tip. Hissing, he dropped his gaze to where Nav was wrapped around him intimately.

Trick usually struggled to give up control, even with something as simple as a hand job. He craved to direct every movement, every touch—how hard, how soft and how long he had to wait to come.

But he could give control to Nav, if only for a moment. *It's what he needs. He's struggling, even if he won't let it show.*

Trick gripped the steering wheel, nearly missing their turn as he stared straight ahead. Familiar signs and advertisements whipped by the window, but Trick barely noticed them. *I can do this without killing anyone.*

Tree. Car. Sign. Shit! Turn.

He tried to focus, willing the throb to withdraw, but his body didn't listen. Nav wrapped his warm lips around him and instantly shot his remaining control to hell. He veered over to the side of the road, clicking his blinker on at the last second and slamming the brakes as the tires fishtailed onto the gravel shoulder.

"Fuck." He slammed his head back into the seat as he turned the car off and gripped the back of Nav's head, pushing him down. He barely managed to keep his hips from bucking up as Nav took him down his throat, sucking him like a goddamn porn star.

He shot off embarrassingly quick with a groan that was too loud in the small space. As Nav leaned back, Trick caught him by his hair and dragged him in for a kiss, sucking his flavor off Nav's tongue.

Trick ran his palm over the seam of Nav's zipper, pressing softly as Nav bucked against the touch. He was so close to ripping Nav's pants off and fucking Nav with his fingers until he came all over the dash.

Instead, he drew back, nudging Nav into his seat before pulling his seatbelt around him and clicking the buckle into place. Nav giggled, throwing his head back as he squirmed.

"Safety first," said Trick, restarting the car and pulling back onto the road. He pushed the pedal to the floor as he finally reached their street. Nav was practically begging to be fucked, and Trick wasn't going to make him wait another moment longer.

Chapter Seventeen

Nav

Which one? Nav looked between the two doors, each identical except for the number nailed to them. He wanted to wrap himself in Trick's scent and roll in his sheets, but they wouldn't just smell like Trick. He wasn't sure if he wanted Trick to fuck him with Theo still clinging to the bed.

He'd done it before with other men, their exes barely out of the door — or not out of the door at all. But Trick was...different. *Everything* was different.

Turning to his own door, Nav fumbled with his key before he managed to unlock it, pushing inside and dragging Trick along with him. He kicked off his shoes, Trick doing the same before they went straight for the bedroom. Nav considered pausing three times as he passed other surfaces that were totally acceptable for fucking. His nuts were ready to bust, but there was nothing like fucking in a bed. He'd experienced some of his worst sex injuries trying to fuck in random places. He did not recommend subway bathrooms.

Trick settled his big hands on Nav's shoulders steps away from the bed, sliding down his chest and tweaking at his sore nipples. Nav arched into the touch, trembling at the line of heat that Trick left behind. Unlike his comforting touches during aftercare, Trick's caresses were now charged with sexual tension and intent.

Trick moved closer, resting his hard chest against Nav's back. Nav tilted his head to the side, begging for Trick's lips on him. A groan pushed through his lips as Trick tweaked his nipple and slid his mouth over his neck.

"Are you sure you're okay with this?" asked Trick. "Sometimes it takes a few days of recovery after you use your safeword." His tongue teased Nav's ear lobe, Trick's breath tickling the inside of his ear.

"This is exactly what we both need."

Trick spun him, lowering his mouth over Nav's and capturing him in a fierce kiss. Nav's knees buckled as they met the bed, and they tumbled back onto the soft sheets, their teeth clacking as they landed.

Trick's taste of darkness had transformed into stale booze, but Nav sucked him in anyway, twining their tongues and teasing, all while waiting for Trick to take control. In the car they had been equals, and it had left Nav feeling more off-balance than he had expected.

Trick dropped down his body, his tongue drawing a wet line on the strip of flesh between Nav's pants and the hem of his shirt. Trick gripped the hem in his teeth before tugging it up, grappling with it until Nav's chest was finally exposed. Sucking on Nav's nipple, Trick pulled Nav's shirt over his head with one hand.

Nav gasped, arching his back and whimpering. His nipples were still bruised from Derreck, and every touch was laced with an ache that went straight to his cock. He was so close already and leaking on the inside of his jeans. At the rate they were going, he would end up an absolute mess by the time he finally got his pants off.

Trick tugged at Nav's shirt until it slid over his biceps, holding Nav to the bed with the light touch on his arms. Instead of sliding the shirt free, Trick tangled the material at the level of Nav's wrists, locking him into a hold that was more intimate and softer than any manacle.

Trick moved one hand to the middle of the makeshift bind, pushing against the mattress until Nav felt the strain against his bruised wrists. A tiny glimpse of pain faded as Trick brought their lips together.

Nav sucked in a gasp. From within the light hold, something had changed. Trick pressed his lips a bit harder, his tongue moving deeper and his movements slowing to match the steady beat of his heart against Nav's chest. Nav's own heart was pumping fast, his lungs screaming for air, despite the greedy breaths he dragged in through his nose.

He had never felt this way before — period, not even in high school when he'd cornered the biggest jock and convinced him to stand still while Nav practiced his oral skills, not when he'd had a foursome during an epic summer vacation in college and definitely not when he'd fucked his ex's dad against the countertop of their main floor powder room as his ex had waited in the living room for him to finish washing his hands.

"Stay still for me," said Trick, his voice deep. The order was softer than Nav had ever heard it, leaving room for something more.

Nav nodded, biting his lip when Trick tugged at the button on his jeans. Trick slid them down quickly, his eyes going dark when he realized that Nav had chosen to forgo boxers.

Nav's cock arched toward Trick, who was still fully clothed but was licking his lips like a dragon who had just discovered a hoard of golden eggs. His blond hair was mussed, and his calm breaths had given way as he took his time, his gaze exposing every part of Nav.

Nav glowed under the attention, parting his legs so Trick could see every bit of him. His body was far from perfect, but he'd always managed to make the best of what he had. Shy wasn't even in his vocabulary.

He choked as Trick went from looking to dropping down on his cock without warning, sucking the tip briefly before shoving himself all the way down until his nose touched Nav's trimmed curls. Trick swallowed, somehow pulling him deeper before he started to suck, pulling the pre-cum directly from his balls.

"Ah. Fuck, fuck." Nav couldn't stop himself from bucking, driving even deeper until Trick gagged around him. His blue eyes were watery, but Nav couldn't pull back. His cock had been up and down so many times in the last few hours that he couldn't hold on for another second.

With one last suck, Nav came, spurting down Trick's throat in an embarrassing amount. He struggled to fight his orgasm, even as it was pulled from him suck after suck.

The last time he'd come without permission, Trick had crushed his balls so hard that they had ached for three days.

But Trick didn't stop or reach for Nav's sac. He swallowed, pulling Nav deeper, even as Nav's cock started to soften and go sensitive. The next suck had a touch of fire that lanced over his nerves, drawing a spurt of cum from him that he didn't even know he had left.

"Fuck." Nav groaned, trying to free his cock, but Trick slipped his hands under his ass, holding him deep while taking long breaths through his nose as Nav's cock shrank small enough for him to breathe again.

Pleasure evaporated into a tickling ache that made him writhe, desperate to free himself from the onslaught. Trick was too strong, his mouth and grip the only force in the world that Nav really respected, but now it was too much.

He kicked out, his heel scraping down Trick's side as he struggled to breathe. Teeth grazed his sensitive flesh — a warning and a threat.

"Too much," said Nav, arching as Trick only sucked him harder, slipping a hand over his sac and kneading his balls at the same time. A thread of pleasure pierced the agony, but it wasn't nearly enough. His dick and balls were going to fall off if Trick kept it up.

If Trick was trying to get him hard again, it was an impossible task. His orgasms were always bone-deep, pulling everything out of his core and leaving nothing behind but a bit of dust.

"I can't, Trick. I really can't." Tears streamed down Nav's face and he dug his fingers into Trick's hair, pulling so hard that a few blond strands broke free, tangling with his fingers.

Trick pulled off with a loud *pop,* surging up and grabbing Nav's wrists to pin them back over his head. *When did I move them?*

Trick's eyes were dark, his lips stained bright red and pressed into a thin line. "Can you be still or do I have to make you?" His voice dripped with disdain and sarcasm as he raised one eyebrow.

Nav's chest heaved, his legs trembling against Trick as he struggled to answer. A burst of sound thrust through his lips as Trick dropped down and sucked his cock deep into his mouth.

Nav groaned, his cock twitching to life, even though he knew he was spent. How did Trick even know how to do this to him? It was as if the man had a manual to his body and his mind — one that Nav had never had the pleasure of reading.

Gripping the headboard again, Nav took a deep breath and held on for dear life. It took most of his brain power just to focus on keeping his hands still and his fingers hooked under the edge of wood. His body thrummed, sweat trickling down to the sheets as his breaths came out in garbled pants that were so close to a scream that he should have been worried about his neighbors overhearing.

"Quiet." Trick ordered, his tone terrifying as he gripped Nav's balls and tugged. Blood flooded Nav's mouth as he bit his lip, the only possible way for him to keep the noises back.

"I can't," Nav whispered, sweat mingling with tears as he shivered. He was so fucking lost, pinned even as he floated under Trick's stare. He wanted to come again for Trick so badly, but he just couldn't. He wasn't nineteen anymore.

I can't. I can't.

"I don't know what you're talking about, Nav. I just want to play with you. Is it so hard for you to be still and quiet so I can play? Besides, you know how to stop me, so don't pretend to be dumb. One little word and all this is over." Trick's lips curved into a malicious grin and Nav's heart thundered, his vision wavering for a second. Both fight and flight were at the forefront of his mind, his body tense and ready.

"Green." The word was strangled, but Nav meant it whole-heartedly. The feeling from the club had already transformed into something so much better. How could he have ever thought that he would want someone other than Trick to take care of him?

When Trick dropped down on Nav's cock yet again, sucking fiercely and grazing the head with his teeth, something snapped deep down in his core. He moved his hands from the headboard, threading his fingers in Trick's hair before tugging hard. *Punish me. Push me.*

Trick let out a yelp, gripping at Nav's wrists until his bruises flared to life. Nav went slack, the resistance draining from his body as he let out a long moan. *Please.*

Trick moved quickly, surging up and grabbing Nav by his hair before forcing him to roll over and pinning him face-first into the mattress.

Nav struggled as he was momentarily smothered, Trick's clothed cock scraping against his naked ass. A slap rang out, and seconds later a path of fire scalded across the same place.

"Fuck," said Nav, biting his tongue to hold back a scream as a second slap hit the same spot. He pushed his face into the sheets, smothering his cries and yelps as the hits rained down over and over, each one as fierce as the first.

It was nothing like the leather flogger whose tiny straps had struck him in a hundred places at once, spreading the impact into a stinging thud. That had been for pleasure, where the slaps from Trick were pure humiliating punishment.

Trick's palm was hot and hard, his hand so large that

one hit consumed Nav's entire ass cheek. He was being beaten like a naughty boy who had stumbled across his daddy's porn stash.

Nav knew his words. They'd never been so clear to him before. But why would he need them? He'd never felt stronger in his life.

"Oh, so now you're trying to keep quiet? It's fine to moan like a whore, but you can't let anyone hear you cry from a little spanking?" Trick slammed his hand down again, the numbing surface of Nav's ass soaking up the blow.

The neighbors. He wanted to remind Trick, but he couldn't quite get the words out of his mouth. Nav bit his lip harder, copper soaking his taste buds. The apartment's walls were thin enough that he could hear when someone dropped a plate or whistled a tune in the shower. If someone called the cops, he doubted they would be very understanding about his suddenly kinky sex life.

"Will you be still?" asked Trick, taking harsh breaths as he smoothed his palm over Nav's ass. "Can you be quiet? Or do you want your neighbors to find out how much of slut you are?"

They probably know already. Nav shuddered as the sudden urge to have someone watching them slithered into his mind. If Derreck saw them now, would he be jealous? Or would he be so hard that not even his zipper would be able to hold him back?

Nodding, he gripped the sheets with his tangled hands. His shirt was close to falling off, but he didn't want the restraint to disappear. It was what he had wanted when they'd walked into the *Still* room. It hadn't been Derreck's fault that he wasn't Trick.

Trick moved, stroking and squeezing Nav's ass like

the fucking sadist he was. Nav barely kept his groans behind his teeth by sealing his lips and breathing solely through his stuffy nose. He shuffled his legs wide as Trick spread his cheeks, his breath ghosting against his hole.

He'd prepared himself in the halfway hope that he would get lucky, despite Derreck's insistence that sex was off the table. *How many times have I heard that?*

Luckily, Nav's two-week stint as a Boy Scout had taught him two things. The first, and most impressive, was how to build a fire in the pouring rain, although he usually cheated with gasoline and a lighter instead of the waterproof matches, dryer lint and tiny bits of kindling that he'd learned with.

The second was to be prepared. As a kid, that meant extra snacks in case he got lost on his short walk home from school. As an adult, it meant a shower and a deep clean if he was going to be within a five-block radius of a club or bar. He was never sure when he would meet Prince Charming or get fucked in an alley by a stranger.

At the first touch of Trick's tongue, Nav almost broke his vow of silence. He tensed as he tried to keep the sound behind his lips, his back bowing as he clenched his fists in the sheets. His bed was a disaster, the fitted sheet already untucked and making its way across the mattress.

Rimming was one of the best things that had ever been invented, but it was surprising how many guys didn't want to do it. Maybe it was the fact that he'd stuck to short-term relationships with guys who didn't want to put their tongue inside someone they barely knew.

Trick didn't seem to have any qualms as he flicked his tongue over the rim of Nav's hole before he pushed inside. It was hot, wet and fucking perfect, with none of the burn that Nav had been expecting when things had started to get heated. He'd half expected Trick to shove his cock inside as soon as Nav had been stripped of his pants, but as usual, Trick had surprised him.

Trick swirled his tongue, seemingly going for it one hundred percent and not half-assing it with two licks before he called it a day. Nav was ready to bare every part of himself to Trick and give himself over whole-heartedly.

Trick speared him with one finger alongside his tongue, then two before Nav could adjust to the first. He waited until Trick was knuckle deep before he clamped down with all his strength, reveling in the aching burn that flared to life.

"Damn," said Trick, letting out a shuddering breath as he scraped his teeth over Nav's sore ass. "Such a good boy."

Nav preened, relaxing and rolling back onto Trick's fingers before clamping down again, as if he could milk Trick's cock through his hand. The sound that Trick made was probably illegal in most provinces.

"Lube and condoms?" asked Trick, as he withdrew and moved toward the nightstand.

"Wait," said Nav, his tangled wrists halting his momentum as he tried to reach the drawer first, sending him face-first into the mattress.

"Condoms are non-negotiable, and I think you deserve lube today," said Trick as reached for the drawer. He closed his hand over the knob and Nav's breath caught.

"That's not it...shit." Nav sucked in a breath as Trick pulled the drawer wide and his blond eyebrows jumped. "I know you told me not to Google search, but

I-I went a bit...overboard. I should know better than to shop when I'm horny."

Groaning, Nav ducked, smooshing his face back into the comforter, and flushing as Trick pulled a leather flogger from the drawer. The strips were genuine leather and the website had claimed that it was for beginners, even though it looked so similar to the torture device that Nav remembered from the club. The real difference was the color — the handle a sparkling blue with dyed leather to match.

"It has a nice weight, but I think you can take more," said Trick, tossing the flogger on the bed as if it were the most natural thing. "I like this, too, but we are nowhere near there yet." A blue studded collar dangled from his fingertips, the shade matching the flogger perfectly.

Nav groaned, attempting to smother himself into unconsciousness or something more permanent. He'd caught a brief glance of a couple at the club — a Master and their pet more likely — and it had instantly intrigued him. He'd wrapped the collar around his neck as soon as it had arrived, and goosebumps had broken out over his skin.

"These are nice. I'm sensing a theme."

Nav glanced up at the string of anal beads dangling from Trick's fingers. They were the same shade of blue, even though he'd purchased them two years before when he'd been going through a drought. There was a matching plug and dildo that had come with it as a set, but he'd moved those to the spare room after the new additions.

"I think this one is my favorite, though." Trick held up the only object that was black in the entire drawer. The plug seemed fairly thin and was definitely easy on the way in. If it wasn't for the bulb that inflated it to an exceptional size, it would hardly be noteworthy.

"What inspired this, slut?" Trick held the plug, twisting the knob before pumping the bulb. His eyes went dark as he watched it expand, doubling then tripling in size as he continued to pump. "You can answer, but don't think I've forgotten about how you broke your promise to stay silent."

A thrill ran up Nav's spine as he wondered what the punishment would entail. Would he be flogged over his already-inflamed cheeks? Or would Trick forget that he ever went to grab lube in the first place? Nav's dormant cock twitched painfully at the idea, still throbbing from the overstimulation.

"I got it 'cause…well I thought that someday — maybe…or maybe not — you and Derreck?" Nav wilted. He was usually so confident, his shyness burned out of his system long ago. Trick always managed to pull it out, though.

"Derreck and I *what*?" Trick asked, his grin malicious. He let the air out of the plug with a hiss, the stretched plastic shrinking back to an unremarkable size.

"Would want to fuck me," said Nav, sinking further. The humiliation was worse than when his mom had found his gay porn stash and had spent three days quizzing him on why he thought he was gay. *"I like dick,"* had not been a clear enough statement.

"I've already fucked you with no prep, and Derreck's not much bigger than me. I don't think you need this for that." He twirled the plug and squeezed the soft, deflated rubber.

"No, I meant, at the same time. You'd fuck me at the same time," said Nav, letting out an exasperated sigh. Trick was just being an asshole.

"I would pound your ass and Derreck would fuck that pretty little mouth of yours if we were fucking you at the same time. That still doesn't explain the plug." Trick furrowed his forehead and Nav held back his curse.

"I wanted you both in my ass at the same time. Two thick cocks stretching me so wide that I needed an inflatable plug to open me up first," said Nav, his voice deadpan as he lost his patience.

"Oh," said Trick, as if he was just finally understanding. *Liar.* "I hate to break it to you, but Derreck doesn't fuck his subs. You'll have to be content with just my dick for now."

Nav flushed hotter, shaking his head. "I'm sorry. I wasn't..." He had only been hopeful that someday something like that would happen to him. After a night of Internet searching and porn, he had made a few impulse buys.

"Don't apologize for something you want, slut, even if it is *nasty*." Trick's grin stretched wide as he tossed the toys back into the drawer, grabbing the tube of lube and two condoms out of the super econo box that Nav had in there.

"I don't have extra-large," said Nav as he watched Trick pull the condom from the package and eye it up. He hadn't wanted to get his hopes up.

"Turn around with your ass up." Trick's voice dropped, all playfulness disappearing as he tugged the zipper on his jeans. It was only after Nav turned around and planted his face back into the sheets that he heard the cap of the lube popping open.

Cool, thick gel smoothed over his hole before Trick jammed two fingers in deep to coat his walls. It was the best lube that Nav could afford, and it usually lasted forever, but he wasn't sure it would hold up against a cock the size of Trick's.

Licking his lips, he leaned back, peering over his shoulder. Trick's gaze was glued to his ass, and where his fingers were disappearing over and over, spreading wide each time to stretch Nav out. He was still fully clothed, with only his cock peeking through the zipper in his jeans, looking bigger and thicker than Nav remembered. He still couldn't believe that he had managed to take it raw.

Their eyes met and the corner of Trick's lips quirked as he lunged ahead, burying his fist in Nav's hair and pushing his face back down onto the bed, twisting to the side so Nav could still breathe. The blunt head of his covered cock lined up with Nav's opening, feeling like it would never fit inside him.

One thrust, and Trick eased into him, stealing the breath from his lungs and driving his cock directly into Nav's prostate with brutal steadiness. Nav let out a strangled cry, before fighting it down, refusing to break his silent promise again so soon. His soft cock dribbled as his prostate was battered and Trick rocked his hips, forcing himself deeper and deeper as he split Nav wide.

Oh God. How did I do this last time? He couldn't have gotten tighter since their alley fuck, but even with prep, he felt like he was on the verge of tearing—like he was some kind of fucking virgin. He pushed back, trying to welcome Trick inside, who took advantage and bottomed out with one last jerk. Trick's zipper scratched against his sore ass, his jeans still clinging to his hips.

"So fucking tight for me. Maybe I should have opened you up with that plug and spread you wide. I bet you would still be tight, clamping your ass down on me to try to milk me dry. You're practically begging for my cum in your ass." Trick stilled, his breath tickling the back of Nav's ear as he whispered filthy, depraved things that made Nav wish he could get hard again.

I can't. I can't. He wasn't in college anymore. One orgasm a day was pushing it, but God forbid he go three days without.

Trick gripped Nav's hips, rolling so his cock slid over Nav's prostate, each sweep forcing a dribble of pre-cum onto the sheets. Nav had firmed up into a semi, but his cock was painful and throbbing in protest.

"You like my cock, slut?" Trick drew all the way out before sliding back in slowly, dragging over Nav's spot with evil precision.

Nav nodded into the sheets, biting his tongue to keep back the whimpers and moans. It was too much, but it only got worse when Trick settled his hips against his ass, his wiry hair scratching against his sore cheeks as Trick's pants slowly slipped down and he humped himself as deep as possible. After another slow pass and dribble of pre-cum, Nav couldn't keep back his pained whimper.

"Am I too much for you?" Trick asked, his pace unchanged.

Nav shook his head, pushing back against Trick to try to take him faster. It was the slowness that was too much. He had been expecting a fast, and borderline painful fuck, but Trick had thrown him for a loop yet again. Slow fucking was for couples—and definitely not for whatever they were to each other.

"Bad boy." Trick slapped Nav's sore ass when Nav tried to meet his thrust again. "You promised you could keep still and let me play. That's two promises you've broken now." Trick withdrew, tugging his pants off and tossing them to the floor before easing back in like he'd never left.

"I'm sorry." Tears prickled at the corners of his eyes unexpectedly, but it wasn't from the pain. He was trying so hard, but he never seemed to be good enough. He was too tight, too loud, and he just couldn't stop squirming. How long would it be before Trick went back to Theo?

"You shouldn't be sorry yet, but you will be." Trick pistoned his cock in and out at slow speed and Nav could feel every inch as it buried itself over and over — every drag, every slick slide and every aching brush against his prostate.

The sounds of the apartment faded, the clock's monotonous clicking a background buzz with no meaning. He wasn't sure how long Trick had been fucking him, but he seemed no closer to finishing than when he had first buried himself inside.

"Have you figured out your punishment yet?" Trick asked, his voice cutting through Nav's drifting thoughts. Nav started at the sound, so lost in the steady rhythm of pleasure and pain. *Am I hard?* It didn't feel like it, but he didn't think he was soft, either.

Nav shook his head, his voice locked away and the answer too far out of reach to even try. His heart slowed and his eyes rolled back as Trick splayed his hands over his back, pushing him down and changing the angle of his thrusts.

"I thought you were a smart boy." Trick chuckled as Nav flinched, his prostate aching and sore. "But I understand that you're too focused on my cock right now. You can't help yourself. Do you even want to know?"

Nav licked his dry lips. It didn't matter. He belonged to Trick, and Trick could do whatever he wanted. If Trick wanted to turn him around and fuck his face while his cock was still shiny with lube, Nav would have taken it without complaint. If Trick wanted to flog him while he was inside so Nav clamped down on him with each blow, that would have been fine. *Anything.*

"I'll tell you before you get too deep. You're already floating now, aren't you, slut?" Trick pinched Nav's ass, fire bursting over his skin. "I'm not stopping until you come. If I can't last that long, then I'll get the plug and fuck your hole bigger and bigger until you come for me. I'll destroy you before I stop, and you are going to take every thrust until you come." As if to prove his point, Trick slowed his pace, the excruciating pleasure zinging along Nav's spine.

"So, are you going to come for me now like a good slut? Or do I have to wreck you first? You can answer." He rocked his hips, popping the head of his cock in and out of Nav's hole.

"Nnn-n." It took everything Nav had to moan before his voice was torn away again and he started to drift. His body was too large for his tight skin, his ass the focal point of the ache. He couldn't take much more before he broke. Or maybe he was already broken— already a little doll for Trick to play with.

"It's okay, slut. I should have known that you wouldn't be able to decide. There's no room left in your head when all you can think about is my cock. All you have to do is take it and let me play." Trick's voice dropped to a whisper and the dam inside Nav snapped.

Color blinked out of existence and sound was barely important anymore. The only thing that remained was Trick.

Tears soaked into the sheets, as Nav heaved with sobs — the sensation so strange that it could have been someone else crying and not himself. Taking a distant back seat, he let go, giving everything he had to Trick.

Distantly, his cock wept, an aching pleasure rushing through his gut as his balls swelled then released. Trick pushed in deep one last time before stopping, the stillness more jarring than any fuck could have been. It had been going forever, but now that it had stopped, his world was crumbling. He floated away, a strange type of unconsciousness settling over him.

"Good boy."

He drifted.

Chapter Eighteen

Trick

"Christ." Trick cursed as he stepped into the bathroom that was just down from Nav's bedroom. He should have been more prepared. He was *always* prepared, until Nav had swept the world right from under his feet. He usually didn't scene with an ounce of alcohol in his blood either, but although he'd sobered, Nav had thrown that off the rails, too.

He'd waited until Nav had fallen fast asleep before he'd used his shirt to wipe them down. Dreading the moment when he would have to pull away and get them a cloth and water, Trick had waited as long as he could.

Nav had fallen so hard into the state that most subs only dreamed about, and Trick had been riding the same waves, almost out of his mind as Nav took each thrust. It had been like no scene he had ever experienced, and he hadn't even lifted a flogger.

Trick had hoped to give Nav exactly what he needed after whatever had happened to him at the club, and he had responded like a dream as Trick removed every trace of Derreck from his body. The bruises had been stripped away, Nav's fleshy canvas stained only with Trick's marks by the time he'd finished.

Leaning against the cool glass of the mirror, he took a deep breath, letting it fog over the glass as he exhaled. His skin was still buzzing, his body itching as adrenaline and serotonin rushed through his veins. The mere thought of curling around Nav again pushed him even higher.

Theo had been so right. What they'd had together had been safe and sexy — two beautiful and like-minded people putting on a show for themselves and others. But that was as far as it had gone.

Every scene with Theo had been a carefully guided dance — one that Trick had gotten so good at that he hadn't been able to see the falsity of it anymore.

If I push Theo's face into the bed, he'll arch his back and wiggle his hips with a teasing smile on his face…

If I slap his ass, he'll wince, the word 'gentle' hidden just behind his teeth…

If I prep him too quickly so I leave him tight enough to split open, he'll beg for me to go slower…

None of that described Nav. Nav was a surprise, wrapped in mystery paper and delivered by a masked man. Trick never knew what he was going to find or how Nav was going to react. Nav's pain tolerance had probably been as low as Theo's until Trick had managed to flip that switch that turned Nav into a god of submission.

Grabbing a cloth, he blinked in the dim light, feeling along the sink and running the water until it warmed.

He crept back to the bed, staring at Nav, who was still in the same position as he'd been in when he'd left.

The single window in the room allowed the moonlight to filter in, casting an eerie glow over Nav's sleeping form. He'd clutched his soft hands to his chest in his sleep, his pale legs exposed to the moonlight. He was so beautiful that it made Trick's chest ache.

He eased onto the bed, moving behind Nav and swiping gently between his ass cheeks. Nav whimpered, tossing his head as Trick tried to scrub the lube from his hole before reaching around to clean his cock that had responded to him, despite Nav's insistence that it wouldn't.

Trick had been ready to go again in the car and could probably go again after a power nap, but Nav seemed to be a one and done kind of guy. *I'll have to work on his stamina.*

It wouldn't be a hardship.

Rinsing the cloth in the bathroom, he scooted back into bed, spooning Nav's warm body against him. Nav's ass was hot from the beating, like a blistering sunburn against Trick's groin. Shuddering, his cock flared to life, the head slipping between Nav's still-damp cheeks.

He would never violate Nav when he was sleeping—at least not without permission—no matter how tempting it was. He had no desire to fuck up a relationship that was still so fresh and new.

Skimming his hand down Nav's sternum, he paused as Nav's chest rose and fell with a long sigh. His hair tickled Trick's face as it fluttered from his breath, his skin so soft that it hardly felt real.

Trick closed his eyes, slowing his own breathing and listening hard. Nav's heart thudded under his palm, the deep sound just on the edge of Trick's hearing. He needed to get closer—close enough to live inside Nav so he would never have to let go.

"Nav." Trick pushed his face into Nav's hair, breathing in citrus shampoo and something deliciously masculine. His chest pulled tight as tears gathered in his eyes. There was no risk of them falling. He had more control over himself than that.

"You okay?" asked Nav, apparently awake, even with his breathing still low and deep. He must've been coming down, but hopefully not as hard as Trick was.

"Not really," said Trick, knowing he had to be honest with Nav as well as himself. "It was really intense for me, and I'm feeling it." He took a shuddering breath, letting the shiver wash over him as he pulled Nav closer.

The guilt was always the worst. *Did I push him too far? Did I force him into something he doesn't want?*

Nav's warmth sank into his limbs, pushing the ice to the tips of his fingers where it could never threaten his heart.

Nav turned in his arms, laying his head on Trick's chest and tangling their legs together. His palm rested over Trick's heart, chilled in the air-conditioned room. It was barely summer, but the window shaker was humming away on maximum.

"Missing Theo?" asked Nav, his voice gravelly with sleep. He shifted, probably trying to get comfortable, and rested his thigh between Trick's legs, the limb brushing against his half-hard cock. Nav grunted, shifting his leg away.

"I don't know," said Trick, trying to untangle his thoughts. "I don't think so. I don't want to be anywhere but here right now, and I don't want anyone but you in my arms." He tightened his hold, cupping Nav's lower back to bring them closer.

"Hmm-m. You know how to make a guy feel special." Nav's lips quirked against his chest, even as a tiny drop of wetness that was probably drool, seeped onto his pec. "I don't mind if you need to take off. I'll probably keep you up by rolling around all night, anyway. Just lock the door if you do go. I don't want any creepy neighbors sneaking in." Nav chuckled before nuzzling his chest.

Trick stiffened. "Did you want me to go?"

If he had been waiting for a hint, that was it. *But why?* Maybe Nav liked his space after sex. Of the many guys Trick had seen go into Nav's apartment, none of them had stayed longer than an hour or two.

"Mm-m, doesn't matter." Nav's voice came quieter, trailing off as he drifted back to sleep.

Trick's sleepiness evaporated into talon-rich smoke. The thought of leaving brought him closer to puking. But staying while he was unwelcome had ice curling in his gut. But maybe Nav had just been talking in his sleep, and he hadn't meant what he'd said?

He shook Nav's shoulder, desperate enough to wake his exhausted sub. Nav let out a long snore, a second stream of drool dropping on Trick's chest.

Letting his head fall back against the pillow, Trick closed his eyes, hoping he would be able to find sleep with Nav in his arms.

Chapter Nineteen

Nav

Nav pulled at his blankets, kicking his legs when they refused to budge. He could barely breathe, his bedsheets somehow wrapped around him and doing their best to smother him. A heart attack was not a great way to wake up.

There was an *arm* over his chest that felt like it weighed about a hundred pounds, and it was sticking to him with a film of sleepy, sweaty grossness. And, of course, he had to pee terribly, as if his prostate had been battered like a motherfucker.

Which it *had*. His memory flared to life at the same time as the ache at the base of his spine. He blinked his eyes open, catching sight of fluffy blond hair — the reason for the pain in his ass.

Trick was facing him, his cheek on the edge of Nav's only pillow, and his arm and leg thrown over him and very effectively pinning Nav and pushing on his bladder, all in one go.

Trick's mouth was wide, his face relaxed in sleep and his breaths slow and heavy with just a hint of a snore. But it didn't matter how quiet the snore was. It was still a fucking snore.

In my bed.

His fucking *sanctuary*, where no one was allowed to stay the night because he kicked them the fuck out.

He *liked* Trick more than anyone he'd ever been with, and the sex had blown his mind and given him the mental reset that he had desperately needed. But it had still just been sex.

He vaguely remembered dropping a huge hint for Trick in the middle of the night, but he'd had fallen back to sleep before he could see Trick out. Obviously, Trick had taken that as an invitation.

Why didn't Trick wonder why there was only one pillow? It wasn't like his place was even that far.

His fiancé just left him. Nav crushed that thought with more force than Trick's knee in his bladder. Trick was fun, cute and had opened up his eyes to an island of sex that had been hidden in the bowels of reality — but he was still just a guy.

One of them was going to get bored.

Nav had money on himself, simply because he had the shittiest track record of any gay man in the province. But maybe it would be Trick this time. Nav was a rebound — something shiny that had dangled its ass in front of Trick while he'd been having second guesses about his engagement.

But did he have to be so...clingy?

Clingy was the opposite of what Nav wanted. Clingy meant attachment, which meant heartbreak, despair and depression when the fun came to its natural end.

Sasha would call him a shallow motherfucker, but Nav had watched his best friend get his heart ripped out by over a dozen women.

How many times had Nav felt that way? *Never.* And he was probably better off for it.

He grabbed Trick's arm, flinging it off him before wriggling out from under his heavy leg. His ass and bladder protested violently, but he gritted his teeth and pushed through it. Standing over the bed, he glared as Trick rolled toward the warm spot that Nav had left behind, effectively blocking off his return and stealing the rest of his pillow.

He glanced at the clock and shuddered at the time. It was too fucking early after not enough drinks on a Saturday morning. Growling under his breath, he grabbed the edge of his pillow, pulling it out from under Trick's head with a jerk. Trick's head dropped to the mattress with a thud, but the blond didn't stir.

Grumbling, he relieved himself before marching to the couch, where at least no one would try to steal his blankets. He *hated* the cold, despite not minding the Canadian climate. His skin prickled as he grabbed his fluffy blanket and threw it over his shoulders, trying to bring back the same warmth he'd had in the bed.

Trick is warm. He shook his head, curling in on himself and pulling the blanket tighter. The cushions were comfortable, but couches were shit for sleeping, especially when the colored leather stuck to every inch of his naked skin. At least he was clean, and even his ass was fresher than it should have been after what they had done.

Nav let out a huff. He refused to be grateful when he was stuck trying to catch a few hours of sleep on his dumpster couch while Trick slumbered peacefully on his very comfortable bed.

The clock ticked above his head, so much louder than it usually was from the bedroom. Each stroke seemed to drag as the black hand jerked over and over. Two and a half breaths for every five ticks—but sometimes six. Was it running out of batteries?

He sighed, rolling into the cushion and throwing his arm over his ear to block out the sound.

Rhythmic thumps struck his eardrums, even through the protective layer of his arm. It wasn't the clock, but something that moved closer with each thump, each louder than the last. The thumps paused, and the sound of a key scraping in a lock broke through Nav's sleepy bubble. A door squealed, then slammed shut with a resounding thud.

He breathed a sigh of relief, until the thumps started again, this time much softer, so he had to strain to figure out if they were real or imagined. They were steady this time and stretched on for minutes until he realized what they were—his own beating heart, keeping him awake.

"For fuck's sake." He threw back the cover, shuddering as cold air stripped away every bit of warmth. Storming to the bedroom, he paused, biting his lip.

Trick was just as handsome as the first time Nav had seen him, his breath catching in his throat as he took in his fill of Trick's naked body. Goosebumps prickled over Trick's skin, tanned even in the glowing moonlight. Tracing his fingertips down Trick's shoulder, he shuddered as his nerves jumped to life. Trick stirred in his sleep, and Nav dropped his hand back to his side.

Stop looking. Nav turned away. He didn't want to get used to the sight of a man in his bed, no matter who that man was. He was letting himself get too carried away with Trick, allowing himself feelings that he couldn't afford.

Like the way that he didn't want to wake Trick up now and kick him the fuck out.

He grabbed some clothes, throwing them on and brushing his teeth in the bathroom before he stomped back to the kitchen. Priority one was coffee, but after that was taken care of, he wasn't sure what to do. What could he do with so many extra hours on a Saturday when every else was sleeping?

Making breakfast would probably just tempt Trick to stay even longer, and it was too early for food, anyway. He huffed, looking around the tiny space of his living room with its worn floors and paint curling on the walls. It had never felt so small before. *Time to move.*

Nav planted his ass on the couch, slapping his coffee on the table next to him before turning on the television. As much as he wanted to crank the volume and wake Trick up as abruptly as he had awoken, he wasn't about to stoop that low.

The infomercial morphed into a nature program as he grabbed his second cup, a white hare darting across the screen as he took his seat. He winced as his ass touched the couch, his prostate still aching.

Setting his coffee back on the table, Nav leaned back, his eyes drooping as David Attenborough droned on in his melodic and sexy voice. For some reason, there was a tiger on the screen. Hopefully he hadn't eaten the hare.

Nav started as the couch shifted, glancing to the suddenly occupied seat beside him. Trick's hair was a disaster, his cheeks flushed pink and his blue eyes watery and bloodshot from sleep.

"Couldn't sleep?" asked Trick, his voice artificially deep as he rubbed his eyes with the back of his hand. He shifted on the couch, pulling the pillow from under him before looking at it with deepening confusion.

Nav grunted noncommittally, watching Trick from the corner of his eye. He couldn't help but feel a little bit bad. He hadn't been clear on what he'd expected the night before, but it hadn't been completely his fault. Trick hadn't let him get a word in.

"Is there coffee left?" Trick asked, still looking at the pillow in his hands.

Nav couldn't stop the glare that he sent Trick's way. His bed, his pillow and now his coffee, too? Next thing he knew, he would be sacrificing a kidney.

"Okay, I get it. You aren't a morning person," said Trick, Nav's glare rolling off him like water. "You're lucky I know the cure for that."

Nav grunted again, looking back to the television screen. *Shit.* The rabbit was probably alive, but a gazelle was dead. His terrified respect for cats went up another two notches.

Maybe Trick would figure out that Nav's favorite cure for a terrible morning was silence and solitude? Nav doubted that. Trick seemed more like the 'offer you food until you pop' kind of guy. Dishes clanging in his kitchen confirmed that idea.

"Do you have eggs?" Trick asked, interrupting his show again. Nav faltered at the bright smile on Trick's lips, his bitter words dropping away.

"No, sorry," said Nav instead, cursing himself internally. Why the hell was he apologizing? It was his house, and he happened to not like eggs unless they were baked inside something that resembled cake.

Blond hair blocked his view as Trick dropped to his knees in front of the couch. He delved into Nav's blanket, grasping his palms and bringing them out to the freezing air. Nav wanted to resist, until Trick brought each palm up to his lips, kissing the sensitive centers. Nav's gut flared like molten lava.

"You okay?" Trick asked again, his blue eyes begging. He stroked the back of Nav's hands with his thumbs, draining the tension that had been building since the moment Nav had woken.

"I'm just surprised you're still here. People don't usually…stay," said Nav, keeping his tone carefully neutral. He couldn't be mean with Trick looking at him like his big heart was pinned to his sleeve.

Get the hint. Nav waited for Trick to pull away and excuse himself, but instead, he pulled Nav closer, wrapping him in a warm hug.

Nav sniffed, cursing his stinging eyes as he took a deep breath of Trick's clean scent that was tinged with the tiniest bit of stale booze.

"Come back to bed with me, baby," said Trick, reaching for the remote and clicking the screen off before Nav could protest.

"Not 'slut'?" asked Nav, not sure why he was asking. He didn't mind being called Trick's slut, but he wasn't really sure about being his baby.

Trick pulled back in alarm, his blue eyes going wide. "You know I don't really think that, right, Nav? Degradation is one of my turn-ons — giving, not receiving. The things I say in moments like that don't really mean anything."

Nav looked down as his vision blurred. *It didn't mean anything?* So Trick had been lying to him all along after all. He was another wolf in sheep's clothing, and more like himself than Nav had thought. *Well played.*

"Shit, baby, I didn't mean in like that. This is why discussions are important. We've jumped into this so quickly together, but I keep forgetting you don't really know much about kink." Trick squeezed his hands before tilting Nav's chin to meet his gaze. "I don't think you're a slut, Nav."

"But I want to be," said Nav quietly, fighting the hold on his chin. He wanted to be Trick's slut, no matter how vulnerable that made him. Maybe he could hold himself back from falling deeper, but he needed another hit of the drug that was Trick.

"Can you be my baby, too?" asked Trick, refusing to release his hold. "I like to punish my slut, so they remember they belong to me, but a baby needs to be spoiled, too. They need to be lo—" Trick slammed his mouth shut and looked away. "They need to be adored."

Being spoiled sounded nice, in a generally emasculating sort of way. Being a slut sounded better — powerful. As a slut, he could take anything that was tossed his way, and suck up pain like it was his fucking day job. Babies were helpless, weak and dependent.

"I don't know," said Nav, finally managing to get his chin free. Being spoiled was probably another way to develop those nasty things called *feelings.* At least as a slut, he could be cold.

"Come on," said Trick, tugging his hand until Nav stood. Trick led him to the bedroom and back to the bed that had lost its pillow and sheet. It was the last thing that Nav wanted to see while he still had company, but he was just so tired.

"Lay down, baby."

Nav stiffened at the name before he grudgingly complied. Was Trick even aware that he was still calling him 'baby'? Or maybe he was still thinking about Theo. His chest went tight at the thought, his skin crawling under Trick's touch.

Nav rolled onto his side, facing the wall and one of his favorite canvasses of a bird perched on a dead tree. A single branch burst from the center of the tree, its glowing leaves teeming with life, even as it was surrounded by death.

"Not like that," said Trick, tugging Nav until he was on his back, his head against the sheets and his gaze locked on the stucco ceiling. There were so many shapes in the tiny stained dots that he had mapped over thousands of sleepless hours alone in the bed.

A tug at Nav's pants had him startling. He gripped his drawstring, tugging it tight and barely restraining himself from slapping Trick away. "I'm sore."

It certainly wasn't the worst he'd felt, but he was in new territory, and he was more unsteady than a runaway train.

"I'll be careful with you." Trick held his gaze, his blue eyes sucking him in and draining the strength from his soul. Nav dropped his hands with a sigh, flopping back on the bed. *Why am I fighting what I want so much?* Once more, then he would ask Trick to leave.

His pants disappeared before Trick tugged at his shirt, leaving Nav naked and shivering in the cool air. The air conditioning clicked on again, but he had no desire to get up and turn it off. His skin prickled as

Trick's gaze blazed into him like a heated caress, his muscles going tense as he fought his instincts to flee.

"You are so beautiful," said Trick, reaching to skim his hand over Nav's belly. The tip of his middle finger sank into Nav's navel, tickling the tiny bud that was hidden away. "I could look at you all day and I'd never be bored. Your skin is so soft, so flawless and perfect for cherishing. The only marks on you are the ones I put there."

Nav flexed his wrists, the bruises aching as he moved. Shifting on the sheets, he cut back a groan as his ass flared to life. Trick had left his mark on every part of him.

"I like this part here," said Trick, circling Nav's shaft and tugging him to hardness. "Your cock is the perfect size for sucking — and curved so it fits down my throat just right. It's tasty too — a bit salty and a bit sweet."

Nav snorted, unable to hold it back any longer. "Cum is worse than day-old coffee dregs, but you make it sound like expensive cheesecake."

"Maybe I like the taste," said Trick, licking his lips as he stared at Nav's cock.

Whatever. Nav rolled his eyes. Whatever Trick was up to, he hoped it would be over soon. He could hardly keep his eyes open as it was. He needed a solid eight hours to be a functional human, and he was running with less than half that.

He grunted as Trick leaned down and sucked him into his mouth, slurping and licking as he traced up and down his shaft. His body responded for him, even if he was half-asleep and shivering, flexing in Trick's mouth as his balls went heavier with each swallow.

Trick drew back, and Nav could only whimper as cold air hit his cock, draining the heat away from his skin. Shifting up his body, Trick slotted their lips together, settling between Nav's legs as their cocks brushed.

It was *sweet* and soft, with a hint of Nav's own taste lingering in Trick's mouth as their tongues entwined. Despite the pool of heat in his groin and the feeling of Trick's cock against his own, there was no rush.

Heat slowly built in his core until sweat beaded on his skin, driving away the goosebumps and cold, and leaving something else in their place — something that he couldn't identify.

Nav couldn't remember the last time he had made out with someone. Perhaps when he'd been in high school, before his first time taking a cock. Once he'd discovered sex, there had always been a rush to the main event, and by the time it was over, he had always been ready to move on.

Nav bucked up, but Trick refused to move faster, barely grinding as he mapped out every inch of Nav with his hands, leaving no freckle or sweet spot untouched. He found spots that Nav hadn't even known about, like the patch just under his arm where his skin prickled as Trick gently pulled his nails across it. Or the dip of his lower back, where Trick's curled his fingers, sending bursts of pleasure straight to Nav's groin.

Gasping, Trick pulled away, his eyes blown wide and his hair mussed from Nav's hands running through his tresses over and over. Nav let them fall back to the bed, not knowing when he had reached for Trick. His heart was pounding, his breaths coming fast and hard as pre-cum slicked their cocks.

Trick smiled, his swollen lips stretching over his perfect teeth, before he leaned back in, his kiss landing against the column of Nav's throat. Nav let out a loud gasp as Trick explored him with his tongue and his teeth, sucking a likely mark beneath his ear, then soothing it again. He never stopped moving his hands, the combined sensations pushing Nav closer to his peak and to panic.

I feel cherished. Fuck. He groaned and pushed the thought away. The sound spurred Trick on as he dropped to Nav's nipple, teasing the bud to hardness before sucking it into his mouth. His teeth gently nibbled it next, tugging until Nav thought he might come.

"I can't," Nav called out between panting breaths. He couldn't take it much longer — the completeness that he'd never realized he'd been missing. Sex was one thing, but what Trick was doing wasn't just sex.

Nav hoped that Trick would shush him and tell him to take it, but instead, Trick moved back to Nav's lips, stealing his breath and his thoughts and draining the last of his resistance. Something in him broke and a wave of pure want washed over him.

He wanted sex, but not just sex. He wanted Trick, too — every part of him.

He wrapped his legs around Trick's hips, pulling their groins together as Trick settled firmly between them. Trick shifted, thrusting a hand between them to adjust their cocks until they slid together, his skin searing against Nav's.

It was as if Trick was everywhere at once. Every place Trick touched prickled with heat, bringing tears to the corner of Nav's eyes.

"Fuck me," he begged, unable to last another moment without Trick inside him. He didn't care if it was fast or slow, but he needed it. He needed the fullness, and the drag of Trick's perfect cock so deep that he knew he would never forget how it felt. He was ruined. No other man could touch him this way and worm their way inside of his defenses at the same time.

Trick leaned in, shaking his head and bringing their lips together. His touches were achingly soft as he spread Nav's legs apart, trailing his fingers over the inside of his thighs as they strained wide. Nav's nails cut into Trick's back, which flexed under his touch.

"I'm going to do what I should have done last night," said Trick, his stubble prickling Nav's skin as he nuzzled his neck before sucking the spot into his mouth again. He made his way to Nav's ear, licking the lobe as his breath tickled the shell.

Nav arched into the touch, his heart ready to burst and his lungs burning for air. It felt like he'd been running a marathon with a hard-on, and he was way beyond the ten-kilometer mark.

Groaning and cursing, Nav slowly broke as Trick teased every part of his body. He nibbled at his kneecaps and kissed his inner thigh, before moving between his legs to his prize. He only lingered for a moment before he was moving on to Nav's entrance, then gently biting his ass cheek. When Nav begged for more, Trick slowed down, pulling every aching syllable from his body.

Nav whimpered as Trick finally started to slowly prepare him, taking his time with his tongue and his fingers until there was no ache, only shuddering pleasure.

Sliding home, Trick let out a breath between them, bringing their lips back together again. Nav was so far gone that he could hardly stand the tiny hitches of Trick's hips, too focused on his lips and his tongue. His orgasm was nowhere in sight, even with so much pleasure caressing every nerve.

Trick pushed himself deep, and suddenly Nav was right there at the edge. The fullness and the pressure on his prostate would have made a lesser man come immediately, but Nav held on with his nails in Trick's flesh. As terrified as he was, he never wanted the moment to end.

"Come for me, baby," said Trick, his hips shuddering one last time.

Nav's orgasm crept up on him like a tsunami, so innocent at sea but rising fast as it slammed into the shore. He cried out, the sound caught between Trick's lips and tongue, as he clutched at the blond like he might lose himself if he let go. He clamped down, milking Trick's cock as he came inside of the condom with a quiet groan.

As Trick pulled out, discarding the condom on the ground to be dealt with later, Nav forced himself to swallow the tears that suddenly threatened. He usually wasn't one to cry, but Trick seemed to tear it out from his soul, tossing his barriers aside like he hadn't spent his lifetime building them.

If Trick saw his tears, he didn't say a word. Grabbing a discarded shirt, Trick cleaned the cum from their bellies, before lying back on the bed and pulling Nav onto his chest. His sweat cooled against Nav's cheek as his heart pounded under Nav's ear.

There was no way that Trick felt the same thing that Nav did — the mind-numbing terror that threatened to consume him.

"Can I stay a little longer?" asked Trick, his voice soft and his eyes closed against the dawning sunlight. Nav nodded.

Please stay. Please don't leave me. He tugged Trick closer, hiding his tears among Trick's sweat.

"Thank you." Trick leaned down, placing a single kiss to the top of Nav's head.

Nav's heart broke. He would never be whole again.

Chapter Twenty

Nav

"This is what happens when you ghost me, man," said Sasha as he guzzled down his third beer, licking the foam from his lips before slamming the glass on the table. "I know I was out of town, but you should have called me weeks ago. Where the fuck were you, anyway? You look like shit."

Nav swirled the sweet cider around in his glass, sucking the cold from it with his palm. He was still on his first drink, and he planned on keeping it that way for as long as possible. If he managed to get drunk, he was going to say a lot of shit that he was determined to keep buried deep.

"I was busy," he finally answered, taking a small sip. The liquid was almost room temperature and coated his tongue with a film of sickly apple sweetness.

"Busy getting fucked? Or busy getting fired?" asked Sasha, a touch too loudly for the quiet bar. He tossed back his fourth beer, waving the bartender over for another before he'd even finished swallowing. "The last time I saw you like this was when you got an academic suspension in college."

Nav grunted, looking off to the bar to scope out the crowd. *The professor's dick was worth that suspension.*

Sasha had dragged him to a straight bar, but there were always pickings, even if they were slim. He skimmed over a few guys, dismissing them all without a second glance. He paused at a brunet perched on a barstool, his face stormy and his grip on his glass white-knuckled.

Not tonight.

"Seriously, man, what the fuck?" Sasha dragged Nav's attention back like a weak magnet. Having straight friends was great, until you felt like someone had driven a sixteen-wheeler through your chest. Then they were too loud, too invasive and downright assholes.

Maybe gay friends would have been the same, and he might have known if he hadn't fucked and fled from every one.

"I met someone," Nav ground out, staring at his drink as he swirled it again. The music from the bar smashed against his eardrums, even though it was still quiet because of the early hour.

"You meet someone every week," said Sasha, snorting into his beer. Nav could almost hear Sasha's thoughts. *'You're a man, get over it and find someone else to fuck. Real men don't have relationships. Real men don't get attached.'*

"You are being a pretty shitty friend right now. Maybe that's why I didn't call you for a few weeks." Nav set his glass back down, knowing that there was no way he was going to be able to stomach another sip.

His couch was calling his name, along with a new series he'd started binge-watching.

"I'm being an honest friend right now. You meet people all the time, you have your fun, then fuck off. You are living every man's dream. All the pussy, but none of the commitment or gifts. It has never bothered you before, so what's different now?" Sasha blinked slowly, his eyes slightly glassy as he winked at a passing lady. She was way out of his league.

"This guy is different," said Nav, letting out a sigh. Even thinking about Trick made his chest ache. When had his life become a teenage drama? He'd thought he'd left that shit behind after prom.

"Does he have a big dick?" Sasha let out a belch, not even pausing to apologize. "Not that I really care about that shit, but you do."

"Fucking huge," said Nav, a smile tugging at his lips. His best friend was so disgusting, which was probably the reason why the thought of fucking him had never entered Nav's mind. The brief image alone made him nauseous. "You shouldn't be asking about another guy's dick. That's awfully gay of you."

"Nah, fuck it," said Sasha, sipping at another beer that had somehow landed in front of him. *Do bartenders still cut people off?* "I peek in the urinals every once and a while. I mean, I gotta size up the fucking competition and see what them chicks are looking for."

Well, they aren't looking for a drunk idiot. Nav kept the smile on his face, even as Sasha drained another beer. He caught the bartender's eye, shaking his head while glancing to his friend.

"So, he's got a big dick. What else?" Sasha counted off one finger while staring at Nav, his voice getting progressively louder.

"He's gorgeous, sweet as fuck but so dangerous that he just gives you the shivers." Trick's hands could probably kill, or take whatever they wanted, but Nav had never seen him lose an ounce of control.

"Dangerous? What the fuck? He's not like one of those back-alley rapists, is he?" Sasha's eyes went wide, until a passing redhead caught his eye. His lips transformed into a sleazy smirk as he leaned back in his chair, spreading his legs wide.

Nav swallowed. His friend's aim was as direct as it always was. Trick wasn't a rapist, but he was a fan of consensual non-consent, and Nav happened to be, as well. Just thinking about it made him want to call Trick and break his own vow of silence.

"Holy fuck." Sasha whistled as he looked back to Nav, who was chewing his lip. "You caught yourself a serial rapist. If he's threatening you, I'll fucking kill him. You tell me where to find him, and I'll take care of it. Nobody forces my boy." His voice rose and a few concerned glances were sent their way. Nav slapped a hand over Sasha's mouth, stopping his rant before it could get any worse.

"He didn't do anything that I didn't want." Nav felt himself flush. *Except for the last time.* The last time when he'd wanted to be fucked and left alone, and Trick had cherished him instead, as if Nav had been worth something.

Sasha squinted, tilting his head. "He hurt you, yeah?"

The bar seemed to go quiet, as if everyone was listening in. Nav dropped his gaze, the flush on his face burning ferociously. He nodded, chewing his lip as his heart pounded. Trick had hurt him so fucking good.

"Then I'll kill him," said Sasha, pushing his chair back as he leaped up. Nav surged from his seat, grasping Sasha's wrist while leaning precariously over the small table. A few gazes cut their way, the bartender eyeing them like he was about to call the bouncer over.

"I wanted him to hurt me," said Nav, leaning in close so he could whisper. "It's a kink thing." He looked around the bar to the others that seemed to be invested in their conversation. "Let's get out of here and go to my place."

Sasha shrugged, grabbing his wallet and fumbling to pull out a few bills before tossing them on the table. Nav checked them, adding another twenty to the pile before he trailed after Sasha. He glared at a giggling brunette that had been pointing their way. Bars were only slightly better than clubs for serious conversations.

"Like whips and stuff?" asked Sasha when they were barely out of the door, the music still floating through the exit. Nav shushed him, looking back at the bouncer and giving him an apologetic smile.

Spring had almost given way to summer, and the humidity had responded in force. It also meant that the street was scattered with other couples and a few more of the nefarious sort. Nav kept his gaze on the sidewalk as a drug deal went down feet from them. Sasha barely seemed to notice as he stumbled on nothing before grasping a lamppost to right himself.

"Yeah, and other stuff, too. Sometimes it's just his hands, holding me down and making me take it," said Nav after they'd turned the corner and the street went quiet. He touched his pocket where his slim canister of pepper spray was tucked away.

"And it hurts?" asked Sasha, his voice echoing along the old crumbling buildings.

"Well, yeah," said Nav, grabbing Sasha's shoulder when he almost took the wrong turn. Of course it hurts...sometimes. It just wasn't supposed to hurt inside, too.

"And you like it because it hurts?" Sasha threw his arm over Nav's shoulder, his body spray almost overpowering.

"I don't like it because it hurts. I like it because it's him who hurts me." Did that even make sense? He *did* like it when Trick hurt him and made him burn, but the gentle caresses were too much.

"That's pretty fucked up, man, but you do you." Sasha shrugged, stumbling again and threatening to keel over. "They need to fix this fucking sidewalk."

Nav glanced around. They were only a few blocks from his place, and it was a hell of a lot closer than Sasha's. There was no way they were making it to the nearest bus stop, and he didn't trust Sasha to make it home himself, anyway.

"You wanna show me your kinky shit?" Sasha laughed once before he paused, his face paling. "I dunno, man. I think I gotta draw the line there. I don't think chicks dig that stuff."

Nav snorted, shaking his head as they approached his building. He fumbled with the key, pushing his friend through the door as Sasha tried to look at his reflection in the glass. Sasha had few redeeming qualities, and humility was not one of them. Most ladies weren't impressed that Sasha took more time to do his hair than they did. Short relationships were something they had in common.

"The kink club I went to was packed with ladies," said Nav, as turned to the staircase. Out of the nine kink rooms, he'd only been in two. What glorious things awaited him in the others? *If only.*

"There are fucking *clubs*?" Sasha yelled, his voice echoing in the small space.

"Shut the fuck up," hissed Nav, slapping his hand over his friend's mouth. "It's almost ten o'clock." There were a few moms on his floor who would not be impressed with them yelling past their kid's bedtime.

"You gotta get me in," said Sasha, launching himself at Nav as they moved through the doorway and onto Nav's floor. Nav wilted under his friend's weight, trying to throw Sasha's arm off his shoulders, but it was no use. Sasha spent too much time in the gym working on his physical appearance.

His stale, alcoholic breath fluttered against the side of Nav's face, and Nav had to laugh. "I can't get you in. I was there as a guest, and it's members only. I don't think you want to go in there, anyway — not unless you want a lady to put you on your knees and make you beg."

He might have been stretching the truth a bit, but Sasha in a kink club would be worse than a bull in a china shop. He didn't know how to be confidential or discreet, and he would probably manage to offend half the people there in the first ten minutes.

Sasha swallowed, groaning as he laid his head down on Nav's shoulder. The move pushed them against Nav's door, squishing Nav against it with Sasha behind him. If it had been anyone else, Nav would have probably been getting hard from the compromising position, but with Sasha, he couldn't have been more turned off.

"Fuck off, you're too heavy," said Nav, shooting back an elbow that struck his friend directly in the gut. Sasha deflated, wrapping his arms around Nav and pulling him close, before nearly crushing Nav with his full weight.

"You don't love me, do you?" he asked, way too loudly in the narrow hall. "Radio silence, and now you won't even let me into your fancy club. What do I gotta do? I could pay some guy to give you a blow job, 'cause I ain't fucking doing it."

"Get off," Nav hissed, looking up and down the hall. Someone definitely would have heard that. He tried to get along with his neighbors, even if that was impossible sometimes.

The sound of a lock scraping followed by the squeak of a doorknob sealed his fate. He tried to turn to the sound, only to have Sasha squeeze him tighter, the apology on his lips dying as he choked. If it was Denise, she would never forgive him. Her young son had colic and some nights it took hours to get him to sleep.

"Nav?"

Nav cursed, pushing Sasha off him with more strength than he thought he possessed. Sasha stumbled back a few steps before he caught himself on the wall. Turning to Trick, Sasha eyed him up.

Trick was standing in his doorway with nothing more than a pair of pajama shorts slung low on his hips. His golden abs were on display, along with his mouth-watering pecs and little round nipples that looked so suckable.

Nav's thoughts stalled as he stared at Trick's chest, his gaze dropping to the treasure trail that led to the most fantastic pot of gold. Licking his lips, he eyed the bulge in Trick's pants. He'd mourned for that cock just as much as he'd mourned for Trick.

Clearing his throat, Nav dragged his gaze back to Trick's face. The blond's lips were pressed into a thin line, and he was looking between Nav and Sasha. He narrowed his eyes, dragging a hand through his messy hair as he let out a shaking sigh.

Shit. He looks pissed. "I'm sorry, Trick. We didn't mean to wake you up." Nav stumbled over his words, his chest constricting when Trick's frown only deepened.

Sasha pushed himself off the wall, grabbing at Nav's hand. "Give me your fucking keys, man. I hope you didn't change your Wi-Fi password or I'm gonna beat your ass." His eyes sparkled with amusement at his own little drunken joke while Nav's stomach plunged three stories down into the creepy basement full of spiders.

Sasha grabbed at Nav's pocket — thankfully the one that didn't have the pepper spray in it — before plunging his hand inside and pulling Nav's key free. Nav grimaced, as everything reorganized itself in the wrong way.

I'm going to kill him. Nav bit his lip, staring after his *friend* as he stumbled into the apartment, slamming the door like he owned the place. That was the last time he was letting Sasha get past four beers. Sasha was usually a decent guy — or at least passable — but he was a dick when he drank.

"Sorry, Trick," said Nav, his face flaming as he waited for the floor to swallow him. *Sorry for waking you. Sorry for my friend who is an utter asshole. Sorry for ghosting you for the past three weeks.*

Would Trick think that Sasha was making fun of him? Probably. Kinksters already had enough negative bullshit to deal with without another asshole belittling them.

"It's okay. I thought... Well, I guess I was wrong," said Trick, his gaze going hard. "Enjoy your evening." He turned away, shutting the door quietly and leaving Nav standing in the hall alone.

What? Shaking his head, Nav turned back to his door, twisting the knob in his hand. It stuck half-way, refusing to turn any farther — which meant that it must've locked automatically after Sasha had stormed through it.

He knocked gently, whispering his friend's name through the door. Knocking a little harder, he called Sasha's name again, cursing with the need to throttle his friend. He was probably already passed out on the couch, or worse, on the bed. There was probably no way that he would answer unless Nav woke the entire building.

Grabbing his phone, he called Sasha, tapping his foot as he held the phone to his ear. It clicked once, then went straight to voicemail.

He typed out an angry text next, wilting as he heard the quiet ping directly on the other side of the door. Sasha had probably dropped his phone on the ground right next to the fucking keys.

Sighing, he leaned back against the door — so close, but so far away.

Chapter Twenty-One

Trick

So, this was what a broken heart was supposed to feel like? Just when he was convinced that he was made of stone for feeling nothing when he'd lost Theo, he got his heart ripped from his chest by a doe-eyed beast.

Nav hadn't made a commitment to him. Hell, he hadn't even called Trick in weeks, but Trick had been determined to give him some space. The lifestyle could be a lot for some, and he'd needed to give himself some time to process what Theo had left him with.

But Nav had apologized — like that made everything okay, like Trick hadn't made love to him and held him while he pretended not to hear the tears and feel them dripping down his chest. He hadn't been sure what they'd meant, so he'd just held Nav tight and hoped that everything would be fine in the morning.

He'd seen a lot of men go in and out of his neighbor's apartment, but none of them had clung to him quite like that. None of them showed a familiarity that suggested a relationship longer than just a one-night stand. And none of them made him want to pummel them into the wall and turn his rage into blood and heat.

Dammit. And Nav just stood there, looking like a bunny about to be run over by a steroid-riddled blond that reeked of cheap body spray.

How could I be so stupid? Nav wasn't a rebound, but Trick had gotten so deep so fast, and now he was drowning. He hadn't realized that it was something more than lust until he'd woken up alone in Nav's bed, longing for him to be back in his arms.

They fit so perfectly together, and Nav was so sensitive that it was unreal. Every moment Trick was with him, it was like he was on fire, burning for more. The moment they'd parted, Nav had been all he'd thought of. His unanswered texts from the day after had him lying awake in bed, staring at the glowing screen of his phone and wondering why Nav hadn't responded. *Is he working late? Is he sleeping?*

He hadn't guessed that Nav was out picking up a new guy—or maybe not such a new guy.

The guy had been tall, built—with twenty pounds or so on Trick—and handsy enough that Nav could have filed a sexual harassment suit. He was also loud, rude and pushy enough to grab Nav's keys like they'd belonged to him—from his *pocket.*

Everything about the guy rubbed Trick the wrong way, and when he had opened his mouth, rage had bubbled up from Trick's core, consuming his better judgment.

Nav had told Trick that he had never really scened before and that he didn't know much about kink, but had that been a lie? That *guy* had seemed comfortable enough with it to make jokes.

It would explain why Nav had told him his safewords and gave him the green light in the alley, when he'd apparently had little experience. How much of it had been faked?

Trick's stomach heaved and he gripped the counter, taking a deep breath. He could still smell Nav's cologne from the hall with a wisp of booze and the unfamiliar aftershave from his friend.

I have to get out of here.

Stomping to the bedroom, Trick shed his pajama shorts, pulling on the closest matching jeans and T-shirt from the floor. There was a small stain on the shirt where he'd spilled his dinner, but it didn't matter. If he stayed any longer, with Nav's presence looming so close, he was going to do something he would regret.

Grabbing his keys, he reached for the door before throwing it wide. The knob slammed into the plaster in the hallway, digging a circular hole into it.

The superintendent would be pissed, but Trick couldn't bring himself to care. He was nearly blind with fury, his tunnel vision focused on the door across from his and the curved numbers labeling it.

He dropped his gaze and his heart nearly stopped. Nav was crumpled in front of his door in a way that was so reminiscent to when they had first introduced themselves. Nav's eyes were wide, and he clutched the scraggly carpet.

"I think you broke the wall," said Nav, his voice soft as he peeled himself off the floor and moved down the wall, giving Trick a wide berth.

Trick swallowed, his rage caught between confusion and heartbreak as Nav leaned over to inspect the spot where the doorknob had crushed the plaster. Nav reached out, his thin, unmarked wrists so delicate as he traced the divot.

"I won't tell if you won't," said Nav, a small smile on his face. "I don't think the super will notice if no one points it out."

How could he be smiling? Did he feel nothing? Trick quaked under the weight of the one-sided lies between them.

"What are you doing?" Nav asked, stepping back to his door and sliding down the surface until he was sitting again, his head tilted back to look up at Trick.

"Going to the club," said Trick, trying to keep the growl out of his voice. It was exactly what he needed — a place he could let off steam and cherish someone who would actually appreciate it. Once he calmed down, of course.

"Oh, cool," said Nav, his gaze dropping and a blush rising over his cheeks. The flush only made him more beautiful, and Trick longed for him, despite his cruelty. "I'm sorry about what Sasha said, about the *beating*. He's an asshole when he's drunk, and I never should have told him about the kink thing."

Oh. Trick swallowed. Maybe some of it had been true and maybe he had judged Nav too harshly. But he'd still had another man that wasn't Trick, pushing him against the door with his cock pressed to his ass.

"Have fun, I guess," said Nav when Trick didn't answer. He closed his eyes, his lashes so long and dark against his pale cheeks that only had a few faint freckles.

"What are you doing?" Trick looked down the hall when Nav made no move to get up. He cleared his throat. "Shouldn't you be with your...friend?" *Lover. Boyfriend. All the things that I'm apparently not.*

"I'm locked out, because I'm pretty sure he passed out in there. It's not the first time I've had to camp out in the hall. I'm just lucky it's Saturday and not a work night." Nav shrugged, closing his eyes again before letting out a sigh.

"You're just going to sit in the hall all night?" asked Trick. "Why don't you bug the super?"

"At this time of night? I like living here, thank you very much." Nav chuckled. "That woman is out to get me, I swear. Ever since she found out I was gay, she's been looking for an excuse to kick me out. For some reason she thinks that gay people are in the same group as child molesters."

That was new. Trick had spoken to her exactly once, on the day they'd moved in, and he hadn't thought twice about her scowl when he'd introduced Theo as his partner.

"Won't she kick you out for sleeping in the hall?" asked Trick, wiping his clammy palms against his jeans.

"Shit. I never thought of that." Nav looked around frantically, as if she would emerge at any moment. "Fucking Sasha. If he gets me kicked out of here, I'm going to trash his place."

"Come on," said Trick, letting out a deep sigh before cursing his bleeding heart. "You can stay at my place tonight." *Bad idea. Such a bad idea.*

Nav's eyes went wide, and he peered over Trick's shoulder while nibbling his bottom lip. Trick had seen Nav bite his lip dozens of times, and it never failed to get a rise out of his cock. It usually seemed to mean Nav was nervous about something, which happened to make Trick's cock even harder.

"Theo's not here. He's staying with his sister until he gets his own place. Most of his stuff is gone already." Trick had come home from work to find the closet and living room emptied of Theo's things. Their movie collection remained untouched, but Theo had left a note on the television remote that he was planning on changing the password to their streaming services. *Ouch.*

"The painting?" asked Nav, his gaze dropping to the floor.

"Is still here," said Trick. *What the hell does it matter?* Theo had sent a text claiming that he didn't want it, and Brian was taking his sweet time picking it up. As far as Trick knew, it was going back to some gallery in the city because it was apparently worth a lot of money. Trick didn't really give a shit, seeing as the whole thing was a blatant lie.

"Come on. I don't want you to get kicked out for getting locked out of your own apartment." Trick crossed his arms when Nav didn't budge from his spot on the floor.

"But you were going to the club. I don't want to ruin your night." Nav didn't lift his gaze, a blush flaring on his cheeks. *What is he thinking?* Trick would have given anything to know.

"Get in the apartment," said Trick, unable to keep the growl from his voice. He was barely holding on to his composure, and Nav was poking his fingers in every imperfection in his shield. The first thing he needed was a scene, and the last thing he needed was to be in the same room as Nav, but sometimes life was crappy like that.

"I'm missing out on a scene with a very desirable sub, so I expect you to be on your best behavior," said Trick, pushing down the guilt from the lie.

Nav blinked, something clouding his vision for a moment before it disappeared. It didn't matter. Nav wasn't his, and Trick didn't owe him a thing.

Nav slowly rose to his feet, stepping past Trick and into his apartment. Nav's gaze was trained on the floor before he glanced at the rack of shoes which had two of Trick's three pairs on it. Pulling the door shut, Trick slid the lock home, the sound like a nail in his coffin.

"I could..." Nav started and trailed off before wrapping his arms around himself.

"You could *what*?" asked Trick, prowling closer until his skin prickled from their proximity. Nav was so close, the heat of his skin almost within reach. Trick pushed his anger and grief to the forefront of his thoughts. He was not about to be manipulated again.

"I could sub for you, if you need it," said Nav, flickering his gaze up, then back down to the floor. Shifting from foot to foot, Nav tugged at his sleeve, glancing at the door.

"Who says I want you?" Trick's anger surged, even as regret instantly overwhelmed him. Nav had been with another man minutes before, and now he was throwing himself at Trick again? His mouth went dry as his stomach churned.

Nav turned away, but not before Trick caught the shiny tears in his eyes that threatened to spill and the way he slumped his shoulders with defeat. It sent a bolt straight through his chest. *I can't do it. I can't hurt him.*

"But I might be convinced to change my mind," said Trick, moving that tiny bit closer until he could smell the thick, masculine scent that was Nav. There was something sweet about him, like he'd been sucking on an apple instead of another guy's dick.

"I'll be good…if you want me." Nav dropped to his knees with a shuffle of cloth and a burst of air.

Trick let out a groan, looking to the stained stucco ceiling for some sort of guidance. The stain that looked like a toad offered none.

Why did Nav had to be so perfect? *One of a kind. Flawless but utterly unreachable.* But how could he resist?

"Go to the bedroom. It's the second door on the left, same as yours. I expect you to be naked and kneeling when I get there." Trick bit his lip, letting his eyes fall shut as Nav scurried from the room. He was never going to make it out in one piece.

Chapter Twenty-Two

Nav

"Who says I want you?"

The words continued on repeat as Nav stumbled through Trick's apartment, which was an upgraded echo of his own. The flooring was smooth beneath his feet, his socks sliding over the polished surface after he discarded his shoes along the way. The paint on the walls wasn't peeling, and the decorations were tasteful to the point that they must've been from a picture in a magazine.

The place looked *loved*—unlike his own temporary abode and unlike *him*.

Peeling his clothes from his body, Nav's heart raced and a chill settled in his body that was from more than just the air conditioning. His T-shirt dropped from his numb fingertips, before he struggled to slide his jeans from his hips.

The bedroom was so unlike his. It had the same square footage, but the walls were dark turquoise instead of standard peeling beige, and the curtains were bright yellow with white geometric designs. A pile of fancy pillows was on the floor next to the queen-sized bed that had been made to perfection. It was intimidating, to say the least.

Nav settled on the floor, his knees aching after only a few seconds. He glanced at the pile of pillows, wondering if he should grab one before his knees seized up. But he didn't want to break the rules — not when Trick was so close. The idea of Trick touching him had him hard already.

What was I thinking? He was supposed to be putting space between them, not offering another round. Ten minutes passed on the bedside clock, then another ten. He'd made it three weeks, but as soon as he'd seen Trick again, he'd thrown himself into his path.

"Who says I want you?"

Was it supposed to hurt that much? Nav had thought that he had put up some barriers, but Trick had squirmed his way deep inside, haunting his thoughts and his dreams for weeks. The painting in the front hall resonated through the apartment, even without Theo's presence, sinking its cold fingertips into his mind.

His knees were aching, and he could hardly feel his toes. Shifting, he eyed the clock, blinking with surprise. Trick had left him for almost an hour. *Is he even coming?*

He stayed still. He had offered himself, after all. The thought of Trick with someone else, giving them the pain that belonged to him, made him sick and kept his knees planted on the floor. Trick had acted like being with Nav would be a chore, but Nav ate it up anyway, exposing himself in a strange bedroom with dark, unfamiliar walls.

Worthless.

"Nav."

Nav looked up at the sound of his name. Trick was standing in the doorway, his hair straight and freshly brushed. His blue eyes sparkled, his pupils dilating as he dragged his gaze over Nav's crouched form.

"Why are you here?" asked Trick, his voice soft. Nav knew how brutal Trick's voice could be, and how it could twist his mind and make him feel things that he never could have imagined. The softness he couldn't stand, though. It was the softness that broke him.

Nav looked down to his folded knees, touching the old bruise on his thigh from when he'd run into the corner of a table. He had no idea why he was kneeling on the floor with his knees aching beneath him, the line between two laminate slats digging into his bones. He swallowed, looking up at Trick and begging for the man to understand.

"What I mean is, why are you here and not across the hall? Why do you kneel for me when you have him? Does it matter who fucks you? Or are you just a desperate hole, needing something inside of you to make you complete?" Trick stalked toward him as he spoke, his words carving like a knife over Nav's skin.

Slut. Tears prickled in his eyes as the thought consumed him, this time refusing to bring him an ounce of heat. His cock went flaccid between his legs, his sac shriveled from the cold. He wasn't even sure who Trick was talking about, but it didn't matter. Nav had been with so many men that he couldn't have told anyone the number, even at gunpoint.

"Already spent so soon, I see. That's fitting for your punishment," said Trick, a smile spreading over his face that didn't meet his eyes. He pulled his shirt over his head, tossing it to the side of the room.

Something isn't right. Nav shifted on the floor, his knees aching. Trick had never undressed during a scene, only sex, and the wrongness of it made Nav swallow dryly. Trick's clothes gave him power, and Nav's nakedness deprived him of it.

The only time he'd seen Trick's body was during aftercare, or the times together in Nav's bed when he'd been fucked and cherished. Biting his lip, he shook off his thoughts. He would give Trick whatever he needed.

"What is your safeword, slut?" Trick hissed, dropping his hands to his belt before fumbling with the buckle.

"Red," Nav whispered. He wouldn't use it...not with Trick. Trick always knew exactly what he needed.

"And if you need me to slow down?" Trick held the belt in his hand, folding it over on itself until it morphed into a menacing strap of solid leather.

"Yellow." Nav shivered as he stared at the belt. The leather was thick and broad, and the stripes it would make were bound to burn like hell. But he could take it...for Trick.

Trick crouched, fisting Nav's hair and roughly tilting his head back. A few hairs caught between his fingers, tugging from Nav's scalp and leaving a trail of goosebumps on his skin. "Just so you know, I won't be slowing down, slut. You're here to be punished and you'll take whatever I give you. Get on the bed with your face down and ass up."

Nav's breath hitched as Trick stood, and he scrambled to comply, a drop of real fear settling into his belly. It was the same way they had played before, but Trick had never looked at him like that.

He reached out to touch the bed with his fingertips before the leather strip cracked over his skin, sending him sprawling onto the sheets as the back of his legs flared with heat.

Nav couldn't hold back his yell as he reached for the sensitive spot that Trick had struck. He hadn't been ready.

"Quiet, slut. I wouldn't want the neighbors to know how weak you are. They already know that you bend over for every cock that you see, but do you want them to see you like this?"

Nav shook from the quiet lash of Trick's words as he crawled onto the bed. Shock and pain were already receding to a dull throb, but Trick's degradation was more painful than any strike.

He planted his face into the bed as another stripe landed over the back of his thighs in the sensitive area just beneath his ass cheeks. He howled into the sheets as the edge of the leather bit into his sac, skimming the sensitive surface.

He bit back a shiver. He could do this – *for Trick.*

Hits rained down on him and he choked back every groan and whimper, even as his sac was struck more than once. Fire turned to numbness, even as Trick found new spots to tan, until Nav could hardly feel the blows. Adrenaline shivered under his skin, and for a moment, he was absolutely invincible.

But he couldn't let go. Trick needed him. *Hold on.*

Trick shoved a finger into his hole, startling Nav from his rhythmic trance. Trick was dry, and the burn lit his body anew, pushing a yelp through his lips. It had been weeks with nothing but his own fingers, and even those moments had been brief.

Gasping, Nav shoved his face into the sheets as Trick circled Nav's cock with his other hand, cupping his flaccid dick and squeezing.

"You really are fucked out, slut. Did he fuck you dry? Or maybe you sucked him off and came on the ground like a whore. You're too tight to have just taken a cock. I know you could take mine, though." Trick shoved in a second finger, and an ache lanced through Nav's body.

He couldn't do it — not dry. This new Trick was dark, and something told Nav that he wouldn't be there to pick up the pieces.

"Yellow," said Nav, his voice shaky but clear.

Trick stilled, his panting breath brushing over the back of Nav's neck as he slowly withdrew, leaving an empty burning ache.

"Did I hurt you?" Trick's voice was shaking, his breath coming faster over Nav's skin. His hand trembled where it touched Nav's ass, the coolness lancing the heat from Nav's flesh.

"I can't take you dry. You can do anything else, but not that." Nav shuddered as tears started to flow, soaking into Trick's pillow that he must've grabbed. He hugged it, shivering as the cold fabric touched his sweat-covered chest.

"I thought you would have been stretched out already — or did you two not fuck yet?" asked Trick.

Ice swept over Nav as the ache of his ass and thighs transformed into something unbearable. He bit his lip so hard that he tasted copper, but it did nothing to help. "What are you talking about?"

The bed shifted as Trick pulled away and the ice solidified. His teeth chattered.

"Your…friend. In the hall. You two had just fucked…or were just about to. He was all over you, and you were giggling like a bitch in heat, letting him feel you up and everything."

Nav looked over his shoulder as Trick's voice faded. The blond paled as he backed away, sweat dripping down his skin as he panted. The belt hung from his hand, looking nothing like the threat that it had before.

"Sasha is my best friend. I'd never fuck him." Nav slowly rolled over to face Trick, hissing when his ass touched the bed. He was going to be so fucking sore in the morning.

"Then why aren't you hard?" asked Trick, his forehead furrowing as he glared at Nav's dick.

Nav closed his legs, whimpering as the small movement stretched his delicate skin. It was like a welt on top of sunburn. There was a spot where the belt had curled around the side of his leg, a purple-black streak painting an echo of its touch. He blanched, fisting the sheets as he trembled.

"Because it hurts." He managed to keep the tears back, but the ache only got worse as he looked at it. It was supposed to be beautiful, but it felt like more of an accident that Trick hadn't intended.

Trick slowly stepped to the bed, dropping to his knees as he reached Nav. His blue eyes were wide and expressive, and it broke a tiny smidge of the ice off Nav's heart.

"I've hurt you before, and you've come from it." Trick reached out with a shaky hand, his fingers hovering over Nav's leg where the purple welt marred his flesh.

"Not as a punishment." Nav shook. That was the difference. Trick's disappointment had never been so real before. Goosebumps burst over his skin, prickling his oversensitive nerves. Trick's face paled, the dark lines under his eyes standing out.

"Why are you here? Why didn't you say something before I punished you?" Something flooded Trick's face, and it wasn't rage.

"Because you needed this. I can take your pain if it helps you. You can hit me, fuck me and break me, and I'll take it all if that's what you need. If you need me to go, I can do that too." Nav shuddered at the thought of standing in the hall and waiting for Sasha to wake up and find him. But he could do it...*for Trick.*

"Fuck." Trick bit his lip as he swore, closing his eyes. "I hurt you." He stumbled away from the bed, his back hitting the bedroom wall before he slid down and crumpled to the floor. His head hung between his splayed knees, his hands flat on the spotless laminate. His face had gone so pale that he looked close to fainting.

"Trick, it's okay," Nav pulled himself off the bed, crying out as the movement had every nerve in his body cringing. His vision wavered as he hurried to Trick, his ass and thighs glowing from the beating. He would be lucky if he would be able to move by Monday.

Kneeling should have been out of the question, but he did it anyway, landing next to Trick with a thud that made him swallow. The ache was all-consuming, and it felt like he'd been held over an open flame for too long. Circling Trick's neck with his arms, he held on, trying to offer what comfort he could.

"I'm so sorry," said Trick, shaking his head as his body trembled. He shrugged Nav off him as he crumpled in on himself.

Nav's strength disappeared, and he lay against the cool floor, hooking his nails between the tiny cracks. Maybe he should have stayed on the bed instead of trying to get to the man who had ripped his heart out and decided to play. The ache receded to a low throb as he held still, the sound of Trick's heavy panting like a metronome.

"Trick," said Nav, his voice impossibly steady. "Trick, I want to hold you, but I can't move. I need you to help me."

Trick trembled beside him, his leg tapping Nav repeatedly as he shook. Trick needed him in the same way that Nav had needed Trick the morning after the alley. *But I can't move.*

"Trick," he said as loud as he dared without waking the neighbors. Trick blinked once, peering through his bangs with bloodshot eyes. His eyes went wide as he noticed Nav beside him, their bodies barely touching.

"Nav, shit. F-Fucking coward, get it together," Trick growled, lunging at Nav, even as Nav flinched.

Gasping, Nav relaxed as Trick touched him, moving his hands so gently that they were like butterfly kisses on his skin. Trick was cold, his palms sucking the heat from Nav's sweaty skin.

"Can I carry you to the bed? I need to look at you. You might need to go to the hospital." Trick sucked in a breath and Nav rolled his eyes.

Men are so dramatic sometimes. Going to the hospital for a bunch of welts was as ridiculous as trying to shake off a broken collar bone.

"I don't need a hospital. You hit me with a belt, not a baseball bat. Just get me to the bed." Nav cringed, a yell pushing through his lips as he was lifted to Trick's chest. *Okay, maybe it's more than a bunch of welts. It feels more like thousands.* He panted as Trick lowered him to a cool spot on the bed, urging him to roll until Nav was on his belly with his ass exposed to the room. His skin prickled under Trick's gaze.

"It's really bad," said Trick as he bit his lip. Nav glanced over his shoulder, watching the emotions play over Trick's face. "I should never have hit you that hard. You should have safeworded." Trick glared at Nav's ass, his brows drawing together.

So, it's my fault now? Nav grabbed Trick's pillow and shoved his face into it as a wave of grief washed over him. Taking Trick's pain was one thing, but Trick's shame was another entirely.

I could have been better for him. What the fuck is wrong with me? Or maybe he should have stopped Trick that first night in the alley, then his life wouldn't have been spiraling out of control into a dark pit that had no way out.

The first cool touch to his skin was agony, and he couldn't stop the scream. He tried to bite it back and muffle himself in the pillow, but it was no use. If the neighbors weren't awake already, they would be very shortly, and somebody was going to call the cops.

"I'm so sorry, Nav."

Nav couldn't look, he could only bury himself deeper as the bed shifted and Trick's presence withdrew. Trick didn't even want him here.

"Why are you here?" If that hadn't been a hint to get out, Nav didn't know what was. How had he missed it? Trick had told him that he wasn't wanted, but he'd invited himself in anyway.

Nav forced himself to roll over, tasting a fresh wave of blood as he bit into his tongue. Grabbing the edge of the bed, Nav held on as he reached for his clothes that were just in reach from when he'd tossed them as he'd stripped.

Taking a deep breath, Nav pulled his jeans up one leg, groaning as the rough material clutched his skin. They still smelled like the bar, and the stale cider he'd been sipping, and they soaked the sweat from his rosy skin. He caught sight of another welt, the red line not looking half as bad as he felt inside.

"What are you doing?" asked Trick from the bedroom doorway, his voice a grumbling growl that made everything in Nav want to submit.

"Leaving." He clutched the bed, tugging his jeans over his other ankle and grinding his teeth as he dragged them slowly upward. How long would he have to wait in the hall until Sasha woke up in a drunken stupor and realized that he wasn't there?

"You need aftercare."

"You need to fuck off." Nav whirled, grabbing the bed as he stumbled. A cloth hung from Trick's hand, and the sight of the blond's anger only fueled his own.

"You don't even fucking want me to be here." Nav's voice cracked as he looked down at his pants, which were tangled around his ankles and apparently inside out. Righting them seemed like a monumental task, but he could only imagine what the pocket designs would do to his sore ass if he didn't fix them.

"Why would you think that?" asked Trick, slowly stalking to Nav.

Nav chuckled, wiping the tears from his eyes before they could fall. "You told me that you didn't want me, and it's obvious you don't, even when I give you everything I have. Just let me leave, Trick. I'll get out of your hair, and you can go to the club to find a sub that you want."

His chest cracked as Trick touched him, the heat of his palm driving away the cold even as he ached. He willed his feet to move, but he was frozen and barely able to stand. Hours of agony waited for him in the hall, but it would be better than staying with Trick.

"Please stay, Nav." Trick touched his chin, meeting his watery gaze. "The only reason I wanted to go to the club was so I could forget about the way his hands looked on you. I can't stop thinking about you. You're all I want, but I keep hurting you and pushing you away. I've never felt this way about anyone before, and I feel like I'll lose myself without you."

It's not true. It couldn't be. How could Trick feel that way about him? The guy who fucked anything human with two and a half legs, and who had no redeeming qualities to speak of. Trick could have anyone and any sub he wanted. He was perfect, beautiful, witty, and he made Nav's heart pound and his chest tight, even when they'd first met.

"I can't stay," said Nav, taking a step back. The bed met him halfway, thudding against his sore ass and pushing a groan through his lips. He watched Trick's gaze fall to the cloth in his hand as he tightened his grip.

"That's okay, Nav. Let me take care of you one last time, then you can go. I'll never bother you again if that's what you want, and I'll never hurt you again, either." Trick reached out, sliding his fingers along Nav's shaking wrist.

"I want you to hurt me," said Nav, holding fast to his only support. "I want you to break me and build me back up again over and over, but I can't let you. I'll never be good enough for you, Trick. I'm a slut, a whore and a needy bitch who likes to get fucked and gets bored too easily. I can't hurt you like that, not when I lo—"

Nav slammed his mouth shut, pulling his hand back. What the fuck did he almost say? Love was not a part of his vocabulary, and it never would be. He didn't love his parents, who had abandoned him the moment that he'd come out at the eager age of fifteen. He tolerated Sasha, who had been there from the beginning and had kept him from living on the streets. There was no love and there never would be.

"I love you, too."

The room went deathly still at Trick's words. Even Trick seemed stunned, blinking as his forehead furrowed. A smile tugged at Trick's lips, his eyes going bright.

"Don't." Nav shuddered as Trick enveloped him and he collapsed into the heat and the warmth. There was nothing like it. "Don't." He couldn't stop the tears.

It was the bliss of wrapping himself in a blanket that was fresh from the dryer with the scent of laundry detergents still crisp and fresh. It was the satisfaction of a summer rain with lightning streaking across the sky and snapping into his dreams as water crept across the window glass in his bedroom.

He never wanted it to stop.

Trick laid him on the bed, kissing him on his wet cheek before he touched the damp cloth to Nav's wilted skin, giving it new life that had never felt so good.

The ice in Nav's body melted in drips and bursts, tendrils of heat stretching over him until the first curl of arousal stirred in his gut. Trick never stopped speaking as he slowly, and oh so carefully, wiped the sweat from his skin until Nav finally felt clean. Smearing a cream over the welts had Nav throbbing, the pain bleeding away to pleasure as the marks went numb.

If Trick had noticed his hardness, he hadn't said a word, and Nav was content to exist, his mind floating as he let himself be loved.

Chapter Twenty-Three

Trick

Nav loved him. Nav *loved* him.

Nav hadn't actually said the full word, but Trick knew how hard those four little letters could be because he'd said them to Theo exactly once. It had been very early in their relationship after a scene that had been more intense than most. The word had slipped through Trick's lips as he'd held Theo to him, bringing them both down.

With Theo, it had been a fabrication of Trick's mind, but with Nav, it was true. He'd never been so certain of anything in his life.

But he'd hurt Nav, even as he loved him. The wounds were twisted and shaded with furious blurs of purple and red. If he had used a whip instead of his belt, Nav would have been bleeding and broken. And Trick wasn't sure if he would have been able to stop himself if Nav hadn't said his word.

Ten years' worth of frustration had burst forth, and

Nav had taken it to his breaking point. The marks were the very picture of his full strength on Nav's pale flesh, and it could have been so much worse. He was lucky that he'd taken an hour to calm his boiling rage.

I need help. Nav grumbled in his sleep, his legs drawing up to his chest as Trick soothed his back. Easing away, Trick stood from the bed, staring at the colored skin before him. It didn't even look real — like someone other than himself had done it. Pulling a sheet over Nav's form, Trick turned from the bed.

I've never lost control. Ten years as a Dom, and I've never even come close.

He grabbed his cell phone from the kitchen counter, staring at the screen and the list of contacts. There were few that he was comfortable calling and even fewer who would understand the situation. The phone call would put his lifestyle at risk, but he had to make sure Nav would be okay. He had to make sure there were only welts and bruises and that he hadn't done any deeper damage to Nav's body. He wouldn't chance it.

Trick had wanted Nav to writhe with pleasure and confusion, giving in to lust as Trick tempted and tested every part of his body. He never wanted fear, only the illusion of it. Consent had always been first, even when they'd been virtual strangers and Nav had been nothing more than a happy mistake who'd shown Trick what true submission was.

Theo had tried so hard, but he had been right. Trick had never been honest with Theo because he'd never been honest with himself. There had been a reason that he'd never collared Theo or had a proper contract with him.

Taking a deep breath, he pushed the call button on the contact at the top of the list, his hand trembling as he held the phone to his ear in time to hear the first droning ring.

Clint had always answered, whether it was because of a sense of duty or because of a general sense of worry, Trick wasn't sure. In a way, Clint had almost been a father to Trick when he'd first discovered kink, showing him the ropes and helping him to find his first sub.

"Hello?" Clint's voice was thick with sleep as he answered on the third ring. Trick glanced at the clock. It was three o'clock in the morning and long after the club would have closed for the night.

"I need your help," said Trick, clutching the phone as it threatened to slip through his fingers. He dropped his head into his hand as he slid to the floor. The cool kitchen tile seeped into his naked legs, stripping him of his last remaining bit of warmth.

"Trick? Fuck, what's wrong?" asked Clint, his words followed by a loud thump and a jingle.

"I fucked up." *That's the understatement of the year.* Trick glanced toward the bedroom. Bile burned in his throat as he thought of going back into the room and seeing what he'd done.

"I'll be there. Where are you?"

"Home." Trick trembled as the line went dead and he dropped the phone.

He was in his forties, but sometimes he still felt like a teenager facing a closed-door society with more questions than answers about his sexuality. His parents had still loved him after he'd come out, but they probably would have had him committed if he'd confessed his desires to dominate.

A soft knock on the door startled him from thoughts and he glanced at his watch. He hadn't moved in the last twenty minutes.

A key scraped in the lock when Trick didn't answer — his own emergency key used against him. The door swung wide, and Clint stepped through, haloed by the light from the hallway. His light hair was disheveled, and his eyes were bloodshot with dark bags under them. It didn't seem to faze him that Trick was on the floor as he flicked on the light and let the door fall shut, turning the lock so it slid home.

"What happened?" asked Clint as he pulled his leather coat off, his scarred chest heaving as he hung it on the hook where Theo's used to reside. His pajama pants were barely hanging onto his hips, the mottled scars that stretched across his torso dipping beneath the waistband.

"I was wrong. I punished my sub when he didn't deserve it," said Trick, his voice still shaking. Curling his arms around his knees he pulled them tight to his chest.

"Show me." Clint tugged his pajama pants up his hips, tying the drawstring in a knot fast enough to make a world-champion calf-roper jealous.

Trick pulled himself off the ground, hardly noticing that he was still naked, his cock slightly shrunken from the cold. He took the few steps from the kitchen to the bedroom, pausing in the doorway as his heart pounded. "He's sleeping. I didn't tell him I was calling you, and I don't think he knows who you are."

Clint's scowl deepened as he pushed the bedroom door wide, the hinge squealing.

Nav was so beautiful, the lamplight showing every bit of his softness with his dark hair fluffed against Trick's pillow. One arm was tucked under his head while the other was tossed out to the side with his narrow wrist on display. The thin sheet hugged his body and had slipped between his legs while Trick had been away, displaying the curve and tuck of his ass.

Trick sank to the edge of the bed as Clint moved to stand next to him, eyeing Nav with something akin to confusion. He had probably been expecting Theo.

Biting his lip, Trick tugged at the edge of the sheet that covered Nav's body, watching Nav's face for any sign of discomfort. His breath caught as he pulled the sheet free, tossing it down to cover Nav's ankles.

If anything, it looked worse than Trick remembered, fresh bruises developing in spots that Trick could have sworn were pale before. Purple, red and black swirled together, no place untouched from knee-level to ass. It could have been beautiful, but not when every stripe showed him how wrong he had been. He looked away, his eyes burning.

"Look," Clint growled as he stepped closer, grabbing Trick's chin and pinching it tight as he forced Trick to look. "You look at your beautiful sub and see how strong he is. Don't you dare look away."

He stared long and hard, until he knew he would remember the sight for the rest of his life. Clint dropped his hand as he leaned closer to Nav, hovering his palm over the stretch of brutalized skin.

Clint had spent years as a nurse until he'd settled down with his husband and they had poured everything they'd had into Unkinked. Even after his husband had passed, Clint still maintained everything about the club, using his medical knowledge to teach new Doms and subs basic first aid.

"I don't think there will be any permanent damage, but there might be scarring here and possibly here," said Clint as he hovered over two dark welts where it looked like the top layer of skin had broken. "Did you treat your sub with anything?"

Trick grabbed the tube of cream off his side stand,

shoving into Clint's hands. It was something he'd rarely had to use with Theo—not that Theo had been able to tolerate the pain once the scene had ended, but because Trick had rarely pushed Theo to the point that he would have needed it.

"This will help a bit, at least." Clint hummed. "I assume it was a belt. Did you clean it first?"

"No." Trick shook his head. "I was wearing it before the scene." He glanced at the floor where his belt was curled into a lifeless loop.

Clint followed his gaze, his lips paling as they pressed together. "Do you have peroxide or a gentle cleanser? We should disinfect the area, just in case."

Heart pounding, Trick stood from the bed. He would do anything and everything to make Nav more comfortable and try to mend his mistake.

Clint gripped his shoulder, and Trick's steps ground to a halt as he flinched. Although Clint was on the shorter side, he packed a mean punch, and he dug his fingers into Trick hard enough to leave bruises behind.

"You need to wake up your sub first and introduce us. I don't want him to be frightened or upset if he wakes up without you. And trust me, he *will* wake up."

Trick flinched under the weight of Clint's glare. *I'm screwed.* He could kiss his kinky ass goodbye. Everything he'd ever learned and ever stood for had fled under the weight of his guilt.

Leaning over the bed, Trick touched Nav's cheek with the back of his hand. Nav was warm, his cheeks rosy from sleep. His expression flickered as Trick softly traced his cheekbone, dipping down to his chin and the exposed corner of his lips. His heart nearly broke when Nav's forehead furrowed, a groan pushing through his lip as he came awake.

"Nav, wake up, baby," said Trick, wiping the tears from his own eyes with the back of his hand.

"Am I your baby again?" asked Nav, his lips curling into a smile as he blinked awake. He still looked half-gone, his gaze cloudy in the way that only happened with subspace. Trick could hardly believe that Nav had still managed to slip there, even after everything he'd done.

"Such a good boy for me, Nav." He pushed his fingers through Nav's hair and Nav practically purred, his body going limp and a sigh pushing through his lips. "I called my friend here, baby. I hope that's okay. He owns the club and he used to be a nurse. I know you said you didn't want to see a doctor."

"Where?" Nav asked, grimacing and going still as he attempted to turn over. "Ow."

"I'm right here," said Clint, speaking up as he moved into Nav's line of sight. "It's nice to meet you, boy. How do you feel?" The change was startling as Clint smiled, placing his hand on the bed within Nav's reach.

"Uh, don't talk about it," said Nav, hissing as he shifted. "It's not so bad when I don't move, but yeah, not great."

"Do I have your consent to touch you, or would you prefer if your Dom treated you? Your wounds need to be cleaned, and I won't lie to you and say it's going to feel nice. There are also a few places that might scar."

"I-I don't know," said Nav, his eyes going wide as he paled and bit down on his lip. "I don't know if I can take much more. Trick?"

"It's okay, baby. You are such a good boy for me." Trick moved in front of Clint, dropping to his knees and cupping Nav's hands in his own. Nav trembled at his touch, fluttering his eyes shut as he started to pant. "We

227

can still go to the hospital and get you pain medication. We can make you feel so much better, baby. It's your choice."

"No," said Nav, shaking his head. "I just...please don't make me go. I just want you, please." Nav reached for him, twisting and groaning in his effort to reach Trick.

"You can do this, Nav. You are so good for me and so damn strong. You're the strongest person I've ever met." Trick moved to Nav, settling on the bed with his back to the headboard before pulling Nav to his chest. Nav grunted once before he settled between Trick's thighs, his breath filtering over Trick's belly.

"He can touch me, but please hold me," said Nav, gripping Trick like a lifeline. "Don't let me go."

"I'm never letting you go," said Trick, the truth resounding in his words. Nav melted against him, letting out a soft sigh as Trick hugged him close. He flicked his gaze up to Clint, nodding his thanks as Clint returned with supplies from under Trick's bathroom sink.

"This might sting at first," said Clint as he opened a bottle of peroxide, his voice low and calm. "The tricky thing about peroxide is that it is great for cleaning wounds the first time, but not more than that. It kills the bacteria and anything else that's on your skin, but it also kills some of your skin cells. If you use it over and over, it just keeps killing more and more of your cells, and you will never heal."

Clint poured the bottle over Nav's skin, the liquid bubbling in a few spots as it met the tiny tears Clint had pointed out. The air filled with a distinctive chemical smell, tickling Trick's nose as he watched it drip onto his sheets.

Trick didn't care that he would probably have to replace his sheets. He would throw out his entire bed if it helped Nav feel better.

"It's warm," said Nav, squirming against Trick's lap. His gaze had clouded again as he slithered back under the veil of subspace. *So beautiful.*

"Does it sting?" asked Clint as he gently dabbed at the marks, sucking the fluid up with a clean cloth that he must've pulled from the drawer in the bathroom.

Nav hummed, shifting his hips as he clutched Trick tighter.

"He's still under," said Trick, rubbing his hands over Nav's impossibly soft skin. "He didn't go under for the scene, but when he safeworded and I started aftercare, he slipped really deep."

Clint hummed, dipping his head closer to inspect his work and following Nav's squirming body with a professional detachment that Trick couldn't help but be thankful for. Jealousy had already sent him over the edge once in the last few hours.

"Trick," Nav breathed against his chest, his pupils blown wide. Flexing his hips, Nav ground against the bed with rhythmic purpose.

"Are you hard, boy?" asked Clint, a smile stretching over his lips when Nav nodded. "Well, don't stop on my account. Let your Dom make you feel good." He flicked his gaze up to Trick. It wasn't a question. It was a demand.

Trick swallowed. Clint had guided him as he'd taken his first steps into the lifestyle, but he'd stomped over everything that Clint had taught him in one short scene with Nav. He wasn't sure if Clint was angrier because Trick had lost control or because he had left Nav afterward, terrified of what he had done. *If Clint weren't here…* He didn't even want to think about it.

"Can you get up on your knees, baby? I want to touch you." Trick slid his hands under Nav's belly, helping him as he struggled to his hands and knees. Nav's head hung down, his cheek still pressed to Trick's chest. He could probably hear Trick's pounding heart.

"So good for me," said Trick, trailing over the very edge of the welts that he could reach. Nav's cock was solid between his legs, hanging with its beautiful curve and leaking onto the sheets. Nav groaned as Clint continued wiping the peroxide from his skin, his cock flexing and dribbling with every touch.

Trick stared, taking in every single inch. He memorized the way Nav's arms trembled under his own weight, the thin muscles standing out under his soft skin. His hair was sweaty, clinging to the back of his neck where it had started to grow a touch longer — the perfect length. Nav licked his lips, his eyes half-lidded and glazed. It was everything that Trick had wanted — everything he could have dreamed of.

I'll never hurt him again. I'll never lose control.

"Can you stay still for Clint? You can come whenever you want, but I need you to stay still." Trick tugged Nav up his chest, taking some of his weight and gasping as Nav latched onto his nipple, sucking hard.

"Fuck." Trick cursed as his cock filled. His nipples had never been overly sensitive, but he'd also never had someone suck them like that. How many times would Nav open his eyes to things he'd never even known he desired?

"You like that, baby? You like sucking on your Dom's chest?" His breath shuddered as Nav nodded without letting go. "Keep going, baby. You take whatever you need from me. I'm going to make you feel so good."

He moved for Nav's cock, twisting his body a bit so he could reach the throbbing flesh that fit so perfectly in his hand. It flexed as he touched his fingertips to it, pre-cum drooling from the slit.

Jerking him quickly, Trick shuddered as Nav tensed, coming into his hand with no warning. He sucked fiercely as Trick eased him through it, slowing his movements as Nav came down.

"Trick." Nav whimpered, releasing Trick's swollen nipple that glistened with spit. "Trick, I need more. Please." His cock was quickly going soft as he went lax, his weight settling against Trick. Trick caught him, supporting him so Clint could continue to work.

I can't give him more! I can't hurt him! He held Nav tighter, looking to Clint. To Clint's credit, he was still at work, cleansing the area with the antibacterial soap he'd found, despite the tent in his pajama pants.

Clint was a rock and would have never given into his anger or lust, unlike Trick.

"What do you need, boy?" asked Clint after the silence had stretched a moment too long.

I should be asking that. What is wrong with me? Trick stumbled mentally but scrambled to gather himself. *I will not fuck up again.*

"I'll give you anything you ask for, Nav," said Trick, taking control of the situation and running his fingers through Nav's hair. The strands were slick between his fingers and sweat plastered against his skin where Nav touched him.

"I want to suck you," said Nav, whispering against him.

Trick throbbed, his cock leaking against his thigh. He'd been fine ignoring it where it was squashed between his leg and Nav, until Nav had mentioned it and his lust had surged like a lightning strike.

Pride burst through his chest, and he could almost feel the glow on his own skin. He'd offered Nav anything, and his sub had chosen his Dom's pleasure. Nav was *his* sub, and he was never letting him go.

"So perfect for me," said Trick, shifting so he could help Nav move down his body. Clint supported Nav's haunches as he shuffled down, a wet spot on the front of his pajama pants. Clint's chest had flushed, his scars standing out like northern lights against a dark sky.

As soon as Nav caught sight of Trick's cock, he sucked him inside his mouth, taking him so deep that he should have gagged. Somehow, he didn't, getting all the way down until his nose was pressed to Trick's blond curls. He took Trick's cock like he was made for it, then he held himself there, despite his watering eyes.

"So good for me," said Trick, holding still, despite his longing to buck even deeper. He tugged Nav's hair, lifting him off so his sub could take a deep breath after holding himself down for so long. Nav whined, pulling against the grip on his hair, as if he were desperate to take Trick again.

"It's okay, baby. Breathe for me, then you can have more." Trick waited until Nav sucked in a breath before he relaxed his grip and let Nav sink down on him again. How he accommodated Trick's cock so easily was beyond him. Trick was hefty, and although Theo had managed to take most of him in his ass, he hadn't come close with his mouth. A big cock was usually a blessing and a curse, but with Nav, it was nothing but a blessing.

Even Clint looked impressed, which was a feat in itself. Clint had been there, done that and seen more ass than a porn director.

Trick held himself back as long as he could, pulling Nav off to breathe periodically when he realized that his sub seemed to have no interest in breathing on his own. The heat, pressure and the scent of Nav was too much.

He let Nav sink himself down one last time before the heat built and broke in his groin. His orgasm hit him on the edge of a groaning breath, and he spilled down Nav's willing throat.

Nav sucked him through it, holding him deep until he softened enough that Nav could still breathe without letting him go. It was a lot to take, especially when Trick quickly became oversensitive. But he let Nav continue to suck him, until he was sure that he would get hard again soon. Only then did he ease Nav back, curling down to bring their lips together.

"So perfect for me."

He watched as Nav drifted, then fell into a deep sleep, his skin cleaned and the cream reapplied. Clint had moved to the edge of the bed, waiting as long as they needed.

"A word," said Clint quietly. Trick nodded, setting Nav gently on the bed before pulling the sheet over him, making sure to avoid the spots that were damp with peroxide and cream. Flicking one lamp off, he followed Clint into the hall, leaving the door open so he could look back at Nav. If Nav awoke, he would only have to open his eyes to see Trick watching over him.

Clint turned away, stepping into the kitchen where the light was infinitely brighter. Trick looked over his shoulder once before he followed, Nav's smell still clinging to his skin. His limbs were loose, the terrified uncertainty drained away to nothing.

The tent in Clint's pajamas looked so out of place with sleep clinging to the edges of Trick's thoughts. Trick dropped a glare to the peaked flesh hidden behind thin fabric, a surge of jealousy wisping over his skin. The feeling was gone again in seconds. Clint was his friend and hadn't done a thing but help them.

Clint crossed his arms, raising one brow as Trick lifted his gaze.

"You're hard," said Trick, immediately wishing he'd kept his mouth shut. It was one thing to be honest but not when he sounded like a pouting teenager.

"I'm a man not a saint, and your sub is…something special." Clint looked to the side, something passing over his gaze before he snapped his attention back to Trick. "You ready for that word?"

Trick nodded, wishing he had stopped to put on boxers. Getting yelled at in his own kitchen in nothing but his birthday suit was not his idea of a good time.

Clint smashed his fist into the side of Trick's face, his knuckles thudding into his eye and cheekbone with enough force to send him to his knees. His head whipped to the side and a gasp pushed through his lips. Gripping his cheek, Trick stared up at Clint, his thoughts whirling.

Clint hit me? Clint, who never touched a soul without three levels of consent? Who had taught him everything he knew and had been by his side from the beginning?

Clint was panting, clenching his fists over and over as he glared down at Trick. Every muscle in his naked torso was at attention, his arms flexing as he licked his lips. Trick was strong, but naked and kneeling, he wouldn't stand a chance against Clint.

Trick scrambled to get to his feet, his survival instincts cutting in as his cheek throbbed.

"No, you stay on your knees. You don't deserve to stand right now. I understand that you dropped *hard,* but that's not an excuse," Clint growled, the tendons in his neck going taut.

Trick could recall one instance when he'd seen Clint pushed past the brink of rage. A Dom had ignored his sub's safeword at the club, and luckily, the sub had hit his panic button. Clint had handed the Dom's ass to him, literally throwing him out into the pouring rain. Trick and the dungeon master had been there to back Clint up, but they hadn't needed to step in.

"What the fuck is wrong with you?" Clint seethed, his voice low. "Were you trying to beat him until he called red or just trying to prove a point? No sub deserves that. It's no wonder you dropped."

"I lost control." Trick flinched, ready for another blow. His knees ached from the hard kitchen floor and his nose was stuffed up from where the edge of Clint's knuckle had caught it. Goosebumps broke over his skin.

"You don't lose control, Trick. You know that better than anyone else, because I fucking mentored you. This is what you do with what I taught you? That's what limits are for — yours *and* his." Clint paced the kitchen, each step a resounding blow to Trick's ego.

"How many strikes until he said his safeword? I know he felt every one," Clint growled, and Trick struggled not to drop his gaze. Trick was a Dom through and through. He didn't kneel to anyone, not even Clint. Struggling to his feet, Trick faced Clint head-on.

"He's so much stronger than you give him credit for. He didn't safeword from the strikes." Pride surged through him. Nav had taken *everything* — well, almost everything. Trick knew he had been way out of line, but his sub was like none other. He had to make sure that Clint knew that.

"I know that boy is stronger than you or me, but not for the right reasons. You can't even see it you're so

235

fucking blind. Answer the question, boy. What made him safeword?" asked Clint.

"I...I was going to fuck him dry. It was a... punishment. He called 'yellow' and I stopped right away. I realized that I had been wrong, and I had no reason to punish him in the first place." *It sounds even worse out loud.*

A slap resounded through the room, stinging worse than the punch as it landed over the opposite cheek. Trick took the blow without flinching. He deserved worse.

"Do you know how fucking dangerous that is?" Clint roared. Any louder and he would wake Nav. "If his limits don't restrict scenes like that, then yours should. I know your style, and how rough you are. If it had been a cane or a whip, you could have landed him in the hospital. Did you respect his limits, at least?"

"We've never discussed them," said Trick with a dawning horror. The last time they had talked limits was when Derreck had guided the scene. Before that, and after, they had never been discussed. He swallowed, blood draining from his face. He had thought that he was a good Dom. He *knew* better.

"I could ban you from every kink club in the country, boy." Clint could. He had more pull in the community than anyone Trick knew.

His life...his *everything* would be gone with a few words from Clint. His heart pounded. Trick couldn't live without kink in his life, not when it drove so much about who he was as a person.

But he had abused the privilege as if it were nothing.

"I've been with Theo so long, Clint. I used to know what he was thinking, and I just assumed that I would know with Nav, too. I hurt him so much." He forced back the tears, even as he trembled and clutched the wall for support. "Nav is so different from anyone I've ever met," said Trick, staring pleadingly at Clint as he told him of how they'd met — not the cute stares in the hall, but their first time in the alley when he'd finally found someone that he could love — someone that could handle all of him and take pleasure in his darkest thoughts. "I was trying to show him that he was mine, but I forgot that I'm his, too. He'll never forgive me for this," said Trick, sliding until his ass met the floor.

Clint had stopped pacing and had grabbed a chair as Trick spoke. His anger had cooled, his eyes going wide when Trick had vividly described the alley. He worked his jaw, shaking his head as he stared at Trick, silence stretching between them.

"Theo never would have gone through with that scene," said Clint, leaning back in his chair. "That boy loves restraint and praise, but he can barely tolerate pain."

"I know," said Trick. He had always known. "When I met Nav, it was like everything I'd been holding back for ten years suddenly came rushing out. And he took it so well, so perfectly — until I got jealous and fucked it all up."

"You listened when he told you to stop. If you hadn't, you wouldn't be conscious right now," said Clint. "Your membership is suspended for one year," he went on, leaning back in his chair. "I trust you not to try and go to any alternate clubs, but if you do, then you will no longer be welcome anywhere."

Trick's chest twisted. It was a slap on the wrist compared to what he had expected, but it still hurt. Kink was such a big part of his life that he didn't know how he would survive without it for one month, let alone twelve.

"I expect you to attend the club four times per month as my guest. You will only have one room available for your use, and it will be under my supervision or the Dom of my choice. You will not participate in any scenes at the club without my express consent and you will only get that once you prove that you've had a detailed discussion about hard and soft limits." Clint let out a long sigh, suddenly looking weary. "That boy deserves the world, and you will give it to him."

There was only one thing for Trick to say. "I promise."

Chapter Twenty-Four

Nav

Nav awoke in the type of agony that should have been reserved for hell. Perhaps his parents had been right all along, and he was there now, his flesh stripped from his bones as he was sodomized by Satan. He snorted.

Ever so slowly he moved one leg, then the other, the muscles stiff and his skin tight like he'd slept in the sun for forty-eight hours. Stretching, he took a few deep breaths as his legs and ass started to feel better with every movement, except for a few spots that cringed like evil in a barrel of holy water.

The air was warm, the bright light filtering along the unfamiliar and dust-free walls an indicator of just how late he had slept. His memories were foggy and distant, featuring the man he had tried for weeks to stay away from.

Trick. He sat up, his ass twinging against the soft sheets. Other than the single blond hair on the pillow beside him and the scent of Trick clinging to the air, he was alone. Pulling the sheet back, he looked down, tracing his finger over the edge of a welt that had wrapped along the side of his leg. Strangely enough, the touch almost felt *good*, like a sensitive bruise that he couldn't help but poke.

The thuds of the belt were still echoing in his memory, his hands aching from how hard he had grasped the sheets. But after — when Trick had held him close, letting him suck on anything he could get his mouth on...

Nav flushed. He had sucked Trick's nipple...and it had felt so good. Was it just another part of the kink world that he was discovering in leaps and bounds?

"Trick?" Nav called out into the apartment, keeping his voice low so that it didn't carry through the thin walls. How many of the neighbors had heard him as he'd cried and came? He'd hold his head high, regardless.

Standing from the bed, Nav twisted, trying to get a view of his ass. *I look like a fucking Christmas tree.* There were what looked like hundreds of stripes, in so many colors that he looked downright festive. They were sure to stay just as long, if not longer than the marks left by Derreck. Something about that warmed his empty belly, even though he was alone.

"Trick?" He grabbed a pair of discarded pajamas that were a few sizes too big and pulled them over his hips. The fabric scratched against his ass, despite their softness, and he half-considered tossing them off again. Stumbling around the apartment was one hundred percent fine while naked but walking across the hall would probably get him kicked out.

When he stepped to the doorway, the scent of bacon caught his nose and his stomach rumbled. He rounded the corner, following the noise of spattering grease before pausing at the edge of the kitchen.

Trick was standing in front of the stove with tongs in hand, fully dressed, with an apron stretched over his tank top and tied behind his back. Bacon splattered in the pan like nobody's business, jumping a few times as Nav watched. The table was already set with two glasses of juice and two plates with buttered toast and orange slices perched on the edge.

Nav's heart thudded. It was terribly domestic. *Run!* First came breakfast, and the next thing you knew, you were taking off work to attend their best friend's wedding and sucking off three drunk groomsmen.

Not falling for that again. Nav shook his head as he glanced at the door. "Trick?"

Trick whirled, a smile blooming on his face as he spied Nav. A drop of grease chose that moment to drip from the tongs to Trick's leg and the blond cursed, slapping a hand to his leg as he dropped the tongs. Grease went flying, a stray drop managing to land on Nav's toe. It was still hot.

"Crap. Sorry, love. I was going to wake you up, but you looked so beautiful," said Trick as he bent for the tongs, rinsing them off in the sink before thrusting them back into the pan. The oil erupted as the water touched it, the sound almost deafening.

Nav froze. *Love.* Trick had said that he loved him after Nav had almost spilled the terrible word. Nav didn't— He *couldn't* love Trick.

His eyes went wide as he realized what was banging around the inside of his chest. *But I can't.* It was a morning after, but he didn't even *want* to leave. He would rather sit at the table — or stand — and eat breakfast with Trick.

What the fuck is wrong with me? Nav tried to clamp down on the feeling, but it was already too late. It rushed through him, his skin prickling and his eyes suddenly wet as it got its first taste of freedom.

"I thought we could talk over breakfast," said Trick, apparently now impervious to the plethora of grease bouncing his way. "I hope you like bacon."

Nav grunted, making his way to the table with his heart in his throat. Of course he loved bacon, as long as it wasn't paired with eggs. But he had his own bacon in his own fridge. He just had to scrounge up the energy to go get it.

He paused at the table, looking to the door one last time as he pulled the chair back. Glancing down at the seat, he glared at the flat, unforgiving surface. There was no way.

"I got this chair ready for you," said Trick, pulling a different chair out from under the table — one with the overly domestic orange juice in front of it. On top of the seat there was a fluffy white pillow that beckoned Nav's ass like a lighthouse. He cringed as he slowly sat in the chair, relaxing into the pillow as he settled down. It was uncomfortable, but manageable.

"When did Clint head out? I wanted to thank him," said Nav, reaching for the juice when his voice came out scratchy. "And apologize to him, too."

"He left after we had a chat. He knew we needed some time to talk," said Trick as he returned with two plates. As he moved into the light above the table, Nav caught sight of the glowing bruise on Trick's cheek that he had thought had been a trick of the shadows.

"He hit you," said Nav, leaning forward against his will to touch the bruise as Trick sat beside him. His skin was hot to the touch and slightly swollen. Guilt pooled in his gut. "I hope that wasn't because of me."

Nav jerked his hand back, looking down at his plate when Trick reached for him.

"No. You were perfect," said Trick. "He did it because I lost control and hurt you. It was my fault."

"But I wanted it," said Nav, cringing as he eyed up the eggs. He couldn't understand some people's fascination with butt-nuggets. Chickens were the only animal that shit breakfast — and Nav wanted nothing to do with that.

He turned his plate, putting the bacon front and center. "I asked you to hit me, and I'd ask you to do it again if it helped you. You stopped as soon as I said yellow, and you took care of me."

"We shouldn't have done any of that," Trick hissed, reaching for Nav's hand and holding it tight when Nav tried to pull back. "I'm not denying you or telling you that you did anything wrong. You couldn't have been more perfect. *I* was in the wrong. I'm the experienced one who should be guiding you through discussions and limits and discovery, but I fucked it up. I really hurt you, and I could have harmed you because I set us up for failure."

Nav slowly drew his hand back when Trick released him, standing from the chair. His ass ached as his appetite disappeared. "I'm not naïve, Trick. If I'd wanted you to stop, I could have stopped you at any time. You're not the first guy I've fucked who wanted to slap me around a bit. It's okay, I kind of like it."

"I could have hurt you, Nav!" Trick slammed his hand down on the table. The dishes clattered and a few drops of juice spilled over onto the smooth wooden surface.

"It's not the first time that someone's hurt me, and it won't be the last," said Nav, rolling his eyes. "You aren't the first guy to fuck me dry or to fuck me without prep or to hit me, but at least you give a shit about me. No one has ever made me feel the way you make me feel." Nav's voice rose along with his hackles. He wasn't weak, no matter what Trick had to say about it.

"You don't get it." Trick crumpled, dropping his elbows to the table and resting his head in his hands. "This isn't just some passing phase for me. This is my life. A Dom is the only thing that I am and the only way I can ever be. If I fuck this up, I lose everything."

"Oh," said Nav. So it wasn't about him at all. It wasn't about Theo — or losing control or loving him. It was about Trick and only Trick. If Nav didn't play by the rules, then Trick would find someone who did.

"Thanks for breakfast but I think I'll pass." Nav stepped away, the painting catching his eye as he paused at the front door. It called to him like a lost siren, begging him to stay. If he looked hard enough, it could almost be him on the canvas and not Theo.

"Nav, stop," said Trick, leaping from his chair. The dishes clattered again, Trick's orange juice tipping on its side as he knocked the table. The stream of juice trickled onto the floor unchecked. "You can't leave when you're still hurt."

"You wanted to give me aftercare, and I stayed for it. You have no reason to hold me here now." Nav shook his head, tearing his gaze away from the painting. That would never be him. He could never look at Trick that way. "I can take care of myself. I don't need you and you sure as hell don't need me."

"What? No. Why would you even say that?" Trick reached for him, but Nav sidestepped, his ass glancing against the door. Nav hissed as his bruises flared to life.

"You will listen to what I have to say," said Trick, his voice a low growl as he stalked toward the door. His eyes flashed and his lips curved into a snarl as he slapped his hand against the door, pinning Nav without ever touching him.

Oh God. Nav trembled, his eyes falling shut as his cock hardened. *This* was Trick, not the bacon-cooking sweetie who went pale at the sight of a few welts. This was Trick the Dom, who Nav could hand the reins of his mind and body and let go. There was no question, no concern, only pure sensual confidence that spoke to Nav on every level.

Nav nodded, swallowing against the lump in his throat. Tilting his head back, he offered himself to Trick. *Take what you need. It's yours.*

"Enough, slut," said Trick as Nav quaked. "Get on your knees and show me how sorry you are for trying to walk out on me again. Take me into your mouth and apologize in the only way you know how."

Nav dropped to his aching knees, his heels hitting his ass and sending a burst of sensation straight to his cock. Pre-cum dripped from the tip, soaking into the fabric of his borrowed pajamas.

"I expect you to pay attention to what I say, because you'll have to repeat every word," said Trick.

Nav nodded, bringing his hands up and pushing Trick's apron aside. Trick's cock tented his pants, not quite hard but getting there quickly. Nav touched the waistband, only to be slapped away a moment later.

"Use your mouth, slut. I don't want your filthy hands on me." Trick tore his apron off, the fabric tie ripping apart.

Nav's cock ached as he leaned in, nuzzling Trick's drawstring before clutching it between his teeth. The loop pulled free, the fabric squeaking between his teeth as his mouth watered. It was a good thing that Trick had opted for track pants instead of jeans. Nav had a dexterous tongue, but popping a button on a pair of Levi's would have been a Houdini act.

Tugging them down over Trick's cock, Nav frowned at the sight of yet another layer of cotton between him and his prize. He grabbed the elastic in his teeth, gripping it tight and freeing Trick's cock in an award-winning move.

Every inch was hard for him and ready for the taking. Trick's cock was already weeping, a few pearly dew drops gathered at the head that called to Nav like cotton candy at the fair. He cleaned them from Trick's cock with his tongue before sliding his lips over the head and toying with Trick's slit.

Nav looked up to Trick, expecting to see his cheeks flushed and his lips open in a pant. Trick glared down at him with one brow raised. If it hadn't been for his dilated pupils, he could have been sitting in a coffee shop, sipping at a latte.

Challenge accepted.

"I neglected a few very important things, slut, including talking about our limits," said Trick, his voice calm and even as Nav sank down his length. "When you leave here today, I expect you to think about your limits and text me about your hard and soft ones within one hour. If there is anything that makes you uncomfortable or you want to ask me about, that will be your opportunity. Anything that is not on your list, I will consider trying, whether you like it or not. Do you know what that means? You can nod." Trick gripped his hair, pulling Nav off him. Nav nodded his head, lost in the lingering taste of Trick and his desire for more.

"That means that if an enema isn't a hard limit, I will bind you to the wall and fill you until you are bursting. I'll make you hold it until you are begging me to let you release, and just when you are about to break, I'll fuck you hard, my cock the only thing keeping it inside of you."

Nav shuddered, fluttering his eyes shut at the image. Cleaning himself was a routine that he took seriously for his own comfort as well as the comfort of his partner. He'd never considered playing like that and the idea was...interesting. His cock throbbed in agreement.

Trick didn't give him time to reply. He pulled Nav back onto his cock, slamming all the way to the back of his throat. Nav fought the gag, swallowing and holding Trick deep inside. The fuzziness was starting to surround him, but he pushed it away. He had to pay attention.

"I think you like that idea," said Trick, laughing as Nav squirmed. "I'll consider it as a reward for good behavior then. But I need you to be clear. Everything that is not your limit is on the table. Now I'll tell you my limits. Are you paying attention?"

Nav gagged as he nodded, tears streaking down his cheeks as his throat was brutalized. He dug his fingers into his palms, refusing to let his mind wander. He had to focus.

"I will never be your 'Daddy', because that's not who I am. I am your Dom. Calling me 'Daddy' would be a hard limit. My other hard limits are ball crunching, needle play, watersports, scatplay and photography.

My soft limits are breath play and sensory deprivation. I would be willing to put my hand around your throat but I'm not going to choke you out."

Trick pulled Nav back until just the head of his cock was in his mouth. Nav sucked at it, trying to get every drop of pre-cum as it beaded up. The pre-cum was the only sign that Trick was even affected by anything he was doing, and Nav drank it down.

"What are my limits, slut?" asked Trick, popping Nav off his cock. Nav repeated them, lunging for Trick's cock when he'd finished listing them off. Trick ran his hands through his hair and Nav sank deeper, letting his eyes fall shut.

"Good boy," said Trick. "As a reward, you can make me come and swallow every drop. Then I'm going to check your marks and you'll eat breakfast at my feet."

Endorphins flooded his system as Trick's cum coated his tongue, his flavor mixing with his single sip of orange juice. He sucked it all down, searching for more with a groan of loss when Trick ran dry, his cock going soft. Nav moved to Trick's firm sac, sucking one ball into his mouth, then the other. *Give me more.*

"Get up and lean over the table," said Trick.

Nav scrambled to obey, his own neglected cock throbbing as he leaned over the cold surface, his fingers dipping into the puddle of juice that had drifted over the surface. Trick didn't seem to care that their napkins were ruined, the floral placemats soaked.

Tugging at Nav's pajama pants, Trick slowly peeled them down, sliding the fabric over his aching ass and thighs. Nav curled his toes, a moan pushing through his lips. How could anything that was supposed to hurt feel so fucking good?

His ass felt as if it were blazing hot as he was bared to the room, a dribble of pre-cum falling to the floor as Trick skimmed his palm over his ass. "Oh, God. Trick, please." He wished he could see the marks and Trick's tanned hand against his ass in contrast. He would kill to get his hands on a full-length mirror. Trick pinched him and Nav choked as he nearly came.

"Kneel."

Nav floated, staring at Trick's feet as he kneeled next to Trick's chair. His ass throbbed as he squirmed against his heels, scraping over his welts just to feel the zing. His cock was curved toward his belly, weeping steadily as his balls ached with the need to come.

"Eat." Trick held a small piece of bacon to his lips and Nav took it without question, licking and sucking Trick's fingers clean. As soon as he'd finished swallowing, Trick held another piece to his lips, over and over until his stomach finally stopped grumbling.

Nav had never been truly content before, but for the first time he could see himself staying — see himself with Trick for more than just a series of kinky fucks and awkward avoidances. It should have been scary, but he couldn't bring himself to care.

Chapter Twenty-Five

Nav

Nav slipped into his apartment, the door thankfully unlocked when he turned the knob. He touched his face as he shut the door behind him, tracing the smile on his lips. When was the last time he'd smiled after sex? Not that they'd had sex. No — what they had done had been more intimate than any sexual act he'd ever experienced.

He was still swimming, even after Trick had held him close for hours — long enough for Nav's cock to go soft, his balls aching like he'd been kicked. Trick had dressed him in a fresh set of clothes, walking him across the hall and delivering him right to his door before he'd retreated with one last reminder to Nav.

Please be alone. The television was on, but Sasha tended to get up and walk out of a room, despite what was still running. He crossed his fingers as he rounded the corner into the living room. He had homework to do, and he needed privacy to do it.

Nav cursed under his breath as he noticed Sasha waiting for him on the couch, a scowl on his lips as he looked up from the blaring television. There were two beer cans sitting on the coffee table and two more on the ground. One had tipped over, a pool of beer leaking out of the can and onto the floor and probably seeping right through and into the underpadding.

"Where the fuck were you?" asked Sasha, thankfully turning the volume down. Nav caught sight of a few Formula One cars rounding a bend on the television, the whistling hum especially ear piercing after the calm of Trick's apartment.

"Out. Why did you drink all my beer? You already had more than enough last night," Nav shot right back at Sasha, leaning over to pick up the cans off the floor. The move made the fabric of his pants tighten over his ass, but he was still somewhat numb from the cream Trick had applied before he'd left. Something in his chest glowed as he thought of his Dom taking care of him.

"Don't change the subject," said Sasha. He looked Nav up and down, pausing on the track pants that Trick had given Nav. Nav imagined that they had probably belonged to Theo at one point because they fit him perfectly, but they were his now. "Those aren't your pants."

"No, they aren't," said Nav. "And I need you to get the fuck out so I can do some research. It's gay research, so you wouldn't be interested." He slowly eased down onto the couch beside his friend before he pulled out his phone.

There had to be websites that listed common kinky limits for him, and he already knew a few that he would text to Trick.

"If it's kinky gay research, then I'm sticking around," said Sasha, leaning over to look down at Nav's phone. "What the fuck is a violet wand?" His breath reeked of stale beer and nachos.

Do I even have nachos? Nav spied an empty chip and salsa container that had been tossed onto the ground. *Not anymore.*

"I have no idea," said Nav. He clicked on the link, shrugging Sasha off before he could lean on him any harder. His ass could only handle so much extra weight. "Oh, interesting."

"Tell me," said Sasha, leaning right back in.

"Sasha, you are my best friend, but I will boot your ass out the door myself if you don't fuck off," said Nav, ignoring Sasha's snort and eye roll. "I'm horny, and I need to focus on this. It's important."

"That sounds like too much work." Sasha let out a sigh, flopping across the couch and squirming his feet into Nav's lap. Sasha had definitely not had a shower. Good news for Nav's loofa, but bad news for his health.

"Get out," Nav hissed, pinching Sasha's toe. Sometimes he wondered why he hung out with Sasha at all. He told himself that it was because looking at Sasha's disaster of a life always made him feel better about himself. But then he remembered everything Sasha had done for him. Beneath his slob exterior, Sasha was a decent human being.

"Nah, I'm gonna watch this race. You do your thing and I'll do mine, but I don't want to see any dicks." He cranked the volume back up, the sound of zooming car engines peaking. "By the way, you're out of beer."

"Fucking dick," Nav hissed under his breath, bringing up the webpage again. There were a few kinks that he knew would be out right away, so he sent them off to Trick.

Doing research. Hard limits so far. Needles, bloodplay, bodily fluids and permanent scarring.

Nav sent the text, going back to the webpage again. There were a few he had to look up, but most were self-explanatory. Orgasm control — *yes, please.* Ball torture — *thanks, but no thanks.*

His heart raced as his phone pinged with a text from Trick.

I'm sorry that I violated one of your hard limits if that welt scars. Thank you for telling me, good boy.

Nav preened, a smile stretching over his lips and his chest warming instantly. He could almost hear Trick saying those words to him, his voice low and soft as he ran his fingers through Nav's hair. *Good boy.* He loved being Trick's slut, but being his good boy was even better. He sent a text back to Trick.

I don't think I'd be into armpit worshipping because deodorant tastes terrible. I'll call that one a soft limit. Age play, too, because I don't know if I want to go there. Breath play makes me a bit nervous and inversion bondage sounds terrifying. Do people actually do that? I'd pass out.

A few seconds later Trick responded.

They do. We have a rope master at the club, and he's probably one of the best in the country. If you ever wanted to try it, I would invite him to one of our scenes.

Nav's heart pounded as he thought about doing another scene with Trick. Would it be the sensual terror of the alley, the beautiful torture that it had been with Derreck or the enveloping agony of Trick's bedroom? As long as Trick was there for him after, the scene itself didn't matter.

Some of this stuff sounds pretty interesting. Have you ever tried puppy play? It sounds fun and sweet.

Nav hit send, smiling as Trick responded right away.

Yes. It is sweet, and I would love the opportunity to be your owner. Are those all your limits, good boy?

Nav nodded to himself, reading the online list carefully again before he sent his reply.

Yes. If something comes up and I decide I don't like it, can I change my mind?

Trick responded instantly.

Of course, that's what your safewords are for. We will discuss our limits before each scene to make sure we are always on the same page. That is non-negotiable, along with condoms and lube from here on out. I'm not going to risk taking you dry again, baby.

Nav let out a sigh of relief. Getting fucked dry hurt like a bitch and it could be really dangerous. Getting a tear was just asking for an infection, and he did not want to have to explain that to a doctor. He glanced down at his phone as another text came through.

You got all your limits to me in fifty-eight minutes, good boy. You can have a reward now for good behavior. I want you to make yourself come. You aren't allowed to use your hands or any toys, so you'll have to hump something like the slut you are.

Nav swallowed, his mouth going dry. He'd had a semi since he'd grabbed his phone but instantly he was aching and leaking. Trick had kept him on the edge all day, and he knew it wouldn't take him much to come.

Sasha's still here.

Nav sent the text, looking up at his friend whose mouth was open wide as he stared at the screen. Nav doubted he would even notice a fly if it buzzed in there.

Go to your bedroom and close the door. You'll have to stay quiet, slut.

Nav stood from the couch, making a quick excuse to Sasha, who didn't even look up. He raced to the bedroom door, slowly closing it behind him before looking back at his phone.

Okay, I'm in the bedroom. Should I get on the bed?

He looked at the expanse of his messy sheets where Sasha had definitely slept the night before. *Is that another bag of chips?* He would have to sterilize the sheets before he touched them again. Sighing, he read Trick's text.

Don't be so vanilla, slut. You have a tall dresser — the one with the white knobs. Rub your cock against it like you're a bitch in heat.

Nav flushed as he looked at the dresser. The wood was light and delicately carved with deep shadows that could never be replicated with anything but age. He'd had the dresser since he was young — one of the only things he'd managed to smuggle out of his parents' house.

He pushed his parents from his mind. They were the last people he wanted to think about when he was trying to get off.

Lining himself up with the corner of the dresser, he braced his arms on either side to hold it and himself steady. The corner pressed a line across his cock, already uncomfortable. He gave an experimental thrust, wincing as he dragged his cock over the seam of the corner.

It hurts.

Nav sent the text off, his hands shaking as he kept moving his hips. Heat was building in his gut despite the uncomfortable edge. He had been too close for so long that it didn't seem to matter.

Good thing you're a pain slut.

He shuddered when he read Trick's reply. He didn't like pain — not really. He'd once cried over a papercut, although it *had* been from cardstock. He didn't like stubbing his toe and even plucking his eyebrows made him curse.

But it was different with Trick.

Can I come?

He sent the message, begging through the phone while biting back his whimpers. The television was loud, but who knew what Sasha was up to.

No. Pull yourself off the dresser now.

Nav whined, slapping a hand over his mouth to muffle the sound as he pulled back. His cock throbbed from being denied again, his balls so heavy that he wasn't sure that they'd ever been so full.

His phone stayed achingly silent for two long minutes before it finally buzzed again. Nav let out his breath in a rush, his skin thrumming.

Did you come?

Nav shook as he replied.

No, but I was so close. Please let me come. You promised, and I've been so good.

His phone was silent for another minute and Nav sank to his knees, the twinge of his ass pushing another drop of pre-cum from his cock. His borrowed pants were ruined and effectively claimed.

Good boy. Get your cock out and rub yourself against the rug.

Nav whimpered as he freed himself without touching his cock, dropping his pants to the floor. Trick had told him no hands, and Nav would follow that to the letter. Crawling to the rug he had at the side of the bed, he rested his cheek against it before slowly lying down. The rug was comfortable on his feet when he got up on a cold morning, but it was scratchy against the rest of him.

He gasped as he slowly hitched his hips, the dry carpet dragging against his cock and threatening to burn. At the slow rate, he wouldn't be able to come, but any faster and he'd end up with rug burn on his cock.

It's not enough.

Nav sent the text on the verge of tears. He was throbbing so badly, but he couldn't get there — not like this. And any stain in the fibers would be there for life. There was no getting cum out of shag.

You can come whenever you want, slut, but only from grinding on that carpet. I want to see the stain the next time I'm in your bedroom, so I know how helpless and needy you are. You'll fuck anything, just to get off.

Heat exploded at the base of his cock as he read Trick's words, surging upward as his balls drew tight. He shuddered and went still as his orgasm washed over him, his sore cock jerking and painting the purple shag. He smothered his face into the carpet as he cried out, tangling his fingers in the fibers.

Did you come?

Trick had left the message at some point while Nav unraveled on the floor, humping his cum deeper into the carpet as he recovered and spreading the wet stain for Trick to find. Would Trick get hard just from seeing it? Would he force Nav to his knees in front of it and call him a slut as he plowed into him from behind? God, he hoped so.

Yes. Thank you, Trick.

His hands shook as he typed the reply before he grabbed the track pants, wiped the remnants of cum from his groin and tossed them into the laundry. Grabbing a fresh pair from his drawer, he pulled them over his aching ass.

Perfect boy. Go back to Sasha now. I'll see you tonight.

Nav waited until his heart calmed before he stepped out of the bedroom, pulling the door shut behind him. Sasha was staring at him from the couch with one raised eyebrow. Sniffing himself, Nav smirked. He reeked of sex, but it was better than Sasha's beer and feet combo.

"What were you doing in there?" asked Sasha, lowering the volume on the television again.

"Fucking myself on the rug while I texted my Dom," said Nav, refusing to be ashamed. He laughed at the blush that bloomed over Sasha's face. *Prude.* "You still want to get into kink?"

"I think I'll pass."

Chapter Twenty-Six

Trick

Trick looked away from his phone, his hand sticky with cum and his cock still throbbing. Nav's face was fresh in his mind, his imagination filling in the gaps as he thought of Nav writhing on the floor of his bedroom, struggling to get release with his ass aching and his cock grinding against the rough carpet.

"Fuck." He shook his head, running a hand through his hair. He hadn't lasted an hour before he had Nav back on his knees again, and it was perfect.

Trick was rarely able to express himself outside of the club, and never in the way that he really needed.

Theo had tolerated it to an extent, letting Trick dote on him and even hand feed him sometimes. He had understood that Trick had needed it, not just in one place but as part of his entire life. But those occasions had been rare and saved for special dates.

His life had never been an extension of the club, the scene stretching and filling the missing gaps in his life until he was whole.

But Nav had gone willingly to his knees without question, taking food from his hand as if Trick had been feeding him chocolate and not little pieces of bacon. He hadn't complained, hadn't resisted and had been completely at peace, just as Trick had been.

It wasn't something he could just turn off with Nav, but he owed Clint his honesty. He grabbed his phone from where he'd set it on the still-sticky table, clicking onto Clint's contact and hitting the call button. He waited until the line connected before he began speaking.

"No toys and no impact play without supervision. I'm still going to put him on his knees as I see fit. You can't stop me from doing that." Trick paused, waiting for a response.

"Good afternoon to you as well, brat. The conversation went well, I presume," said Clint, letting out a sigh and a groan.

"No. He didn't want to talk limits, so I put him on his knees and made him listen instead," said Trick, his spent cock twitching as he remember exactly what they had done.

Clint snorted. "Can't imagine how you managed that. As long as it worked and he's not hurt or bleeding."

"I'm not a shitty Dom." Trick swallowed. Maybe he was. Maybe that was the reason he had lost control. Maybe that was why Theo had left him.

"That's not what I'm saying," said Clint. "This boy has you on edge in a way I've never seen. He's throwing himself into your path and giving you the reins. I need to know you can control yourself before you try to control him."

"I'm in control." Trick nodded to himself. He'd never felt more in control of himself. He would *never* hurt Nav again. He couldn't bear the thought of it. "I'm coming to the club tonight with him so he can thank you properly for your help. If you'll have us, of course."

Clint grunted. "I'm getting too old for this shit. My kind of thank you or your kind?"

"Get your mind out of the gutter, old man. He's not sucking your cock. That mouth belongs to me," said Trick, forcing down the growl that threatened to rise in his throat. He had shared Theo with other Doms, but not Nav—maybe for a non-sexual scene, but not for a fuck or a blow job. Now that Nav was *his*, he would never let him fuck another man unless Nav begged him prettily for something Trick couldn't give him.

"Fine, brat, I agree to your terms. But remember, as soon as his ass is healed, I'll be there to oversee your scenes. Don't think I won't enjoy myself." Clint let out a breath.

"I was counting on it. I've always loved a good audience." Trick smiled. He couldn't wait for Nav to heal. He had so much to show him—and so many ways to take him apart.

He would be there to pick up the pieces next time. He was determined to be there for Nav, no matter what.

Chapter Twenty-Seven

Nav
A few weeks later

Nav grumbled as the bed shifted, pulling him from precious sleep. Thrusting out one arm, he searched for Trick's heat between the covers. He'd fallen asleep alone and was unreasonably chilly with the air-conditioning humming away in the window.

Nav's lips curled up as he struck Trick's biceps, coiling his palm around it and squeezing. Trick—no. his boyfriend—spent less time at the gym than Nav had expected, and instead spent hours during the week configuring himself into yoga poses that made Nav instantly hard.

He hadn't been able to keep his eyes open another moment to wait for Trick, though, not when his hours had doubled over the last few weeks, even though the gala had come and gone. Business had never been better, especially since a certain canvas had made its way back to the studio and people had flocked to it like buzzing flies to a carcass.

When he'd seen it displayed on the other side of his desk as he'd walked into the building, he had blanched. His new boyfriend and his boyfriend's ex had stared at him from within their entwined fuckery, like they were guarding the entrance to a red room. He had glared at it, hatred seeping through his pores until the most embarrassing moment of his life had occurred.

A small girl had stepped into the studio a few minutes after he'd arrived, clutching her mother's hand fiercely with her tiny fingers. In her other hand she'd held a lollipop that had looked like it was covered in a mixture of carpet fuzz and cat hair.

Nav had taken the mother's name, sorting through a stack of invoices and pointedly keeping his gaze on the desk, before a tiny voice had called out.

"Is that you?" the little girl asked as she stared between the painting and him. Her candy had fallen to the floor as her tiny, curious eyes had gone wide.

Where was a curtain when he'd needed it? They should probably have had one if there were going to be any minors in the building. The painting wasn't exactly explicit, but the suggestion behind it made it very clear that the lovers were having a great time.

The woman hadn't missed a beat, giving the canvas a long look before she'd stared at Nav's flushing face, a smile twisting her lips.

"I believe it is, sweetheart," said the woman. "Very good eye, honey. Now pick your candy off the floor and wait by the door, please."

Nav's face had turned into molten lava, and his stack of papers floated to the floor. The woman had chuckled, leaning close once he had gathered himself again.

"You are very lucky to have someone so much in love with you," she'd said, her smile falling. "My Tina's father cares more for his money that he does for her. May I inquire on the price?" She had forced the smile back on her face.

Nav had stuttered through his response and his hatred had turned into something else.

Trick *loved* him. Trick called him after a long day and lay beside him on the couch, holding him tight just because he could. Trick had pestered Nav for a solid week until Nav had finally agreed that they could call each other 'boyfriends'.

Boyfriends. It still sounded ridiculous.

But what mattered was that the face in the painting was the same face he saw every time Trick didn't think he was looking. They were the same lips that stole his breath and the same eyes that stole his soul.

"You in dreamland?" asked Trick as he settled in the bed, breaking Nav from his memories with his cold hands. A kiss slipped against his forehead before Trick gathered him in his arms.

"Just thinking about how much I love you," said Nav. *How is it so easy to say?* The first slip-up had nearly given him a coronary, but the follow-up a few days later—also said by accident—had been almost natural for him. Trick had bent Nav over the counter to check his welts and it had slipped out of Nav's mouth, landing like a bomb in the middle of Trick's apartment.

He crawled up to place a kiss on Trick's lips, lingering to taste him and the fresh toothpaste that loitered on his tongue. Trick moved his hands to Nav's hips, guiding Nav between his legs and to his awakening cock.

"Everything set for tomorrow?" asked Nav as he pulled back, his sleepiness starting to fade. He blinked in the low light, grinning at the sight of Trick's blond hair against his purple pillowcase.

As Nav's welts had recovered, Trick had revealed so many things to him that they could have done differently to keep them both safe. Pain wasn't the only way to break Nav into pieces, and there were other ways that left Nav's mind at peace in a way that it never had been.

But the following day was their first real day back at the club, their scene under Clint's supervision long overdue. Clint was busier than ever with his business thriving, and he had pushed Nav to the edge of his patience.

It had given them time to plan their scene down to the last tiny detail, going over limits and boundaries until Nav was sure he had them memorized. And he'd never felt more comfortable about the idea of losing himself to Trick. He fucking trusted him, which was something he couldn't say about any other man.

Trick nodded, sliding his hands down to Nav's ass before squeezing his cheeks and spreading them wide. Nav let out a soft gasp as he ground his cock down into Trick's, his heart picking up with the tempo of his thrusts.

"You don't want to wait?" asked Trick, obviously knowing that Nav had the recovery time of a fucking dinosaur. Trick had said that he planned to "*work on it*", whatever that meant.

"Maybe I want you to make me wait," said Nav, giggling as Trick rolled them over until his head met the pillow. So, maybe Nav had a thing about orgasm denial, but who didn't?

"You'll wait, slut—even if I have to cage your cock so you can't come for a month," Trick growled, bringing their lips together in a quick peck. "Go to sleep."

Nav's cock surged against Trick's, completely unaware of the order. Nav shuddered as Trick rolled off him, spooning into his side and placing a hand on Nav's belly. Not coming for a month was probably one of the most unappealing things that Nav had ever heard of. Pressing his palms to the headboard, he hooked his fingers around the edge.

"Good boy," said Trick, laughing at Nav's whine.

"You are so unfair." His cock was aching—a familiar sensation when he was around Trick.

"You love it." Trick nuzzled his hair before kissing Nav on the cheek and rolling over.

Nav took a shuddering breath, closing his eyes even as his groin thrummed. *How many sheep do I have to count to get a hand around here?*

* * * *

Nav shielded his eyes as he stepped out of the car, the sun carving straight down in a path of early summer. His stomach rolled as he spied the door to the club, its nondescript surface putting him instantly on edge. Spontaneity was one thing that he couldn't fuck up, but he didn't want to ruin their carefully laid plans and get them both kicked out of Trick's place of solace.

"What if I fuck up?" asked Nav, looking up and down the street as he slid his hand into Trick's. His skin was vibrating, and his cock was half-hard in his loose jeans. He'd wanted to wear something tight to show off his ass, but he'd settled on comfort over appearance. Hopefully he wouldn't be wearing them long, anyway.

"There's a reason we are coming so early, baby," said Trick. "We'll have as much time as we need to get comfortable, and there will be no one around to distract us." He leaned in closer, whispering directly into Nav's ear. "There will be no one to hear you scream, either."

A shiver traveled down Nav's body, and his stomach calmed a bit. Trick would take care of him, and Trick wouldn't *let* him fuck up.

Trick reached the door, sliding his key card out of his pocket before tapping it to the sensor. A tiny beep later, they were inside, Trick shutting the door behind them and locking them in place.

His cock hardened as the sight of the curtain and the empty chair that blocked off the rest of the club. Even the bouncer was absent. *No one to hear me scream.* He gulped as Trick pushed the curtain wide.

Quiet music played overhead, calm jazz in a place that was usually bustling with rock, techno and sex. The lights were much brighter than Nav remembered, and the place was desolately empty except for Clint, who was standing behind the bar. He flushed as Clint looked up from his phone, sending a grin his way.

"Ready to do this, Trick?" asked Clint, easing from behind the bar. "Or should I say, are we ready to do *you?*" He turned to Nav, his grin going wide as Nav's flush deepened. "I've got a room ready for us. I thought *Still* would work best."

Trick nodded, following Clint as he led them to the back rooms. Nav's stomach bubbled as he trembled. He could remember the last time in the room with Derreck and the types of restraints that they hadn't even touched.

Nav and Trick had discussed the scene endlessly, but he didn't think Trick had informed Clint of their plans. What if Clint tried to intervene? Or what if he had an issue with what they were doing? Would he still kick Trick out? Nav's breathing picked up as he followed them to the back of the club where the music was quietest and the air cooler.

Nav would be fine if he never stepped a foot in Unkinked again. He didn't need a bar and a bunch of rooms to tell him what he needed sexually, but Trick was different. Trick had told him about the time he'd spent in the club, and how much he had relied on the building and the people over the years. They had got him through things that Nav couldn't have imagined, and they showed him that he wasn't a bad person for wanting to torture his subs a bit.

Clint opened the door and flicked on the light. Nav followed at a slower pace, letting his memories of the room wash over him. His gaze fell on the place where Derreck had pinned him. He had never even apologized to Derreck about using him so poorly. Derreck hadn't signed up to get manipulated by someone like Nav, and Nav had crossed a lot of lines, even if he hadn't intended to.

Given the chance, he would have ignored Derreck's hard limit and tried to tempt him for a fuck. Trick would probably think up a terrible punishment for Nav if he ever found out—which he probably would.

Trick touched Nav's lowered chin, tilting his gaze until he met those crystal blue eyes that were the first thing that made him realize he was really in love.

Trick's gaze searched his own before he nodded and turned to Clint.

Clint had taken a seat on the couch that was a twin to the one in the *Impact* room. It was big enough for four people to fit comfortably close, with enough kneeling space for twice that. He crossed his arms, leaning back with an air of relaxed comfort.

"Let's talk limits," said Trick, looking around the room before settling his gaze back on Nav. He cited off his limits, including the ones that he had listed before, along with a few additions. Nav beamed. *No permanent scarring* was among them.

Trick moved around the room as he spoke, pushing the restraint table against the wall before tossing small lube and condom packets around in a way that one would always be in reach, no matter where they rolled to.

Nav dropped to his knees when Trick rounded on him, listing off his limits with his gaze lowered. It was an exercise that they had perfected after many tries. Nav had trouble talking about limits when he was looking at Trick because he would do literally anything for him. On his knees, he could focus on himself and not just on Trick.

"Good boy," said Trick when Nav finished, smoothing his hand through Nav's hair before tugging it gently to pull Nav back to his feet. "Any questions?"

Nav nodded, looking at Clint, who had tossed his feet up on the couch. "Do you have any limits...Sir?" He had no idea what to call Clint, but he had to be a Dom, so 'sir' was probably a safe bet.

A grin stretched over Clint's lips and Trick let out a pleased grumble that sounded a lot like, 'Good boy'.

"Mine are the same as Trick's, with a few additions. Receiving penetrative anal sex is a hard limit for me, but I'd love to watch you two go at it." Clint stretched before, relaxing back into the cushions.

No getting dicked in the ass? Oh, this poor man. There was a prostate for a reason, and that reason was for it to get slammed by a dick. But Nav couldn't judge Clint's limits, just like he expected the other two not to judge his own.

"Does that sound good, slut? Do you like the idea of me fucking you hard? I'd loosen you up for Clint, here. He's got a thick dick—even thicker than mine. We could fuck your ass together and ruin that tight hole of yours like you wanted." Trick tugged on his hair, his nails scratching over Nav's scalp.

Nav's knees trembled. The scene had already begun, even if Clint didn't know it. Clint seemed intrigued, leaning forward a bit with his mouth open, his tongue sweeping across his lower lip.

Nav shook his head, pulling against the grip Trick had on him and clutching Trick's wrist. He wanted to melt into the hold, but what was the fun in that? He dug his trimmed nails into Trick's wrist, drawing red lines over the tanned surface as Trick tightened his grip.

"I don't know, Trick," said Nav, trying to take a step back as he looked over at Clint. Objectively, Clint was hot, but Nav had no desire to fuck him—which was strange, if he thought about it. Maybe it was the room or Clint's steady gaze looking at him and pulling a flush from deep within him. Maybe it was the fact he was about to get graded like he had some kind of kinky report card. "Does he have to watch?"

Trick growled, releasing Nav and dropping his hand to his side before clenching his fist tight. "I can fuck you here or fuck you at home. It makes no difference, slut. You'll spread your legs for anyone, so why not Clint? He let you in here out of the kindness of his heart. You should get on your knees and thank him properly."

On his knees with Trick in his ass and Clint in his mouth? *Yes, please!* His cock throbbed, his balls heavy with the need to come. Clint's pupils had gone wide, matching Trick's.

"What makes you think you have a choice?" asked Trick quietly.

Nav shuddered at those eight words, pre-cum slicking the inside of his jeans. Trick lunged at him, pressing Nav to the wall with one hand wrapped around his throat. His grip was barely there, just enough to remind Nav that Trick had control—that Trick would take care of everything.

Chapter Twenty-Eight

Trick

Trick was so hard that it hurt, the heat from his groin spreading all the way to his chest. Nav was so perfect for him. *I'm so lucky.* Trick had nearly purred when Nav had asked Clint's limits.

He had been worried—not because Nav was anything less than perfect, but because his inexperience was often obliterated by his overwhelming confidence. Sometimes it made the victory all the sweeter when Nav finally bent and submitted to him completely, admitting that Trick knew what was best for him.

He pressed his thumb against the frantic beat of Nav's pulse as his sub looked to Clint, his eyes wide. There was no mistaking the tent in his loose jeans, or the way he licked over his bottom lip in anticipation of a brutal kiss.

Trick smirked as he held himself inches away from claiming Nav's lips. He wasn't prepared to do anything that Nav expected or asked for. *I know what's best for him.*

"The first time I saw you, I knew I wanted to fuck those lips, but now I want them wrapped around something else. Go to Clint, slut, and show him how good that mouth of yours is."

And there it was — the hesitance and confusion. He could imagine what Nav was thinking. *Is he serious? What about the plan?* He had created the perfect scene with Nav, but it was too false to be real. They needed a plan that he could shatter to pieces in a place that was safe, so Nav could let go and Trick could take control.

"What?" asked Nav, as if he hadn't heard Trick properly. His gaze flashed to Clint again as he frowned.

How far can I push him? Trick was still in control of every movement and every feeling. He would *never* lose himself again.

Trick held back his grin as he released Nav and stepped back, backhanding Nav across his cheek before he could utter another protest. The blow struck with enough force to make the back of Trick's hand sting and Nav's head snap into Trick's opposite palm where he'd braced to catch him, a cry pushing from his lips.

He caught Nav's wrists, pulling his arms above his head and pinning them to the wall with one hand before Nav could recover. He brought his other hand back to Nav's neck, tapping the fluttering pulse beneath his thumb as tears gathered in Nav's eyes.

Nav started to struggle as the first tear spilled over onto his reddened cheek, pulling his wrists uselessly, then bucking beneath Trick when he couldn't free himself. The movements went straight to Trick's cock, his breath coming faster as Nav's pupils dilated with lust and a spot of wetness dotted the front of Nav's jeans.

Nav's enjoyment was more erotic than the struggles themselves.

Nav was so beautiful stretched out for Trick, his head craned to the side and his eyes wild, his chest heaving as he finally gave in. His lips were wet from his panting, his gaze already starting to cloud as he let go. A safeword was the last thing on Nav's mind, so Trick leaned in, biting into Nav's ear.

"What's your color, baby?" He made sure his voice was soft, like the lull before the storm.

"Green," Nav whispered back immediately.

Trick laughed, his chuckle dark enough that Nav stilled in his arms. "Such a fucking slut for it. Tell me, how many cocks have you let fuck you?"

Nav flushed, trying to pull away, but Trick didn't let him. He didn't really want to know how many guys Nav had fucked—not in the least, but Nav loved being his slut. "What's one more, huh?"

"Shut up!" Nav yelled, breaking one hand free and almost managing to slap Trick. They had decided that open-handed slaps were on the table—but no fists. They wanted to have fun, not end up in the hospital.

Trick dodged the slap, tugging Nav from the wall and flinging him off balance. With a well-placed tap to the back of his leg, Nav fell to the floor on his knees. Trick twisted Nav's arm behind his back as he fell, gently tucking it up along his spine and stopping as soon as he felt the slightest strain.

"You look much better on your knees," Trick whispered directly into Nav's ear, catching Nav's free arm and twisting it behind his back with the other. Grabbing both of Nav's wrists with one hand, Trick reached into his pocket he grabbed the first surprise toy that he'd hidden in his pocket while Nav had been gazing around the room. The room wasn't called *Still* for nothing.

He looped the ties around Nav's wrists, pulling them tight enough that he wouldn't be able to free himself. They were made of soft rope with two loops that tightened with a unidirectional pully system that could be tightened easily but only loosened with the quick release.

Nav struggled, pulling at his binds and rolling to his side as Trick let go. Pushing to his feet, Trick took a step back before circling Nav, watching him writhe and pant, his wide eyes calling to Clint as his chest heaved.

"Are you going to listen now, slut? Or do I have to teach you another lesson?" asked Trick as Nav went still, the pool of pre-cum on Nav's jean spreading.

"Hmm-m." Trick tapped his chin, his cock aching as he stared at his prone sub. He crouched down, resting on the balls of his feet. "I hope you don't like that shirt, slut."

He pulled a small pair of bandage scissors from his pocket. At first he'd thought about a knife for the sheer terror it would cause, but he didn't want to accidentally hurt Nav if he did struggle. His sub had the self-preservation of a duck on the highway, and a knife wouldn't still his struggles for a second.

He sliced the front of Nav's shirt open with a few well-placed cuts, kneeling on the end of the rope binding Nav's hands as he started to struggle. "Be still or I'll cut something I didn't mean to." He closed the scissors, running the dull tip over Nav's nipple before digging it into the erect bud. Nav let out a loan groan, bucking his hips against the air.

"You ready to thank Clint properly?" asked Trick, glancing up to his friend. Clint was leaning on the edge of the couch, one hand down his pants while he stroked himself. Trick's lips curled. He had barely begun.

"I'll be good." Nav whimpered as Trick pulled at the button on Nav's jeans, tugging them down to reveal the pale globes of his ass and his lean legs. His cock was rock hard and leaking pre-cum everywhere. Trick knew how sensitive his sub was. In just a few touches, Nav would be done for the day.

Trick stood and strolled to the cupboard, reaching for the things that he had requested Clint put there before they arrived. He hadn't checked for them, not wanting to give away the torturous surprise.

"I know you will be." He returned to Nav with his presents concealed behind his back. "But I know you can't help yourself, so I'll help you instead." He reached for Nav's cock, slapping the cold pack over it.

It wasn't frozen, merely chilled, but it would have been torture against Nav's heated skin. Nav shrieked, kicking out at Trick and struggling against his binds. "What the fuck?"

He loves surprises. Nav's eyes rolled back as Trick held the pack to his groin, following every one of Nav's movements as he tried to pull away. "Be still, or do I have to chain you to the wall? I can do it. I have the entire room at my disposal. What else do you think I have hidden here?"

Nav groaned, trembling as a few tears leaked from his eyes. His teeth chattered as his cock started to go soft, shrinking away from the cold the only way it could.

"What's your color, slut?" Trick asked, as Nav bucked beneath him, sweat clinging to his body, despite the cold.

"Green."

Pulling the plastic cock cage from his pocket, Trick eased it onto Nav's softening cock before his sub could even protest. Nav's eyes went wide as he realized what it was. Trick hoped his sub was thinking of the threat Trick had tossed at him to place the first seeds of the scene in his mind.

"You'll wait, slut, even if I have to cage your cock so you can't come for a month."

The cage was a flexible silicone contraption that was easy enough to put on, but unyielding once it was strapped over Nav's cock. It encased him completely, with only his strangled balls and the slit of his cock exposed.

"I chose your favorite color. Do you like it, slut?" said Trick as he locked it into place. He had stolen one of Nav's toys from his drawer, taking it with him to the store so the shade matched perfectly.

Nav groaned as he looked down at the cage, trying to shut his legs to hide his squished cock. Trick pushed them right back open, his eyes wide so he didn't miss a single moment.

"I don't want you to come until I'm finished with you." Trick squeezed the silicone cage, taking a deep breath to rein in his own control. Nav whimpered, pre-cum somehow still oozing through the slit of the cage.

"Oh God, Trick. Please fuck me," said Nav, fluttering his eyes closed.

"Will you thank Clint?" asked Trick, tapping Nav's balls just hard enough to sting. Nav shook his head, biting his lip as he caged cocked bounced.

"I don't need to beat you to make you scream, slut," said Trick, dropping his mouth over the cage and sucking it into his mouth. Beneath the strong taste of silicone was pure Nav, his pre-cum salty as it spread over Trick's tongue. He pulled back with a chuckle as Nav cursed.

He could imagine what it would feel like to have his cock trapped while he desperately tried to get hard, the pressure so intense that it was beyond words.

"Is that all you can take, Nav? My poor slut is ready to tap out before I've even touched you," said Trick as Nav whimpered, trying to close his legs again. Nav went taut beneath him as he opened his eyes, pinning Trick with a glare. Trick knew exactly how to get his boyfriend riled and taking advantage of it during a scene was even hotter than he'd expected.

"Is that all you've got, asshole?" Nav snarled, kicking out at Trick, his blow skimming off Trick harmlessly.

Trick gripped Nav by his shoulders, hauling him to his feet before he pressed him face-first against the closest wall. With three clicks, Nav's hands were free of the ties and bound into two padded shackles above his head. He didn't even try to struggle until Trick kicked his legs wide, snapping his ankles into another set of padded shackles.

Nav was completely on display, his cock to the wall and his pale ass bared to the room. His skin was so smooth and flawless. Even the welts that they'd feared would scar had healed to perfection. Trick just wanted to ruin him.

Trick ran his hand down the seam of Nav's ass, teasing Nav's furled hole that practically begged him to sink inside. Nav's breath hitched as he pulled against his restraints.

"Look at this hole," said Trick, making another pass at Nav's entrance before scraping his nails gently over his pucker. Nav hissed, arching his back. "We could do anything to you and there's no way you could stop us. How many times could we fuck you before you broke? The first fuck would hurt the most. Even if I slick my cock, I won't stretch you out. A slut like you doesn't deserve it. Clint likes them tight, too. He likes to ram his cock into places that it normally wouldn't fit. I think we could both slide into your ass at the same time with you bound to that table."

"You'd break me," said Nav, tugging at his bonds. His fear was so beautiful. Whether it was real or an act, it didn't feel false. Nav was in as deep as Trick was. A peace washed over him — something that had only ever happened with Nav.

"What's your color, slut?"

Nav's 'green' was nearly a shout.

He strolled to the cabinet again, grabbing something he had given to Clint along with the cock cage. Grabbing a packet of lube from the many he had strewn around the room, he coated the dark surface with a full packet before he strolled back to Nav, lining it up with his hole.

Nav had shown an interest in toys that was nearly parallel to Trick's own enthusiasm that he'd kept to himself for a long time — another thing that Nav had freed him of. Ten years with only a flogger and some rope, but that was over now.

"I brought a present for you, slut." He started pushing the plug inside Nav, going slow so that he could watch Nav part around the shiny black surface. He paused as he reached the widest part, listening to Nav's moans before he sank it all the way inside. Nav's ass sucked it in like it was meant to be there, closing around the narrow neck that was barely wider than Trick's finger.

"Did you figure out what it is yet?" asked Trick as he pumped the inflatable plug once. With a rush of air, it grew in Nav's ass, splitting him just a hair wider than he had been a moment before.

Nav let out a low groan as Trick pumped it a few more times, watching the narrow base that hardly changed. Inside he knew it was growing and splitting Nav wide with each pump, getting him ready for whatever Trick wanted to do to him. He knew exactly how many pumps Nav could take and just how far he could push him until he broke.

"It's too much," said Nav, crying out when Trick pumped it again, forcing the swelling bulb into every tight place in Nav's body.

"No, it's not," said Trick, pumping the plug twice more in quick succession. Nav was almost at his limit. *So close.* "It's pressing right against your prostate, and I bet that makes you want to come so bad. It's a good thing I caged your cock to keep that from happening."

"Trick, I need to come. I *need* it." Nav pulled against the wrist restraints, sobbing when he couldn't budge them.

Trick tugged at the base of the plug, watching as he slowly revealed the black surface that stretched Nav's hole to its limits. He paused as he reached the widest part, now swollen twice what it had been when he'd first pushed it inside. With a grin, he shoved the plug back inside, pumping twice more so it would swell even larger inside Nav.

He dropped the pump, strolling to the couch before sitting next to Clint. Clint stared at him with a rosy blush across his cheeks—something that Trick had rarely seen.

"He's very different from Theo," said Clint quietly as Trick threw his arm over the back of the couch, admiring how Nav trembled and searched for Trick over his shoulder.

"He's a good slut," said Trick, schooling his expression even when he wanted to beam. He lowered his voice. "I wanted to check in with you before things go further. I know that consensual non-consent isn't one of your limits, but I'm worried I might trigger you."

"I'm good," said Clint, clearing his throat. "I would have a hard time leaving, even if you asked me to." His flush deepened and Trick let out a wicked grin.

Trick nodded before pulling himself off the couch and marching back to his sub. He had an ass to ravish.

Chapter Twenty-Nine

Nav

The pressure was the most intense thing that Nav had ever felt. His cock was being compressed from all angles, compacted into a tiny cage when all it wanted to do was stand proud.

But the plug was the worst part. He'd never used it before, although he'd watched them in use online and had glanced longingly at it a few times. He'd never imagined it would feel like this — like the biggest cock he'd ever taken, pressing on his prostate and milking his cum that had nowhere to go.

And Trick had left him, chatting with Clint on the couch as if Nav didn't even exist — as if he didn't matter. Goosebumps burst over his skin. *Please, let me come.*

He sank into himself, the pressure and the pleasure-pain taking over every sense. He wanted everything that Trick had for him, even if that meant sucking another man's cock. *Do I want to?* Yes. Clint's cock looked thick and suckable through his pants, and he *did* deserve a thank you.

He blinked. Trick was back, the pressure in his ass easing with a hiss of air. Nav lolled his head, resting his forehead on the wall. The chains that connected his cuffs jingled, a distant sound that relaxed him more than it should have. He didn't have to worry about moving and resisting—not with Trick there. Trick would take care of him.

"You floating, baby?" It was Trick's voice, sounding like it was miles away, even though Nav could feel the warm breath on his skin. He nodded slowly, wanting to beg, but unsure of what he wanted to say. Did he want to come? Or did he need Trick inside him more? He couldn't choose.

"Good, boy." Trick pulled him by his hair until Nav's forehead came away from the wall and his back arched. "I'm going to let you go and you will crawl to Clint. If you struggle or try to run, I'll punish you."

Nav nodded in understanding. His ankles were released, followed by his wrists and his calm evaporated in a puff of air. He wasn't going to *crawl* to Clint. He wasn't usually embarrassed, but crawling naked was fucking humiliating.

He rounded on Trick, who was watching him with crystal-blue eyes that were narrowed and analyzing Nav's every move. Nav laughed, swinging his hand for Trick's face. It connected with a sharp ring, the sting on his palm mirroring the sting on his own cheek.

That was *not* in the script, but none of it had been so far. Why the hell had they even planned it? *So he could deceive me. So he could push me and break me.* Nav had to show Trick that he wasn't that easy.

He lunged for Trick, overestimating his adrenaline-fueled strength and sending them both tumbling to the floor. The anti-fatigue mats across the ground took most of the impact, but Trick's head still bounced, his eyes narrowing as he snarled.

Having the upper hand, even if it was only for a moment, was the single most powerful moment of Nav's life. He was on top of a man who never submitted. Nav was in control, and he wasn't going to give it up easily.

Trick rolled them with ease and Nav's back hit the mat, pushing the air from his lungs, all thoughts of victory dashed. Trick pushed Nav's arms above his head easily, clamping down on his wrists as Nav writhed. Trick kicked Nav's legs wide, fumbling with his own zipper and pulling his cock free.

"The hard way, then," Trick snarled, somehow rolling a condom onto himself one handed before pushing Nav's knees up and forcing himself deep inside.

Even after the plug, Trick split him wide, forcing his body to accept an intrusion that it could barely handle. There was enough lube left from the plug that Trick slid in easily, though. Even if Nav clamped down, there was no way to stop Trick from pushing so deep so fast.

His cock ached, longing for release as the pressure built in his balls and Trick slammed into his prostate. Nav didn't stop struggling for a moment. He tried to push Trick out of his body, and when that didn't work, he slammed his heels into Trick's back, bucking his hips to try to break Trick's hold.

Trick didn't budge as he thrust his cock, forcing Nav wide over and over until he was at his breaking point.

Then he was beyond, spiraling and floating and screaming as Trick took everything Nav had to give. It was beautiful, it was perfect and it was everything Nav had ever dreamed of.

When Trick settled his hips against him one last time, he breathed against Nav's ear lobe, sending him so far under that Nav knew he would be lost for days.

"Perfect, Nav. So fucking perfect for me."

Want to see more from this author? Here's a taster for you to enjoy!

It's a Kink Thing: Unkinked
M.C. Roth

Excerpt

Derreck

Derreck killed his car's engine, letting his eyes fall shut as he leaned back against the leather seat. He could barely keep his eyes open as exhaustion pulled at him, sinking into his weary bones until his frame was thinly stretched.

The seat was comfortable enough that he could almost imagine himself drifting off to the sound of gentle ticking as the Mustang slowly cooled. The air conditioning faded, draining his hope for restful peace as sweat beaded on his forehead. Wiping it away, he let out one last sigh before he opened the door.

Even warmer air coated him as he stepped onto the pavement, his sweat drying under the sun almost instantly. A single shriveled maple on the street hung limp, its leaves barely managing to hold on as the sun baked them black. He rubbed his eyes as his shoes kicked up enough dust to blind an army within a few steps.

Stumbling on the curb, Derreck managed to catch himself on the lamp post that jutted out of the edge of the sidewalk. His palm burned as it touched the heated surface, a gasp pushing through his lips.

Usually it wouldn't bother him—the pain. It was a part of life that he could easily ignore or twist into something much better—but not when he'd gone weeks without a decent night's sleep.

He'd thrown himself into his work, pulling more hours than anyone else, all to avoid the enthralling eyes of the sub that haunted his dreams. *If only it had worked.*

"Are you okay?"

He turned toward the voice as it trickled into his thoughts. The street was empty. Even the plant that hung from the lamp post was nothing more than a few dried twigs and a bunch of dehydrated pansies. He paused, raising his hand to block his eyes from the sun's glare.

The voice had sounded close, but he couldn't spy anyone as he looked around before noting the white door of his destination and the Office Depot across the street. *I must be worse off than I thought.*

There was usually no one to see him coming and going in this part of town, which was exactly how he liked it. There were a few other cars parked along the curb, and he recognized them all except the red Toyota next to him.

He huffed, ready to turn away, before something caught his eye. The Corolla's windows were down, the sun baking the exposed gray-cloth interior with heat waves escaping through the openings. It wasn't a car that should have had its windows down in a place with nobody around.

Derreck took a step toward the car before peering through the passenger window. In the driver's seat was a man who must've been one step away from heatstroke, especially with his black sweater that probably soaked up warmth that much quicker. The interior was tidy, except for a few empty bottles of water stacked on the passenger seat.

Derreck had chosen a baby-blue tank top and jeans himself, but he wished he could pull his tank over his head and dunk himself in the nearest swimming pool.

Leaning over the side of the car, Derreck touched the hood, hissing as heat lanced over his palm. *I am going to be useless tonight.* Shaking his hand, he leaned down to get a better look at the driver.

The driver was flushed, his face a healthy pink and his brown hair soaked with sweat so thick that it looked nearly back. His sweater clung to him, the fabric dark in almost every spot on his rail-thin body. The man gave Derreck a broad smile, sending a small wave as Derreck peered into the steaming interior.

"I didn't mean to startle you," said the man, leaning back in his seat and adjusting the strap over his chest. "I saw you stumble and wanted to make sure you were okay."

Okay? Derreck couldn't keep the disbelief off his face. He didn't even have the energy to turn the question back at the guy who was sweating his ass off in a car when it was sweltering, even in the shade. He didn't want to know.

"I'm good, thanks," said Derreck, slapping the top of the car as he turned away. *You should ask him if he's okay.* Derreck bit down on the urge as it rose behind his teeth. He had too much on his plate, and he couldn't take one more ounce of anyone else's shit before he exploded.

But how many times had he stopped things just before they had been about to go to shit? Too many to count.

"You waiting for someone?" Derreck asked, clenching his fists as he paused on the street. The sun soaked into his shoulders, fresh sweat gathering at the base of his neck. Sweet air conditioning was only a few steps away, but this man was so much worse off than him — sitting in his car…in a fucking sweater.

"Uh, yeah." The man looked up and down the street once before he settled his gaze on the familiar blank door that called to Derreck like the sweetest siren. Beyond those doors was relief and relaxation that couldn't be rivaled by anything else in the world. Too bad there wasn't a bed meant for just sleeping.

The door to the club Unkinked had never been labeled, which kept a lot of pointed fingers from finding it. This man seemed to know what was inside the same way Derreck did.

Someone's sub? The guy didn't look like a Dom, although looks were as deceiving as book covers. Derreck had seen twinky Doms control guys twice their size — putting them on their knees and making them beg usually did the trick.

Derreck had it easier. He looked his part of ruthless Dom, and no one in their right mind would ever ask him to be their sub. It would have been their last question with their own teeth in their head if they did.

He turned away, heading to the door and pressing his hand against the cool surface. He could already feel the stress draining from his body, seeping into the beams of the place where his mind and body felt safest. All he needed was a bit of play and he would be set for the next week. If it were good enough, the high might even last a bit longer and he would be able to catch a bit of sleep.

But his highs were becoming few and far between, and the last one had left him wanting — wanting to never step foot in his place of solace again, wanting to leave the lifestyle behind for good, wanting to be *vanilla*. He shuddered at the thought.

After pulling his key card from his pocket, he tapped it against the door's sensor, the light taking much too long to flip over to green before the lock slid back with a clunk. The security was necessary, as was the bouncer on the other side of the door and the dungeon master who was patrolling the club. It kept curious seekers from sneaking their way inside the place where people laid their hearts and souls out in the open.

He nodded at the unfamiliar bouncer, giving him a quick once-over before thoroughly dismissing him. Derreck didn't care if a sub was burly and thick or lean, because he'd long since mastered hitting a target with a touch of jiggle. But he couldn't pull the bouncer away from his duties.

The bouncer was the third fresh face he'd seen in as many months. The owner of Unkinked, Clint, must have been outsourcing his help for there to be so many unfamiliar faces — either that or maybe they got sick of hearing people fuck and not being able to join in.

Derreck let out a sigh as the cool air trickled over his skin, his sweat turning into goosebumps as the summer heat was sucked away. He let his eyes fall shut as he took a deep breath. Earth and mold that always clung to him gave way to sex and desire, dredging up memories in an instant. He had thousands of memories of Unkinked, and some of them were the best days and nights of his life.

The pull of desire lured him a step away from the door. The sharpness of vodka and rum tickled his nose as he stepped to the curtain. *Am I drinking tonight?* A drink meant no scene, and a scene was everything he needed.

There was a subtle staleness to the curtains as Derreck trailed his fingers over the fabric, finally opening his eyes. He pushed them aside, taking in every detail of the dark interior.

Three of the booths were occupied, all by Doms and subs whom he recognized. A few looked up as he entered, one sub blushing and looking back to the floor. Derreck kept his smirk to himself as he nodded to their Dom, Selina. She had allowed him to borrow her sub, after all. It hadn't been nearly as interesting as he had hoped, but he'd still cherished the submission.

The inside of the club was clean and still bright in the early hour—and was likely different than any newbie expected. There was a touch of nudity in the main area, as well as some rocking leather, but the best parts of the club were out of view. Hidden near the back was the entrance to the main stage and open play area, and tucked around the corner were nine private rooms that made even the most stoic Doms salivate.

From the entrance, though, it could have been any other club, with booths along the wall and a bottle-rich bar with wooden stools for those who wanted to socialize and grab a few drinks. The virgin menu was even more robust than the alcoholic one, catering to the couples who wanted to play.

He stepped to the bar, slipping into an unoccupied stool. Brennen was in the next stool over, bent over a shot glass that reeked of vodka and whiskey—a killer combination that Brennen usually stuck with. There were three more glasses strewn around him and his eyes were already glassy.

He wouldn't be playing, and he was a Dom anyway, which was something Derreck never tried to push. He had no desire to change a person's identity, whether it was Dom or sub. Both positions demanded respect.

"Hey, Derreck. It's a hot one today," said Brennen, looking up from his glass just long enough to ask.

Derreck grunted, tapping the bar top. His nails were still crusted with dirt and clay. No matter how hard he scrubbed, they never seemed to come clean. Even the potato scrubber from the discount store hadn't done the trick, although it had stung.

He leaned against the bar as another wave of exhaustion settled over him. The murmur of voices was almost enough to send him straight to sleep, and the ease that always settled over him in Unkinked had him even closer.

"You drinking tonight, Derreck?" asked Clint as he worked his way through the half-dozen others at the bar.

Clint had started Unkinked with his husband, and after his husband had passed, he had taken full responsibility to keep it going. Derreck couldn't imagine keeping the hours Clint did, along with bartending, organizing events and schedules, giving lessons in first-aid and the mountain of paperwork he must have.

Besides the bouncer and the volunteer dungeon master, Clint worked alone, although there were many subs who offered volunteer service as well.

Derreck blinked as he dropped his gaze to Clint's hips when they swayed with each sauntering step when he moved closer. He was attractive and strong, with a wicked smirk that had caught Derreck's eye more than once.

Nodding his head, he peered back over his shoulder. Clint was so far off limits that Derreck shouldn't have even been looking. *One drink. One drink before the fun starts.*

Clint gave him a quick smile before reaching for a bottle of Jameson. "The usual?"

Derreck shook his head, eyeing Clint up as he passed under the bar's light. Clint looked *tired* and from more than just lack of sleep. He looked the way Derreck had felt for the past few weeks. It was another thing that Derreck just didn't have the energy to fix.

Clint was his friend. Maybe not in a traditional sense, but Clint had been there for him more than once. In return, Derreck usually had his back. But it had been weeks since Derreck had stepped inside the bar. Things had obviously not changed while he had been trying to convince himself he could stay away.

"Give me a shot of Jäger." Derreck leaned his elbows on the bar top, sagging as he took in his surroundings. *Ask him if he's okay.* He looked back to Clint and to the tightness around his eyes. *Not here.*

"Must've been a shit day," said Clint as he set the bottle of Jameson down and reached for the Jägermeister instead. His grip was steady, and the liquid didn't slosh over the side as he poured Derreck his shot. *Maybe I'm just projecting.*

"Shit week," said Derreck, surprised that Clint didn't mention his absence. He shouldn't have been surprised. Clint was one of the most intuitive men he knew, and he must've seen the strain in Derreck's every movement.

Derreck's callused palms were red and blistered, his skin dry and still dirty-looking, despite his lengthy shower. His muscles burned, even as he raised his glass to his lips and tossed back the shot. The liquid seared a path down his throat, turning him inside out as it sank into him. It eased the ache in the rest of his body for an instant. A bit of rain would have gone so much further than the shot, though.

"You starting a tab?" Clint grabbed the empty shot glass, setting it on a tray beneath the lip of the bar.

"I'll stop at one." Derreck pushed off the stool, heading deeper into the club without looking back at Clint. If he'd stayed any longer, he would have had to ask Clint if he was okay. *Letting two people down in one day. Must be a record.* He grimaced as his gut throbbed with every movement. Jäger had probably been a poor choice.

He scoped out the bar a second time, slowing his stride until his stomach calmed. His gaze lingered on a couple—two subs—as they kissed over their table. *Kristie and Katie.* It was too bad that they weren't his type, because two subs *were* better than one. They needed a soft Dom, but he needed a sub to torture the fuck out of.

There were a few other couples, despite the early hour. After dark was when the real sadists started to emerge from the shadows, but the lifers didn't care what time of day it was. Derreck was a lifer, too, he supposed, and after more than fifteen years, he should have known that his life was nothing without kink.

He circled the bar area again. There was nothing happening on the main stage or open floor, and he had no desire to just *watch* if one of the kink room doors were open. He spied a Dom who was reclined in the seating area outside of the rooms, her sub at her feet with his head across her shoe. From the blissed-out look on his face, he was still floating.

Derreck needed something more than that. He needed them sobbing with euphoria in his arms after he fucked them up. It was the only way he was going to get a certain sub out of his thoughts.

He clenched his hands into fists, the calluses on his palms like pebbles over his skin. His hands could do a lot of damage to a person, then dig a grave on a moonlit Tuesday. The damage was always consensual, but the grave...not so much.

He slipped down the hallway of doors that led to kink rooms, which held more implements than any Dom or sub could ever ask for. He slid his hand over the engraved gold letters on his favorite room. *Impact.* Even the name made goosebumps burst over his skin and sent a shudder of need to his core. His cock stayed soft, as it usually did, except for those rare occasions when a sub managed to surpass his expectations.

Like Nav. He closed his eyes, letting his hand rest against the carved surface.

Nav had been introduced to him by a fellow Dom, and after their first scene together, he had gone straight home with his hands still aching from holding the flogger tight. Stepping in the shower, he had dropped his hand to his cock, jerking himself to hardness with Nav on his mind.

But Nav wasn't his in the loosest sense of the word, even though he still managed to haunt Derreck's dreams. Nav had safeworded during their second scene together, then had fled back to his true Dom, Trick. The call of "*yellow*" still sounded in his ears as if it had only been yesterday.

Sex was so rarely a part of life for Derreck, but during their first scene, he had watched Trick come as Nav had shot against the wall from Derreck's beating alone. He wouldn't have been a gay man if he hadn't felt *something*.

But Nav had belonged to Trick before the two of them had even realized it. Derreck had seen their looks and had chosen to ignore them, despite his better instincts. It had been a miscalculation that had added to his sleeplessness and had prompted him to steer clear of the club for weeks.

He gritted his teeth, turning away from the closed door and pushing his way down the hall.

He'd come to the club so he could forget his mistake and move the fuck on.

The private rooms were all closed as he passed them, tracing his fingertips over each name. *Play, Spoil, Calm, Wet.* He wasn't sure whether or not there were couples on the other side of each door, but the closed door meant that voyeurism was not welcome. *I'm not welcome.*

He circled back to the main area, sliding into an empty booth, despite invitations from several tables that he passed. He didn't pause for conversation, just tilted his head before he moved on to his own space. Rapping his knucks against the polished tabletop, he leaned back to survey the room once more.

There was no one for him yet, but he was patient. He could spend hours staring at the same spec of dirt, letting his mind drift until he was content. Sitting in a comfortable chair with the hum of music and the smell of sex in the air was paradise in comparison.

He looked up as the curtain to the entrance slid open and another couple stepped off the street and into his world. Derreck got a flash of the bouncer and a few others before the curtain fluttered back into place. The hum of conversation lulled against his eardrums.

His chest did *not* squeeze when he spotted Nav tucked under Trick's arm as they entered the club together. Trick's tanned hand glowed against Nav's pale, naked shoulder, a pair of tight boy shorts the only thing on Nav's body.

It wasn't that Derreck was jealous of his friend, but there was a certain longing at seeing Nav that summoned his darker side. It wasn't very often that Derreck could take himself in hand and come quickly, and a treat like Nav would have made any man salivate.

Trick spotted him first, nodding from across the room before he gripped the back of Nav's neck and pushed him to the ground.

Nav had come a long way since Derreck had last seen him. Dropping to his knees, Nav didn't seem to care how hard he struck the ground or how rough Trick jerked his head back by his hair. His eyes glazed over immediately, going deep without resistance. He was something *special*.

Derreck shifted in his seat, trying to ease the tension in his gut. Nav — *no, Trick's sub* — stayed on the ground as Trick strolled toward Derreck, giving him a smile as he approached.

"Derreck." Trick stopped at the edge of the booth, holding his hand out in an offering. Derreck took it, accepting the handshake at face value. Trick had grown a few calluses on his palm, the surface rougher than Derreck remembered. *Working his sub hard. Good.* Nav deserved someone who would put the effort in.

"Maverick." He squeezed once before he broke contact, smothering the urge to wipe his hand on his pants. Trick's sweat on his palm was like a raw nerve, his touch buzzing under Derreck's skin.

"My slut has something to say to you, if you are agreeable to it," said Trick, glancing back at Nav. Trick's eyes were hard, despite the languid way he moved. He traced the room, eyeing someone up as they moved from a booth to the bar, passing close to Nav. *Too close, apparently.* Trick clenched his fist, his jaw going tight.

Derreck paused, looking back at Trick's sub. Nav had lowered his eyes to the floor, unmoving, despite the way his knees had to have been aching on the hardwood. Perhaps he had done something to not deserve a pillow—or perhaps he preferred it like that.

Nav wasn't beautiful in a traditional sense—too pale and soft to meet the stereotypical desires of most men—but Derreck had seen first-hand how alluring he was after a scene. Derreck valued that more than any beauty.

He inclined his head, sliding his hand over the tabletop as he looked to Trick. "I'm agreeable." His voice sounded more strained than he would have liked, but he'd buried too many people in one week to feel normal. Trick gave him a sharp look, probably seeing straight through him. *I must look worse than I thought.*

Trick didn't say anything, though, which made him a better friend than Derreck gave him credit for. Instead, he called his sub over, Nav crawling on all fours with his head lowered as he approached.

Derreck slid his hand over the tabletop, Trick's sweat on his palm spreading over the surface until he could no longer feel the edge of it sinking into his skin. It left a streaky mess on the polished surface, his fingerprints blatant beneath the light.

Derreck looked up as Nav finally stopped his crawling and kneeled at his feet with his head bowed. His dark hair shone in the low light of the club, looking almost black against his pale skin. A purplish welt peeked through the waist band of his low-riding shorts and Derreck fought the urge to reach forward and press his fingertip to the bruise.

"Speak," said Derreck, keeping his voice quiet. Nav had a very particular brand of humiliation that he desired, and that brand name was *Trick*. Derreck was *nothing* to him.

"I wanted to apologize, Sir," said Nav, keeping his gaze pointed to the floor, despite his steady tone. "I was lying to myself, and to you, when I asked for a second scene. I should have never disrespected you, and I'm sorry for my behavior."

That…was unexpected. Derreck tilted his head, not fighting the smile that tugged at his lips. It was also a huge fucking relief. It had been a mistake, but maybe it hadn't been his alone.

A smidge of his exhaustion uncoiled, his lungs filling easier than they had in a long time.

"Forgiven," said Derreck, fighting the urge to keep his hands to himself for a second time. Trick, having no need to hold back, threaded his hand through Nav's hair, tugging him so he had to crawl a step closer.

"Thank you, Sir," said Nav, tension visibly draining from his body.

So good. Derreck turned his gaze away, swallowing down the words that started to rise. Nav was one of a kind, but Nav was not *his*.

"Clint will be joining us for our scene," said Trick, patting his sub on the top of his head. "You are welcome as well, of course."

Trick's eyes darkened as he looked at his sub, and it wasn't because of the low light. Derreck shook his head. That was not the type of torture he was after tonight. He had no desire to string himself along, gaze at Trick's sub and *imagine*.

"Slut, go get ready in our room. You know which one," said Trick. Nav scurried away on his hands and knees, the bottom of his ass cheeks peeking through the hem of his shorts. Another small bruise caught Derreck's eye and he licked his lips before forcing his gaze back to the table. Trick was staring at him, his eyes hard.

"You're my friend, Derreck, but I've never seen you this distant before—not with me, anyway. You haven't been here in weeks and tonight...you aren't yourself. I know you won't ask for help, so I'm offering it."

Shit. Am I really that obvious? He swallowed the lump in his throat that had formed as soon as he'd seen Nav walk through the curtain. "It's nothing. I just need to find myself a sub and let off some steam."

But will that be enough? It had been before, but Trick was right. He wasn't himself and hadn't been for some time. Even before Nav, things had been...*off.*

Trick hummed before looking around the bar. "There's only one sub who can take what you have to give right now. The offer stands. You can come, watch or get involved again if that's what you need. I'm sure Nav would be open to the idea, too. He's been kicking himself for weeks about what he did to you."

Not his fault. "He's good for you," said Derreck, turning his gaze back to the table. Maybe he wouldn't stop at one shot tonight. His stomach churned at the idea, goosebumps breaking out over his skin.

A smile cracked Trick's face, his blue eyes glowing with the glee and something more. Trick had never looked at his previous partner like that, but Derreck had always wondered how their partnership had lasted so long when their kinks hadn't aligned. *Compromise maybe?*

"He is. He's a good man and a good slut," said Trick.

"The best of both worlds," said Derreck, his voice flat. Maybe Trick was right. There was no one in the club who could take what he had to give. And on a Wednesday afternoon, that wasn't likely to change.

His patience snapped and exhaustion settled over him again like a weighted blanket. He stood abruptly, leaving Trick behind as he headed for the door. Hopefully, the blond would understand. He'd seen enough of Derreck to know when to take it personally and when not to.

Pushing the curtain aside, he grabbed the doorknob without acknowledging the bouncer who had jumped to his feet, sliding his cell phone back into his pocket. The bouncer opened his mouth once before snapping it shut, taking a step back as he looked at Derreck.

Stepping outside, the sun instantly soaked into his skin, blanketing him in warmth and urging sweat from his body in seconds. The sun had barely moved in the sky, blazing down with what must have been record-breaking heat.

He could barely feel his feet as he stumbled his way along the sidewalk to his car, stopping at the lamp post and leaning on it as he took a deep breath. The post seared through his shirt, heat bursting over his flesh until he thought he might erupt into flames. It did nothing to quell his exhaustion.

He'd never let it get quite that bad before, but he'd never stayed away so long, either. He hadn't wanted to face Trick or Nav or anyone else. He just wanted relief. The apology had given him a touch of respite but not enough to calm the restless energy in his core.

"You sure you're okay?"

Derreck looked up and his gaze followed the sound of the voice.

The guy was still sitting in his car, as if it hadn't been almost an hour. He had pushed up one sleeve of his sweater, one thin and delicate wrist exposed, but the rest of his upper body was still covered with thick, black material. The flush on his cheeks and the sweat in his hair told of how hot he must've been, but he was making no move to remove his sweater.

"Still waiting?" asked Derreck, looking back at the club entrance. None of the couples had been missing a third that he knew of. And no Dom would leave their sub in a hot car like he was some sort of oven-baked dog.

No responsible Dom, at least.

The man nodded, flicking his gaze to the door and back to Derreck quickly. His eyes had gone shiny, as if he was just managing to hold back tears. How long had he been there before Derreck had come to the club? How long would he wait?

It pulled at what few heartstrings Derreck had, but it also spoke to his Dominant side.

It pissed him the fuck off is what it did. He clenched his hands into fists, crossing his arms and staring down at the man in his car.

"Who are they? I'll go get them for you," said Derreck. There was no way he was walking away with this guy still sitting in his car as he got closer and closer to heatstroke.

"Oh." The man dropped his gaze, the pureness of his submission pulling Derreck deeper into the strange thrall. His cheeks flushed brighter, sweat beading under his eyes.

Perhaps it had been the wrong question. Some Doms insisted on titles, and Derreck would have no luck if the guy simply said 'Sir' or 'Master'.

"Describe what they look like," said Derreck, taking a deep breath to keep the anger out of his voice. He was definitely kicking someone's ass tonight—just not in the way he'd hoped.

"I—I don't know," said the man, his gaze still fixed on his lap. "I only have his name. Someone—a friend online—gave me his name and said that he might be able to help me. They said he comes to this club, but I can't get in without an invite."

"You can if you're a guest," said Derreck, letting out a sigh. This was just getting stranger and stranger. "Your friend can invite you as a guest, and you'll have a temporary pass."

"Oh, they aren't a member," he said, finally looking up, but only for a moment. "They went to an open house event here years ago, but they don't live in the city. I don't know anyone with a membership."

It was a conundrum that had always bothered Derreck. Privacy came with the price of inaccessibility and exclusivity, especially for subs who were heartbreakingly shy. He would still take his privacy, though. The one-and-done kinksters could fuck off.

He ran a hand over his scalp, scratching the short, tight curls. It was too fucking hot to think, and he had to get off the street before he passed out.

"What's the name, then? I can tell you if they are here," said Derreck. He *wouldn't* give away much, because if this guy was a stalker, which was quickly becoming a possibility, then he didn't want to encourage him.

"Oh, it's... Let me grab my phone. I have it in there." He fumbled with his pockets, finally sliding his phone out from the pouch in his sweater. Why the hell was he wearing so many layers? Derreck was getting warmer just looking at him. "I saved it in here, 'cause I'm terrible with names. The guy's name is Derreck."

Derreck almost choked on his spit when he heard his own name. Cocking his head to the side, he dragged his gaze up and down the guy's form one more time. His first impression had been pure madness, but he never was one to hold on to a first impression for long. He usually waited until the sixth before he really made up his mind.

The guy was in shorts and flip-flops, which Derreck hadn't noticed before. It couldn't have been great for driving, but at least he wasn't insane enough to wear long pants along with his sweater. His clothes were good quality but well worn, so he probably wasn't out to try to kidnap Derreck. He didn't stand a chance either way, unless he had a gun in his pocket.

The man fiddled with his thumbs as Derreck watched him, the chewed edge of his nail vibrant with fresh blood. All his nails were like that—bitten past the quick to the delicate pink flesh beneath.

"How did your friend say he could help you?" asked Derreck, eyeing the guy's cell phone. It was a new model, fresh out of the store with a custom case.

"I…" The man trailed off, bringing his thumb to his mouth and catching the vermillion edge with his teeth. A fresh droplet of blood oozed up, shining against his lip until he slowly dragged it away with his tongue.

"I heard he could hurt me," said the man, so quietly that Derreck had to strain to hear him. "I need someone to hurt me."

Pushing away from the post, Derreck circled around the car and pulled the door open with a jerk. The man's eyes went wide and he drew back, shrinking into his seat as Derreck loomed over the car.

"What's your name?" asked Derreck, lowering himself into a squat. It left the man with a slight height advantage, hopefully easing some of his fear that had sprung up. Derreck reached for the man's hand, pulling his thumb from his mouth. The flesh was burning beneath his palms, slick with sweat and clammy.

"Maddy," he said, letting out a sigh at the touch.

There was no buzzing under Derreck's skin or desire to wipe his fingers clean. It was the rare perfection that always seemed to elude Derreck when he needed it most.

"And why do you want me to hurt you, Maddy?" asked Derreck, watching as Maddy's eyes went wide with realization.

"So I don't hurt myself."

About the Author

M.C. Roth lives in Canada and loves every season, even the dreaded Canadian winter. She graduated with honours from the Associate Diploma Program in Veterinary Technology at the University of Guelph before choosing a different career path.

Between caring for her young son, spending time with her husband, and feeding treats to her menagerie of animals, she still spends every spare second devoted to her passion for writing.

She loves growing peppers that are hot enough to make grown men cry, but she doesn't like spicy food herself. Her favourite thing, other than writing of course, is to find a quiet place in the wilderness and listen to the birds while dreaming about the gorgeous men in her head.

M.C. Roth loves to hear from readers. You can find her contact information, website details and author profile page at https://www.pride-publishing.com

PUBLISHING

Sign up for our newsletter and find out about all our
romance book releases, eBook sales and promotions,
sneak peeks and FREE romance books!